Briar Blackwood's Grimmest of Fairytales

Briar Blackwood's Grimmest of Fairytales

Timothy Roderick

LODESTONE BOOKS

Winchester, UK
Washington, USA

First published by Lodestone Books, 2015
Lodestone Books is an imprint of John Hunt Publishing Ltd., Laurel House, Station Approach, Alresford, Hants, SO24 9JH, UK
office1@jhpbooks.net
www.johnhuntpublishing.com

For distributor details and how to order please visit the 'Ordering' section on our website.

Text copyright: Timothy Roderick 2014

ISBN: 978 1 78279 922 1
Library of Congress Control Number: 2014952386

A CIP catalogue record for this book is available from the British Library.

Design: Stuart Davies

Printed and bound by CPI Group (UK) Ltd, Croydon, CR0 4YY

We operate a distinctive and ethical publishing philosophy in all areas of our business, from our global network of authors to production and worldwide distribution.

Prologue

The spindle, gleaming, cold as winter, had no real feelings, save hunger. It was constructed of malice and fear, the swirling poisons of death, and it had but one purpose. The Lady held it aloft in her icy porcelain fist, tightening, squeezing, awakening darkness to its chore.

A ray of moonlight, just a sliver of pale gray through the tall, lean windows, reached the infant laying in the bassinet. There was no other light in the soaring stone chamber, and when the light-fragment, the shadow of illumination touched the child's green eyes, she instinctively reached a tiny trembling hand upward. She too had her purpose, and she curved her small back, as though aching for the sharp point that hovered just above her.

One solid plunge and it would be done. The Lady inadvertently caught the infant's gaze and her heart shuddered. The cooing little thing was soft, smiling, exposed. She felt suddenly cold, clenched. *But why?* The question needled her. What must be done, must, she knew. She heaved and steadied herself. Certainly, her task was unsavory. But it wasn't less than that done dozens, perhaps hundreds, of times before. And certainly it was the least in her litany of transgressions. Her knuckles whitened again around the spindle, for her task served the Tales. And what served the Tales likewise served the Grand Design.

There were only three of them who stood nearby. Two old fishwives of low magic and spell crafts—and with them stood a skinny upstart youth. Their botched plans ended here in this lonely stone tower caught in the crags of a rocky outcropping spiked high above the midnight clouds. And now, like butterflies stung and cocooned, they stood impotent, with their gummy mouths agape.

Who were they to stop these Tales? The Lady drew a faint

1

smile across her thin ruby lips. She eyed the three and spat on the floor, now a sea of splintered door fragments and shattered glass. It gave the Lady perverse warmth to know that they could do no more than watch the Tale play out to its ghastly conclusion.

The Lady's wolfguard closed in on the three, the fur on their backs stiffened, and they snapped their saliva-drenched muzzles in delirious anticipation of what would come next. Stragglers, knowing they might never taste the first succulent morsels, whined and drew up on their hind legs to glimpse the bloody end.

Time slowed and then stopped.

A droplet or two formed on the Lady's smooth wan brow, she halted and felt her eyes well up. It was all so inexplicable, and she wondered if she had eaten something poisonous. But ill or not, what must be done, must. She steadied her breath, ground her teeth together, and choked down all sensation. She renewed her grip, knuckles whitening ever more around the spindle, and she began mumbling ancient curses in the Old Language.

A plump matron of the three rescuers implored her. "Please," she said. "You can't—you wouldn't do this. Think not of the Tales, but of the tot."

"Be still, sister," hushed her elder female companion. The elder's furrowed chin quivered as she clasped her withered hands around the plump one's to keep her from doing something foolish in desperation. No matter what would come next, she knew—they all knew—that live or die, the Tale would not end here.

The Lady shot a glance of twisted, unreachable madness at the matron, eyes all darkened clouds. "The tot?" she growled. "Think of the tot? Did any have thought of me? No! I was left. And now, now I am—" Her body went slack as though submerged by a wave of profound sadness, her eyes brimmed over. They were not the softening tears of realization, but those born of hatred for a world with little place left for her to go but into destruction.

The dark-bearded younger man of the three steeled himself. "You are one of us," he said. "Have you no remembering?" The two elder women looked at each other secretly. There were too many secrets among them. It was lies, treacheries and secrets that stretched back into a time before any of them could remember that led to this with an infant, a spindle, and an ocean of regret.

"Remembering?" The question seemed strange. The Lady took a far-away stare, as if something was asleep, but slowly awakening. "The child." Her voice cracked, choked with some unfamiliar emotion.

"Yes, the child," the plump one encouraged. She darted a glance at the elder.

The Lady gazed down at the infant, her cheeks now rivers of tears. Her lips shuddered with revulsion. "Who—whose child is this?"

"Her eyes, Orpion, are they not familiar to you?" the elder asked.

"Lady Orpion—Abbey," said the man. His silenced footstep fell a finger or two above the floor and his voice gently caressed the very air. Those of their kind were practiced in the ways of soothing and beguiling and enchanting thusly. "End this madness," he continued. His voice was a droning psalmody. "Come with us. You can spare the child and—"

He stopped when the Lady's eyes drooped, mesmerized, as though a delicious dream had overcome her. She ceased her trembling and loosened her grip again, causing the spindle to slacken a bit. Fighting the magical intoxication, she shrieked "Silence! You would have me break these sacred Tales?" She was suddenly clear-eyed and fixed to her purpose. "And what of the Grand Design? I cannot, and neither can you. It has been written, and so it must be." Her eyes rested fiercely upon the bassinet. The baby gurgled softly and saw nothing of the world, of treachery or plot. It reached a tiny pink foot upward.

The man took another cautious step toward her and slowly outstretched his hand, a flower gently uncurling amid the storm. "Give me the spindle." His voice lulled again. It sounded like music and the sea and sweet birdsong all at once. The wolves became docile and dull; their gnashing ceased.

But the Lady battled the bewitchment with eyes downcast and rhythmically murmured words of her own. Soon the wolves shook off the spell and began snapping again with strings of saliva dripping from their fangs.

"Here it is," she said, taunting. "Take it." She raised the spindle and rushed it into the infant's chest. Screams, chaos—all became a blur in that instant. A white dust cloud burst forth from the plunge-point, blinding the Lady and confusing the wolves.

Seeing her opportunity, the eldest produced a tiny golden rod from her starchy cuffed sleeve. With a flick of her wrist, it pinged and snapped on springy hinges to the length of her forearm. She raised it like a skilled symphony conductor and brushed the air in a triangular design. The dust cloud responded eagerly, blossoming and thickening, filling the high stone chamber.

"Goggles," she shouted to the others as she fitted her own pair of brass and leather down over her eyes.

Unable to see beyond her own hands, the Lady Orpion flew into a wild frenzy of stabbing, her spindle piercing the bassinet again and again, until it plunged through the wooden base.

The white dust cloud cleared in an unexpected flight out of one of the immense stained glass windows that stood agape to the crescent moon sky. The three intruders had vanished. The Lady looked down into the bassinet with the smile of a boa constrictor, knowing that though they had escaped, her work was complete. But that quickly gave way to volcanic fury. There was no babe in the bassinet, no twist of arms and legs amid a slop of guts and gore. No. There was a sack of milled flour stabbed open, the powdery contents scattered here and there like small drifts of snow amid mangled linens.

With an earsplitting scream, the Lady raised her arm and wildly flung the spindle toward the window, but it skewered the neck of one of her wolves. The creature yelped pitifully and collapsed, writhing and scratching with its paws on the stone floor in a widening pool of blood. The others of his pack watched their comrade fallen in agony with their skittish amber eyes. With whines and ears tucked back, some straggled, some limped, but they cleared a path for the Lady and averted their eyes.

The squirming wolf bubbled and choked in his blood, while the Lady closed her eyes and waited a breath to restore her composure. She paced the room and strode to the dying wolf. She tugged several times at the spindle until it finally yanked free. Then she shook the excess blood from her hands, splattering it across the chamber floor. "Be still, dear one," she said. Her voice resonated deeply, her face engulfed by the folds of her dark cloak.

She reached down and stroked his fur, first with one hand—then with two. Finally, her strokes became throttling around his neck. The creature kicked and thrashed; his fellow wolves whined and backed away. What must be done, must.

When all was a black silence, the Lady stood and glided to the high window frame, watching the three fugitives shuttling the babe through the night sky like bats. Her knuckles tightened around the spindle again. But it was time for it to sleep, to dream of the day when it would find satisfaction.

"She shall return. And it won't take much. A nick, a stick, a prick of the finger and then—" Her lips curled into a secret smile. "Yes, and then..."

Chapter 1

*I hope you're not holding out for some lame-ass "once upon a time" shit.
Or worse, thinking that I'm gonna spring some happily ever after crap
on you. If you are, you're going to be sadly disappointed. That's because
I'm dead.*

*Yep—as in stone cold. And I'm not telling you this so you can get
all teary-eyed and feel sorry for the poor little loser girl who died
because she was too stupid to listen to reason. She was too blinded by
the sack she was being fed by the lying-ass fairies to see beyond, to see
where this was all headed. Yeah, she trusted them.*

*And, I hope you're not getting lost here; 'cuz when I say "she" I
mean me. I trusted their manipulative little asses. And before I knew it,
I was in so deep that there was no climbing back out.*

*Oh God, I can see it now. You're all distracted by my use of the f-
word. You know, fairy.*

*Yeah, they exist, and so what? Think about it; I'm dead and I'm
talking to you. Is it such a stretch to imagine that fairies are real? Come
on. You knew they were real when you were a kid, but someone told you
somewhere along the way that they were like some crazy hallucination
or a dream. And you bought it. But you knew you saw them. Out of the
corner of your eye, in the darkness of your room, under the bed, in your
closet, you saw something. A shadow. Movement.*

*Whatever. Live in your little self-protected bubble-world if you
want. But I'm telling you, they're with us all the time, watching,
waiting to draw us into their screwed-up plots. You need to know all of
this because I can't let this happen all over again to yet one more of us
commons.*

*Oh right, you think you're special. You think, "I'm not common."
But that's what they call you—the fairies, that is. And when they're the
really mean ones, the wicketts, who only see you as a sorry ass to be
used, they'll call you a squelch. Oh sure, it's all kumbaya and "oooh,
you're the chosen one," when you're with them. And before you know*

it, you're getting twirked like somebody's little prison bitch.

They look like us too—the fairies. They don't flutter around on gossamer wings. But they can fly and do crazy magic. They might even try to teach you some. Or they'll give you a taste of something else you want, like love that's just out of reach, or the fantasy of some bullshit power. Hooking you is all they need.

Look, our world isn't brave enough to accept you for who you are, really. I'm proof of that. But the fairies, they will. They want you in all of your quirky glory. And then they'll tempt with such sweetness, that it's almost impossible to resist.

Splat!—right in the back of the head. The apple core left traces of cold, wet juice trickling down the back of Briar Blackwood's neck. It wasn't accidental. Oh no, this was meant for her. She kicked at the brown mushy thing lying on the ground with her black calf-high grunge boots like it was the fruit's fault she stood in the back of the school auditorium with the rest of the freaks, waiting to audition for the play. She looked around to see if anyone nearby had witnessed her mortification. What did it matter? They'd seen it all before, she realized. She wiped the sticky mess off her neck while trying not to get sick.

She scanned the far aisle with a smoldering, half-lidded gaze that she hoped would scorch them—or at least warn them that she *knew* it was them. It was always the same group who did things like this to the less popular kids. Trash-cannings, spit-ballings, and garbage-bombings were standard in the arsenal of their kind. And there they stood in a group, in the shadowed side aisle of the musty auditorium, unsuccessfully restraining guffaws through their noses.

"Lucky Boys" and "Lucky Girls" is what Briar called them. They were the ones whom everyone liked. Maybe it was because they had mothers and fathers, and they knew where they came from and where they belonged. Everyone had their sad story, Briar knew it well. But some kids were able to hide it better than others—and maybe that's what made them Lucky. Who knows? But whatever it was, there was a serious, unspoken line between the loved and the lame, and an apple core to the back of the head was a perfect reminder of which side Briar stood.

She tried to adjust her perspective, which was something she had become skilled at over the past ten years of school. In this case, seeing that she was standing amid an entire crew of dweebs, she reasoned that she couldn't be certain for whom the apple core was meant. It didn't really matter. *Seriously*, Briar thought, *I've actually stepped onto the escalator to hell. It better damn well be worth it.*

There was really no way out anyway, now that the Lucky Ones had seen her at the auditions. The best she could hope for was to have an out-of-body experience and float out of the room. It seemed as reasonable a plan as any. So she tried to will it to happen. But, of course, Briar just stood there, going nowhere, looking a bit constipated.

Some dark, heavy, screaming music just ought to do the trick, she thought, as she stuffed in her earbuds and cranked up the volume on her handheld player. But no music could erase the fact that she was there voluntarily, along with Gluteus High School's celebrated assemblage of oddities. Briar may have had her own problems, but these other kids were just plain wrong. And it was outrageously stupid for her to associate with these bizarre outsiders: the theater geeks. Yet, she had to do it. She had her reasons, even if she wouldn't openly admit them to herself.

To cover for her self-consciousness, she fiddled with her outfit: a tattered black satin Victorian gown made of small scallops (like the lining of a casket, she liked to think), cinched up high enough to reveal fishnet stockings that barely covered her moon-white thighs. She unconsciously twisted the long, iron skeleton key that hung from her neck, hoisted it with one finger to her mouth and nibbled it, tasting the tang of metal.

Briar leveled her scowling eyes at the surrounding herd of

nerd and wrinkled her nose in blatant disgust. She had never been to one of the auditions for the annual school play, but they were legendary among the scoffers, side-mouthed whisperers, and hallway chucklers at Gluteus High. And true to the legends, it seemed like every Renaissance-fair-loving, pimply misfit who had ever been a lunch-break target was dying to humiliate himself by dressing as a fairy in *A Midsummer Night's Dream*.

Briar gave them the once-over. *Oh yeah, this ought to do wonders for their reputations. Screw that. What about mine?* She realized it with a snarl of her tar-black lips and a dramatic roll of her crayon-thick, ebony-lined, eyes.

Briar had to keep reminding herself of her purpose. Seeing as it was just weeks away from her sixteenth birthday, she came to the slow, but burning realization that change was necessary. After all, sixteen was reputed to be some kind of magical number. She read about it in a weird old book she found while hiding out among the tall musty stacks of a used bookshop. She learned that you add the digits one and six to make seven. That was a number representing transformation. It had something to do with fire and alchemy and who the hell knows what. It was mostly gibberish, to be honest. And really, the best part of reading a book like that for Briar was the fretful glances she'd get from soccer moms and tea-toddling bookworms.

That being said, the number and its meaning stuck in Briar's head because nothing in her life really worked and she knew that she was due for an overhaul.

She had never really fitted in, even from a young age. But it wasn't really her fault. There were, well, circumstances. True, she was in foster care. She bounced from one home to another since birth, finally landing in one that "took." They kept her for a good ten years now, at a profit.

But there was more to it than that. Sure other kids could sniff out the ones that had the distinct scent of "reject." Foster kids, once they were discovered, often fell into that category. But ever since she could remember, she had always been associated with bizarre occurrences. For example, there was the time in third grade when a Lucky Girl tried dumping her in a trashcan only to end up with third degree burns all over her body. Then there was the Lucky Boy in fifth grade who tried to covertly cut her hair, but instead found himself in the emergency room, needing surgery for snipping his own tongue in half.

No one knew how these things happened. Not even Briar. But there were innuendos. Words like "witch" and "evil" were whispered around her. And as time passed, the other kids pulled further away until there was no bridging the gap. As the years passed, Briar decided that if they were going to call her a witch, she was going to give them the scariest damned witch they'd ever seen.

Her sullen demeanor and perpetual pout, the capes and black lace veils she'd wear around town had become trademarks. Once she overheard some kids in the bathroom referring to her as the "Queen of Darkness." *Not bad*, she thought. *If you're going to be queen, it might as well be of something spectacular, like the dark.* She with her ash-tone rouge, her nose, eyebrow, lip, and tongue piercings and forbidding demeanor—it was social suicide for anyone to venture near her vortex of doom.

Despite its obvious disadvantages, the whole charade had an upside. It kept the wrath of the Lucky Ones at bay for the most part. But despite it all, Briar held to secret fantasies. She imagined that by the age of sixteen, the other kids would have outgrown their distaste for her differences—whatever they may be. Or they might have at least matured enough to politely ignore them. No such luck.

So maybe there would never be all-night texting sessions with scores of girlfriends, or invitations to parties and school dances. Hell, maybe there would never be basic acceptance. But what Briar hadn't planned on in this whole scenario—what made her absolutely crazy—was the fact that there'd probably never be, well…the boyfriend. So cranking up the volume one more notch was always a good solution, she found.

As the auditions progressed, as usual, Briar kept to herself. She tucked herself away in a shadowed seat near the back of the dusty auditorium and glanced toward the rear double doors for the eighty-sixth time. *Where was Dax, anyway?* Her best friend was supposed to meet her by three o'clock, yet an hour into the audition process, still no Dax. Now Briar was solo and sharing floor space with Buck-toothed Braces Girl from science class, that skinny Grizzly Chicken Girl from math, and the really, really short boy who either had no name or nobody ever bothered to use it.

She caught the nearby sight of a couple of goobers rehearsing a love scene. It might have been pretty good had one's headgear not tangled with the other's scoliosis brace. She followed them with an obvious slow-eyed glower as they shimmied out the back doors.

A Juliet who was shaped like a baked potato was in the middle of her onstage fretting when a stagehand signaled to Briar that she was up soon. She felt a knot form in the hollow of her throat and she started to wonder if she could go through with it.

And where was her reason for auditioning in the first place? She hadn't seen him yet. All right, yes, it was a *he*, Briar begrudgingly acknowledged. *Fine.* But where was he? He was probably hanging out there among the Lucky Ones.

He had to be there, or her whole bloody scheme was wasted. She was sure that she overheard him one day telling another Lucky Boy that he was going to try out for the play. Even if it was a joke and even if he planned on turning the play into a running gag for his buddies, Briar saw this as an opportunity. As strange as it seemed, she felt that sharing the stage together with him might just level the playing field and offer her a shot to get to—well, she hadn't actually thought it through beyond trying out for the same play.

She arranged her long limp black bangs so that they hung in front of her eyes. It was easier to spy on the group of them without looking conspicuous, she thought. As if sitting there looking like a reject from *American Horror Story* wasn't conspicuous.

Unexpectedly Grizzly Chicken girl moon-walked up to Briar, probably for the first time ever, and naïvely, innocently, complemented her on her super cool mortician's outfit. "Your little costumes sure make my day," she said sunnily.

Briar hadn't anticipated sinking to a new low this afternoon, yet here it was. How glorious.

"Thanks, butt-munch," Briar replied. "Your braces are pretty cool too."

Grizzly's face caved. "That's the color of my teeth," she mumbled, holding a hand over her mouth. She faded back into the crowd.

Briar threw over her shoulder, "Well, lay off the tetracycline, then."

She bit her black lip and felt her stomach twist with guilt, but only for a moment. Then, feebly attempting to soften the blow she said, "Cuz your skin already looks great—" But it was too late. "Aw crap," she said and slunk lower in her squeaky theater seat.

Just the week before, a couple of Lucky Boys had slapped Grizzly's books out of her hands and tripped her. As Briar stared at the scene from the locker across the hall, she felt a strange heat rising from her stomach. She had never felt that before. She used to think that some of these kids, like Grizzly, kind-of brought on their own persecution. Well, whatever. Even if that wasn't exactly true, she had to protect herself, which meant staying out of little self-esteem crumblers like the one that was unfolding.

But that day, while watching Grizzly dab at her skinned knee and dissolve into silent tears, something in Briar snapped as the two Lucky Boys slapped high-fives at their prank. Her vision distorted, blurred really. It felt like liquid fire burned her gut, and her face flushed.

That was when she threw up on them. It came out in buckets. Honestly, Briar didn't know where all the barf came from. *I guess they aren't lucky all the time*, she thought to herself watching the boys, their faces slimed by her viscous yellow gunk, and they themselves retching in response. Much to Briar's horror, Leon Squire, the hunk, the hero, the—*him*—happened to wander by as the scene unfolded. At the sight of vomit slopped across lockers and splattered on the faces of his buddies, he doubled over and quickly sped away, holding a hand to his own mouth.

Her nickname changed from that day on. It was announced to the school in the usual way, scrawled across her locker: "Hurl Gurl." Queen of Darkness had a better ring to it, Briar mused. But people ought to keep their distance from a Hurl Gurl just the same. After all that, Briar supposed that Grizzly must now have thought they were BFFs or something stupid like that. Whatevs.

She couldn't have Grizzly and her friends orbiting around in her universe for real, or Leon might never make a move. At least in her imagination, he would make some kind of a move. She scanned the sidelines surreptitiously again. Without warning, a few Lucky Boys parted like cherubs flanking a winged God. They stepped aside just enough for Briar to see Leon standing there in all his chiseled perfection. His face, his body seemed straight out of Bullfinch's Mythology.

Shit. What am I doing? Briar thought. She rolled her eyes, covered her face and tried not to hyperventilate. *This will never work.* She tugged on the black hoodie that was loosely draped over her satin Victorian get-up, and she thumbed her handheld, trying to distract herself. She kept her gaze down to keep from hurling yet again. The screen's glow reflected blue onto her powder-pale face.

That's when something unusual caught her eye.

Instead of her expected death rock videos, Briar was surprised to be viewing a peculiar elderly woman dressed in some sort of archaic garb. She was tall, gaunt, and severe in her neck-high, pearl-buttoned shirt and red waistcoat. She had a small black tie encircling her neck, and a matching black velvet band that outlined her thin waist. There was also a black top hat—the size of a coffee cup—that defied gravity, clinging to the front of her pulled back gray hair. She peered out from the screen through miniscule glasses sitting on the end of her nose—like a puckered old librarian from the *Twilight Zone*, Briar imagined.

Briar moved her thumb to the refresh key but hesitated as the woman spoke. Though the download that played was choppy and full of intermittent scrambled pixels, Briar held her breath for a moment, captivated.

"Briar," the elderly said. She looked anxiously left and right, as if checking for unwanted listeners. The transmission became pixelated.

Say what? Briar thought. *She did not just say my name, did she?* She looked around for a moment. *Who would do this?* "You're not funny," Briar said aloud. This stopped Potato-Juliette's soliloquy.

The auditorium went silent. No laughs. No sniggering. *Okay, so maybe it's not a joke,* Briar thought. She sank deeper into her hood, acting as though she hadn't said anything.

She peered again at the screen. The image finally stabilized and picked up mid-sentence: "—a dangerous time for—" The transmission scrambled again. Then it restarted. "The Lady Or—" The image twisted a bit and cut out.

When it came back, the puckered librarian was speaking while petting a fox fur that fluffed around her neck: "A *dillywig* emissary will come—" The screen went black.

Neither the jostling of nearby auditioners nor the metallic megaphone announcement of her name could take Briar's attention from the screen. So absorbed was she that she nearly coughed up her stomach when she felt a pointed tap on her shoulder.

Briar whirled around with horror in her face. "Jeez, Dax," she said.

Dax pulled at his cinnamon winter scarf, plopped down beside Briar, and huffed warm air into his frozen hands. "Someone here needs a major tranquilizer. And here's a hint: it isn't me."

"Do you really have to creep up on people like that?"

"Here's a newsflash: you're at an audition with people all around you. It isn't exactly a haunted house." He looked at the wild variety parading up and down the theater aisles. "I take that back."

Briar looked down at her device. She thumbed it some more, trying to scroll back to what she had just seen, but the screen was now blank. "Dax, you've got to check out what I downloaded. This old lady is totally cray-cray. I swear she says my name. It'll freak you out."

Dax looked down at the blank screen on Briar's player. "Uh, yeah," he said, "love it." Then he took a moment to re-think. "First of all, cray-cray is dead. Okay? Second of all, I think someone's been hanging out with the drama geekards a little too long. Next you'll be ranting about other make-believe topics like time-travel or geometry."

Briar ignored him and continued to search for the video while Dax more thoroughly inspected the odd student assembly. He watched Potato-Juliet waddling off stage dressed in one of those flimsy pre-packaged Halloween costumes. "Wow. So this is your competition?" he asked. He had a pretty dumb stare. "Come on. Let's get out of here before it's too late."

"Don't be an ass," Briar said. She shrugged Dax's hands away. "Besides, aren't your people all about the theater?"

"I ought to slap you with these jazz hands for that. But instead, I'll file your little gem under 'Briar's bigoted comments.' Besides, theater is old-school," Dax said. He spotted a cute guy dressed in tights and wasn't sure if he was turned on or embarrassed for him. Either way, it reminded him. "Oh, that's right." He smiled. "I almost forgot—how's the stalking going?"

"Shut up!" Briar said.

"He's not even here is he? I knew it. And even if he was, what makes you think he would talk to you?"

Briar gave Dax the eye-of-death from beneath her ringed brow, but said nothing.

The director screeched from the megaphone again. "Miss Blackwood!" Unaware the amplification was still turned on, he said to someone nearby, "You mean the witch? *She's* trying out?"

"Fine," Dax said. He crossed his arms and gave up trying to suppress a sour expression. "Let's get this over with before anyone important sees us here." He grabbed Briar by her arm, ushered her toward the stage, and signaled to the director.

"But I'm telling you, freak shows like this have made us the saddest singles in our school," Dax said. "And I would like at least one of us to meet a guy—oh wait, correction: a normal guy—before we graduate."

Walking up the aisle to the stage, Dax noticed a group of boys huddled together in the shadows along a far side wall. The stage lights were not bright enough for him to see clearly who they were. He squinted and then suddenly recognized them as some of the most popular boys in school. "Holy crap." Dax sounded like someone being strangled. He gripped Briar's arm tighter.

The group of boys began nudging each other once they saw Briar about to take the stage. She peeled away from Dax and stumbled up the black steps. A hush fell over the auditorium as she slogged to the center, flat-footed and slouching, with more than a hint of annoyance.

One of the Lucky Boys shouted from the darkness, "Hey, Dracula's Daughter—bite this."

The director, spoke over the screeching megaphone, drowning out the boys' howling laughter. "Miss Blackwood," he started.

Briar couldn't see his face in the shadowy depths of the auditorium. "You do know that this is a production of *A Midsummer Night's Dream*, not *The Phantom of the Opera*."

"Nice tip, Mr. Ziegfeld. Why don't you save that for the Follies? I'd like to read my monologue, if you don't mind."

Chapter 2

Briar stood alone on the bare stage, a trickle of sweat formed on her upper lip, and her chest felt to her like it might explode. She squinted and shielded her eyes to see if Dax had fled the scene. Nope. There he was, standing in the center aisle, arms folded across his argyle sweater as though he were bracing for impact. This audition could become a memorable social disaster for both of them. Well, mainly for Briar. But whatever happened to Briar pretty much happened to Dax too, seeing as the kids viewed them as inseparable.

She winced feeling her present peril in the middle of her gut, but she hoped to pass it off as a sneer. How ironic her current vulnerability, having to recite a monologue in front of the Lucky Ones who hated her most. She couldn't use her badass image now to shield herself from their likely barrage of taunts. It made her stomach churn to know that she was right where they wanted her. *He had better still be there,* she thought. *He better be watching with his eyes on me alone.*

She was roused by the squealing megaphone. "Any time now, Miss Blackwood. I'm losing my hair."

She closed her eyes and held her breath for a moment. She felt something peculiar, but not all that unfamiliar. It was like a shift in her stomach, as though something important, something big were squeezing in. There was a feeling of liquid fire in her gut, just like when she barfed on Leon. Clenching everything down seemed like a good idea, but that caused the heat to fill her whole body. Then something strange happened.

She stepped out of the shadows and into the glow of the lone bulb that lit the stage. She closed her eyes and eased out her deep breath. Her arms hung loose and limp and she dropped her head forward. It was as if she went into a trance. Dax covered his mouth with his hands, wishing for a miracle, but thinking the worst.

Then Briar spoke. She started out mumbling almost imperceptibly through her, black, stringy bangs. But then, she raised her head and spoke with a voice and a look in her eye that was almost unrecognizable as Briar. No longer was she the awkward cynic. Her movements became elf-like, impish, and almost otherworldly. Dax didn't know how Briar did it, but body, voice and soul, she had freakin' transformed into Shakespeare's Puck. Dax pulled out his cell phone and began to video record. It was all so uncharacteristic of the Briar he knew and it was, well, kind of weird.

> *"—that you have but slumber'd here*
> *While these visions did appear.*
> *And this weak and idle theme,*
> *No more yielding but a dream—"*

On and on Briar went, quieting the side-aisle insults from the boys. Now they just stood, some slack-jawed, some blinking in disbelief.

When Briar finished her monologue, she stood for a moment, her eyes searching the faces of stunned and silenced onlookers in the cavernous auditorium. Dax burst with pride. Then from the squealing megaphone: "Thank you, Miss Witchwood—I mean Miss Blackwood. You may step down now."

Briar seemed to be in a sort of daze. She stood frozen in place, even paler than usual, like some wax museum figure. Dax rushed onstage and ushered Briar to the steps. He spoke out to the man in the dark with the megaphone. "Thanks again. And by the way, the bullhorn's a nice touch." Then under his breath: "I'm sure it makes up for one inadequacy or another."

"Next!" The director shouted though his grating amplification.

Dax hurried Briar up the center aisle, giggling. "You did it!"

he said. He tried to restrain the knot of excitement in his throat. "You were spectacular."

But Briar seemed to still be spellbound. Dax sandwiched her face between his hands to get her attention. Her face felt like refrigerated meat. He knew something was terribly wrong. He took her by the shoulders and shook until she suddenly blinked into awareness.

"Did I do that?" Briar asked. She had a strange far-away look in her eyes. "Oh my God, I did do that."

Dax exhaled with relief. "Look, I don't care if you get a role in that jerk-jockey play." He looked in Briar's eyes. She was present now, and what little color she had was returning to her cheeks. "You showed them a side of you that they've never seen before. And frankly, it was amazing. Was it a bit creepy? Yes. But it was also amazing. I got the whole thing recorded. You'll love it."

Briar knew about Dax's interest in capturing footage of anything that he thought was bizarre. And over the last few years he had amassed quite a library of anomalies. It wasn't exactly flattery to be included in this quirky little side-show. But on the other hand, she must have been something extraordinary and that made her at once secretly proud and a little afraid.

They made a beeline up the sloping aisle and almost made it to the swinging doors in the back when one of the jocks stepped in their path. It was Leon Squire. He had broken ranks with the other side-aisle cranks to stop Briar before she left. The rest of the jocks watched Leon with the same horrified silence of an audience watching a slasher movie.

"Hey," Leon mumbled. He raked a hand through his perfectly disheveled sandy locks. His biceps flexed beneath his tight white sweatshirt.

"Oh. Uh. Hi," Briar said. She stared at his arms and noticed that his shoulders were nearly as wide as a doorway. Why was he standing, incredibly, just a few feet away from her? She looked at Dax, who just shrugged. Not knowing what more she could say,

Briar stuffed her earphones into her ears and tried to force Dax out the door. But he stepped in Briar's path, arms crossed, shaking his head. Briar knew Dax would not miss an opportunity to be seen with Leon Squire actually talking to them, even if just for a moment.

She turned back to face Leon and with a tug, she pulled both earphones out. He gave his trademark half-smile that Briar had heard other girls, Luckier Girls than she, whisper about in the locker room showers.

"Hey aren't you that Hurl Gurl?" he ventured. *Oh come on,* Briar thought. *Who in their right mind could ever forget that stomach-churning hallway horror show?* She was thankful for this little courtesy just the same.

"Oh. Yeah. Something must have made me sick," Briar said. She tried to look in any direction except directly at his blinding beauty.

"Well, you're sure not sick today. Are you?" He laughed and casually gripped her shoulder with his wide, warm hand. It felt like summer at the beach, and she suddenly forgot how to breathe for a moment.

Dax saw her drowning and secretly, he motioned for Briar to at least put on a smile.

"Not yet," Briar said to Leon. She pasted on a stiff smile. "But the day's still young." She felt like she was sounding odd now, but she wasn't sure how to pull out of her small-talk nose dive.

"So, where did all of that talent come from?" he asked. He glanced over his shoulder at his friends, who were making motions at their necks to cut off the conversation.

Briar reached nervously for her necklace and spun the dangling black key between her fingers. "That was crazy, right?" She laughed and hid her trembling hand by running it through her hair.

From the shadows behind Leon came a dark, velvety, voice. "Well, take out your holy water and your wooden stakes—if it isn't Beelza-bitch, Queen of Darkness. And what a surprise, she brought her flying monkey."

It was Megan, Briar's shapely blonde foster-sister. Briar could always count on her to make any bad situation worse. And close behind, as always, was Megan's sycophantic sister Marnie. They must have been hiding among the other students in the auditorium, waiting for a chance to strike. And here it was.

"Flying monkey," Marnie echoed. She laughed and stared vacantly into the air. "What does that even mean?"

Dax couldn't help himself. "Wow, I've been practicing my fake laugh all night. Should I drag it out now?"

Megan smirked at Dax. "Well, I don't know. It seems to me that you'd be the drag expert." Then she squared off with Briar.

"Hi Megan," Leon said. "Hi, Marnie," he added as an afterthought. He didn't even glance at her. "Oh, I almost forgot—" He pulled out a small black leather-bound book from his backpack. Briar recognized it was her diary. "Here's that book you loaned me." He handed it to Megan and Briar snapped it away.

"My diary?" Briar said. And it felt like someone had socked her in the stomach.

"What?" Leon said. "Oh jeez. I'm sorry. I didn't know."

"Is that what that was?" Megan asked. "I thought I brought you the collected works of Edgar Allan Poe." She flipped her silky hair with satisfaction. "Oh well. I'm sure it was just as disturbing."

Leon looked at Briar, horrified. "What? No. I didn't even read it."

Briar felt as though she was sinking into the floor. It was common knowledge that Megan had her eye on Leon. And it was a high crime that Briar had even made eye contact with him.

Megan turned to Briar. "We heard that you were trying out for the play, and we had to see for ourselves."

Leon squared his jaw with a patient smile. "Wasn't she awesome?"

"What a shocker, huh?" Megan said. "Maybe she's finally found her niche. Anything would be better than this phase she's been going through. I mean really. With those boots and a corset, I can't tell if she's an army recruit or going to the *Rocky Horror Picture Show*."

Marnie laughed. "Yeah, now that she's getting a life, I guess we can take her off suicide watch."

This was too much for Dax, who by now could feel his fists tightening. "You girls are such a delight," he said. "You're just sugar and spice and barely suppressed rage. Shouldn't you be at home treating your herpes?" He laid his arms around their shoulders. "Oh, sorry. I didn't mean to jostle your silicone."

Megan squirmed away and grabbed Leon by the arm. "Wow, look, Dicks," she snapped.

"It's Dax," he replied.

"Of course it is. Well, first of all *Dax*, these are real, and I frequently lose my balance."

Marnie looked up from her texting. "Yeah...mine are made in Korea."

Megan squinted at Marnie. "...Anyway. If we want your input, we'll be sure to contact you. You're usually hanging out in the men's room, right?"

"That's right, I'm in the stall next to you."

Megan's face turned the color of a red-velvet cupcake. She faced Dax like someone who was going to start a fight, but Leon intervened by grabbing Megan around the waist. He led her to the auditorium doors, and once she was going through, she looked back to toss Briar a wicked grin. Mission accomplished.

Dax stood for a second in stunned silence. "Wow. That bitch out-maneuvered me." There was an awkward silence. "Well, that was uncomfortable," he said.

He waited for Briar's response, but Briar was already marching flat footed in her grunge boots past the wall of misfits, headed for the emergency exit. In her haste, she must have pulled at her necklace, as the strand and the black key clattered to the linoleum floor near Dax's feet.

Chapter 3

Some days simply bite.

When you're dead, it's different. You don't have to worry any more about Lucky Ones, missed chances, love never realized. Pain seems far, far away now. Distant: like some small desert island I can just make out on the horizon. It's funny, 'cause I expected angels or white light or some happy shit like that when I died. But it's really just a whole lot of nothing.

Well, that, and a bunch of re-runs of those last days that play themselves out over and over again. I see it now. And it all makes perfect sense.

I should have stepped up and finally put Megan and Marnie in their place. I should have told Leon how I felt about him that day at the auditions. I should have done a lot of things.

"One door, one use." It still rings in my ears.

One life, one use.

Boo-friggin'-hoo, right?

Briar stomped home along the most obscure side streets she could find with such fury that she thought she might crack the sidewalk. Striding down rows of tidy vintage houses and predictably manicured lawns, she buried her face, wet now with tears and black mascara streaks, beneath the covering of her hood. She had the volume from her player turned up so loudly that passing cars probably heard it.

My diary. O.M.G. Those deranged pom-pom packers actually handed over my private thoughts for Leon and his buddies to peruse over post-football burgers and fries. Briar cooled off briefly, remembering that he said he hadn't actually read the diary. Whether or not he didn't was not the point any longer. She had lived under the regime of Megan, Marnie and Matilda, their mother, for ten tongue-chomping years.

It's not like her social worker was any help either. It wasn't exactly her fault. She was busy keeping a roof over Briar's head and wasn't too interested in rocking whatever boat she could find.

Ugh. Briar hated Megan, hated Marnie, hated Leon, and most of all hated herself.

She got several blocks away from the campus before Leon drove up alongside her in his tricked-out vintage American muscle car.

He shouted out the passenger window, the car trailing her at her own pace, its twin tailpipes rumbling. "Hey, where are you going?"

Briar wiped her eyes with her sleeves and flared a nose-ringed nostril. "Why are you following me around in a car for a loser with alimony payments and a beer-gut?" She sped up and Leon followed her.

He pulled up alongside again and said, "Your friend said you dropped this." He held out her skeleton key necklace.

"Gee, thanks," she said.

"Look," Leon shouted. "Would you just stop for a second?"

"Why should I stop?" Briar said. She couldn't even look at him.

"You know what? Everyone back there sucked. I get it. But don't let them ruin what you did today. You were really—I don't know—special at that audition. I didn't know you could light up like that. I was totally blown away."

Briar stopped and faced him. "So what? Now you suddenly want to get to know me?" she asked.

"Yeah, why not?"

"Oh please," Briar said. "Like I haven't seen a thousand tacky teen movies where the hot jock was dared by his buddies to talk to the sad, freaky girl."

"It's not like that, really. Wait. Hot? Did you say I'm hot?"

"What is it like then, Leon?" she asked. She stepped close to the car now and leaned into the window.

Leon sat dumbfounded, his eyebrows raised.

After an awkward silence, Briar continued, "Yeah, well thanks for bringing the necklace," she said. Her words sounded like someone who had won a battle. But somehow she knew that she had lost one too.

Briar reached in and snapped the necklace away from Leon. "Sorry you wasted your time," she said and turned away.

Seemingly from nowhere, two looming shadows swooshed behind Briar's back. From the corners of her eyes, they looked like two enormous wolves. Impossible. But they were too swift for her to see for sure.

When she turned all the way around, all she saw were tightly manicured bushes rustling in front of the nearby suburban-blah house. Briar felt the now familiar sensation of heat rushing up from her stomach. Her heart fluttered. She worried she might barf again.

She quickly turned to Leon. He grinned at her with a look she had never seen on a boy's face before. She would have found that comforting under normal circumstances. But right now she wondered if she would hear growling if Leon turned off his chugging, souped-up engine.

"Did you just...? Didn't you see...?" Briar asked. She pointed to the bushes but hesitated.

Leon continued to grin. "Didn't I see what?"

Briar turned back toward the bushes and watched as two enormous, drooling wolves crept out on all fours into plain view. She had never seen creatures like this before. They seemed to be almost the size of humans. They bared their teeth, tucked back their ears, and hunched forward. The gray-brown fur on their backs raised with tense excitement.

Briar's eyes widened, and she wrenched the door handle several times trying to open it in a panic, but it wouldn't open. "Let me in!" she said. She peered over her shoulder with wild eyes.

"Let you in?" Leon cupped his hands to make a fake megaphone. "Paging Dr. Jekyll."

"Yeah. Cute. Let me in. I forgive you," Briar said. The wolves were tracking her every move with their narrowed eyes, and they snarled.

"You forgive me? For what?" Leon asked.

"I don't know. I don't care. Just let me in, hurry!" She wrenched the door handle again, and it broke off in her grip. She held it up and Leon looked with wide eyes.

"How did you—? Never mind," he said. He opened the door. Briar ducked in, slammed the door behind her, and rolled up the window. The two wolves loped forward at full speed and flanked the car.

"What's going on?" Leon asked. He craned his neck trying to look at whatever it was Briar seemed to be watching with dread.

"Are you telling me you don't you see them?"

"See what?"

Briar sank into the seat below window level. Why didn't Leon see what was so obvious and so dangerous? It didn't matter. All she knew was that she needed to get them away from there, and quickly.

"Nothing. I made a mistake," she said, and bit her lip.

She popped her head up just in time to see one of the wolves scrambling up on top of the car. Her heart thumped into her throat.

"Leon, please do as I say and drive away really fast."

"Okay—any special reason?"

"You obviously have this car for a reason. Let's see it peel out." Briar tried to sound calm, but she was dizzy with fear.

With a look of confusion, Leon shrugged. He pressed his foot solidly on the accelerator and screeched away from the curb. Briar sat up and looked out the back window. The wolf on top of the car slid down and tumbled to the asphalt. It rolled back up, but this time it stood erect on its crooked hind legs and extended its clawed front legs. *What the hell is that?* It loped along awkwardly like a...Briar dared not think it. It was impossible. But if she were ever to describe it, it seemed like it was a werewolf.

"Can you go any faster?"

Leon laughed. "Faster? Do you want me to get a ticket?"

She looked out the back window and the creature was sprinting, clawing at the air, its eyes ferocious and crazed. It had reached the back bumper and crunched its jaws down into it.

"Never mind," she said. Impulsively, she lifted her leg over Leon's.

"Wow. Okay. You're a fast worker," he laughed.

Briar rolled her eyes. "Flatter yourself much?" she asked. Then she slammed her foot on the brakes. The car squealed with a cloud smoke and the burn of rubber billowing out from behind. The wolf rolled away, but righted itself, nothing but madness and hunger in its eyes. It lunged at full speed.

Between Briar and Leon together controlling the vehicle, the car fishtailed and spun wildly in a half circle. It came to stop, directly facing the wolf. In its wild chase, the creature did not account for the stalling of the car, and it slammed into the front of it, flipped over the hood and landed in the street. The animal twitched and convulsed for a moment and then dissolved into a thick cloud of black smoke. It trailed along the surface of the street like a low London haze until it eventually found its way to a gutter, and then it slipped down into it with the other street filth.

Briar blinked and stared, eyes wide with disbelief, feeling a deep throb in her throat and stomach. She flipped back in her seat to face the front. She pressed against the dashboard and looked in all directions through the windshield, searching for the second wolf. But the neighborhoods looked empty of any movement whatsoever.

"Damn girl. You're a wild one," Leon said, letting out a whoop.

Just then, Briar saw the second wolf stand up on Leon's side of the car. It held its long jagged front claws out to strike, its amber eyes seemed to glow, and it juddered with a deep, dangerous sound.

Briar screamed. She slammed her foot on top of his once more and punched the accelerator to the floor with all her might.

"What the—?" Leon shouted, throwing his head back laughing hysterically.

"Oh my God! Oh my God!" Briar muttered over and over.

The wolf ran alongside the speeding car and began biting at Leon's door handle.

Briar stomped on the brakes again and the two of them lurched into the dashboard. The wolf tumbled for a moment, but then stood up. Unexpectedly, the car engine sputtered, and conked out.

"Jeez, not again," Leon said. He shoved his door open and stepped out of the car.

"Leon no! What are you doing?" Briar shouted.

"Relax. This happens all the time. I'll be right back."

"Are you crazy? Get back in here!" But he heard nothing, as the car door slammed shut.

Briar watched Leon stride up to the hood and pop it open. The wolf loped up from behind, grew to a stand on its back legs, and towered over him with its carnivorous mouth wide open.

A silver comet, the size of a baseball flew up from the south, with a trail of glittering dust. It swooshed over the car, and slammed into the creature's chest. A second later, it emerged from the animal's back. The wolf arched backward and cried in livid agony. It writhed and strained as it crumbled to the pavement.

Briar slid across the front seats, and spilled out onto the street. The animal lay close enough by that she could see the red of its gums, and its long sharp teeth, protruding through its foaming saliva. The monster convulsed and scraped at the ground with its eyes rolled back.

"You are hilarious!" Leon laughed. He came around to Briar and helped her to her feet. But she was still in shock and unable to stand independently. She wobbled, and slumped. Leon caught her quickly and ushered her to the passenger seat with his arm caught around her waist. "I've never met a girl who liked these kind of stunts. Awesome!"

"No. Leon. You don't understand," Briar said feebly. She was going in and out of a hazy awareness, and wasn't sure if she was actually saying anything, or if what she wanted to say was still in her head. Leon slammed the passenger door and strode past the creature, which seemed to be regaining its bearings. Briar gasped and clutched the dashboard. "Hurry, get in here," she shouted.

Leon slid into his seat and closed the door. "Take it easy." He laughed with his nose crinkled. "What are you so riled up about? Wait. Is this more of your acting?"

Briar's eyes were glued to the wolf that stood again, its ears tucked and its muzzle curled into the most repulsive snarl, seeming more determined than ever to destroy.

She reached over and twisted the key in the ignition. The engine just chugged once and then ticked like a metronome. The wolf caught its claws into the top of Leon's window and started to drag it down. Leon looked amazed by the window that seemed to be opening by itself. "How are you doing that?" He laughed.

"Oh no. This is it!" Briar shouted.

Another silver comet from the same unseen source sailed up to the car like a firework shot from a cannon, striking it from behind and causing it to lurch. The engine turned over and purred. Briar clomped her foot down on the gas pedal again and the car sped away. The wolf bayed angrily and charged down the street behind them. Briar turned around in time to see a third comet strike the wolf in the middle of its back. It arched and then fell to the asphalt. Then it too dissolved into a cloud of black smoke that dissipated every which way into the shadows of the neighborhood—beneath trees and under cars. It fled wherever it could find a scrap of darkness.

Briar looked in every direction, trying to understand whatever it was that happened. She felt numb and detached.

"You are a lot of fun. I never knew that about you," Leon said.

"Yeah," Briar said, looking around for any more creatures. "Fun." But nothing came after that.

"How did you do all of those stunts?" he asked.

"I—really don't know," Briar said. She had never acted before with such speed and conviction. "Can you just take me home now?"

Chapter 4

Leon rumbled up to the Saulks, Briar's foster home, with its yellowing, antiqued details. It was truly a paint-chipped disaster with its shutters hanging at a tilt on broken hinges and cracked flowerpots on the door stoop full of ruined stems. Still it had remnants of grand old architecture with its cornices and a spire atop a conical central roof that spiked high into the cloudy sky.

The neighborhood was filled with other turn-of-the-century homes featuring dirt-and-weed lawns, strewn with abandoned shopping carts, jammed between rusty cars on broken weedy curbs. It all stood in stark contrast to the neat rows of scrubbed and clipped prefabs that Leon noticed just across the cement wash.

"Nice...uh..." Leon mumbled. But he stopped himself and tried to change the subject. He gazed up at the low hanging thunderheads. "Looks like a storm coming."

She didn't hear him at all. She stared out the passenger window replaying the danger that Leon couldn't seem to see. It sent her into a spiral of self-doubt. She touched her legs to test if she was dreaming. It wasn't enough, so she grasped Leon's hand, and felt its strength and the soft hair at his wrist.

Leon responded by smiling his crooked, handsome smile. That snapped Briar back to the moment, to the front seat of the rumbly car, to the dreamy guy in her reach. And, as if suddenly realizing everything, Briar inhaled sharply, but could find nothing to say. She had imagined this very moment so many times before, but it was never under such bizarre circumstances. What do you say after being chased by werewolves?

"So, I'd really like to see you again. That is, if it's okay with you," he said. He gave Briar a glance that she read as "smoldering." But since she thought she recently saw werewolves, she wasn't sure what she could trust.

"Huh?" she asked. There was no question that she wanted to see him. But she flashed back to the wolves, their fierce amber eyes and snapping jaws, the danger that they just faced—or the delusion she just dreamed up. Either way it caused Briar to turn away in a dark withdrawal, surveying the area for more of *them*.

"I don't know," she said. She turned to look out the window at her house, glancing up at Megan and Marnie's second story bedroom windows. This was all a bad idea, she realized. Spending even a few moments in Leon's car parked in front of their house, maybe even seeing him again, it had trouble written all over it. "I kind of thought you were into Megan. I mean, she's so pretty." Briar could feel herself biting on her last words.

Leon laughed. "Of course I'm into Megan. I mean, who wouldn't be, right?"

Briar turned back to face him, but her stomach lurched and she felt her eyes begin to well up at his confession. The strange adventure they just shared made her feel as though they had somehow connected. But just like the werewolves, it seemed that there was nothing really there. She should have known that anything she imagined to be between them was little more than a moment of pity for the weird girl and a sympathy ride home.

"Oh—oh. Right," Briar said. She looked down at the floor mats. "Of course. I'm so stupid." Briar felt a flush of heat in her face. "You're into Megan," she said. Then, for the first time, she effortlessly smiled at Leon. "Well, thanks for the ride home." She opened the door and swung her boots out.

"Hey, I didn't know if you knew it, but I auditioned for the play too," he said. He smiled. And in spite of herself, Briar smiled back. "Anyway," he said, "I was thinking that if we both get cast, we could hang out and practice our lines together."

Briar nodded as casually as she could but felt as though a fifty-pound weight had landed on her. She was such an idiot. Of course he was into Megan. Of course he was into featherheaded Lucky Girls. Of course Briar never had a chance with a boy like

Leon, except in her fevered imagination. "Yeah, sure. That sounds cool," she lied.

Briar ducked out of the car, fitted on her old deadpan like armor, and forced indifference. She stood holding the car door open, silently facing the Saulks' home. Out of the corner of her eye, she noticed that the upstairs curtain in Megan's room stirred and a shadow moved away from the window. Her heart skipped a beat and her breathing halted. She wasn't sure it would ever return. *Freak on a stick! Did one of them see me?*

"Check you later," Leon said.

She turned to face him with a feeling of such heaviness that she wouldn't have been able to explain it. She wanted him to stay, even if that meant the werewolves would come back. *Especially* if they came back. She knew that once she closed that car door, he wouldn't be there anymore. She knew that it was all polite and mannered, but he didn't really mean what he was saying. He wouldn't see her again. It was over. Briar felt it. And then she closed the door.

As he drove away, she hoped this would all be forgotten. She would have to lay low for a while, try to blend in at school, get lost among the shuffle so that she would never have to come face to face with him again. *Okay, well, maybe that's a little melodramatic,* Briar admitted. But the whole episode was better put behind her. She walked up to the front door, planning her next move: sneaking into the house without being noticed.

Very carefully Briar opened the front door, taking care not to open it so far that it would hit the familiar squeaky spots. She took off her boots and padded down the hall to the second door. The Saulks had fixed up a bed, a table, and a small dresser for Briar in their basement so that they could keep all of their discarded belongings in one spot.

Briar never said a word about anything—and neither did her over-worked social worker, Mrs. Poplar. Bouncing from one home to another took an emotional toll, and Briar decided that she'd trade the risks for quasi-stability, even if it came at a cost. She knew better than to invite trouble, although, in truth, her very existence in this house—including living among the basement of forgotten things—was always a hair's width away from trouble.

So what were Briar's options except to learn how to live with the damp, the cold, the spiders, and the rats? She learned how to keep her mouth shut, move quietly in the dark, come up only when no one was there, and live as invisibly as she could.

It was always strange to Briar that existing in this way didn't seem to bother her as much as she thought it might. The perpetual basement darkness, the musty odor, the silence, the soft rustling of rodents all became a source of solace and familiarity. At least she was away from the Saulks, and that's all that really mattered.

Briar eased onto her mattress and listened carefully for footsteps. Even when the Saulks tried to sneak up on her, to entangle her in one of their paranoid schemes, the basement steps, warped and rotting, complained as soon as someone stepped foot on them. So they made a nice early warning device.

Briar also developed a series of moves that made coming and going from her basement world possible. Holding the drippy wall moldings, stepping on the far left or right of each stair, and finally swinging off an exposed pipe to miss the last several steps altogether, she was as silent as a midnight ghost.

She listened, holding her breath for a moment. Once she was certain that no one was coming, she fished around for a cell phone she hid between some of the exposed wall insolation near the head of her bed. There was simply no way she'd be able to make it through the night without sharing with Dax what had happened. Although Briar was outnumbered in this house, she still had Mrs. Poplar watching out for her the best she could without jeopardizing the situation. She was the one who bought Briar the cell phone some time ago, providing that she keep it hidden from Megan, Marnie, and Matilda. And Briar fiercely protected the secret, as it was one of her few lifelines to sanity.

Briar dialed and almost immediately she heard the muffled sound of a ring tone from under her bed. She lifted the ragged brown-stained coverlet that hung past the bed frame. There below, amid the crowd of dirty socks and jumbled books, was Dax smiling his goofy I-know-you've-got-a-secret-so-spill-it grin.

"Hey...sorry to scare you like that," Dax said. He squirmed from beneath the bed, and wiped dust clumps off his clingy khakis. "Hoo boy, you really need to sweep under there. One of those dust bunnies had babies right in front of me."

"Dax, what are you doing?"

"What?! Are you kidding me? You hitch a ride with Leon Squire and you think you're not giving me details?" He sauntered over to the chair just below the high window that opened out to the scrubby bushes and crumbled, winter-fallen leaves. He climbed on top and then shut it. "By the way, did you know that most robberies are due to windows being left open and unattended?"

"Nice—" Briar said.

"Hey, what were my choices? Get smothered by Megan and Marnie's pom-poms? Have their little Christ-Brigade burn me at the stake? No thanks."

Briar was only half listening—really bursting inside about the wolves. She had to say something, but wasn't sure how to broach the subject without looking like the cheese in her taco had finally slipped.

Dax flopped backward onto Briar's squeaky mattress. "By the way—do you realize that they called you back for the part of the fairy queen? That's one of the leads! You're gonna have some hallway cred now—well, until they see you in wings and body glitter. Then all bets are off."

"Dax, listen," Briar said. "On the way home, I saw something

I can't explain, but I don't want you to think that I've totally come unhinged."

"Oh you poor confused thing," Dax said. He stroked Briar's raven hair. "It's called a penis."

"No! Stop it. I'm being serious." Briar pulled away and sat up. "I'm not talking about Leon, fool. But what I'm about to tell you—you have to swear that you'll just listen and won't jump to conclusions."

"Okay, I swear." Dax held up a hand as though on a witness stand.

"Because the temptation to judge will be there—"

Dax sat up. "I am trying so hard not to submerge your head in a toilet right now. Just spit it out."

"I saw wolves," Briar said.

"Okay..." Dax raised one eyebrow. "Is that what you kids are calling it now?"

"No, Dax, you don't understand," Briar said. She started pacing back and forth at the foot of the bed. "I saw wolves—or something like wolves. They walked on their hind legs, like humans and they tried to attack us in Leon's car."

Dax had a ridiculous smile on his face. "And what did Leon think...of the wolves?" He burst into laughter and got up from the bed. "What a load of bull crap!" He jumped up and continued to the window. "You will do anything to avoid telling me what happened between you two. Fine. Keep your tawdry tales of vehicular seduction to yourself."

Then he checked his cell phone. "Oh, my parents are gonna kill me. I was supposed to be home hours ago." He hopped up onto the chair stationed below the window. He opened it up, clambered outside and then stuck his head back in. "Oh my God, there's wolves out here." He shook the bushes. "Down boy! Briar, I need a dog-biscuit, stat!"

"Yeah, you got me!" Briar laughed feebly. But it felt like her lungs collapsed. Dax was the only person she could trust, and even he couldn't believe her.

"See you tomorrow," he said. Then he scraped by the low, dry branches. "And next time, bring a chew toy for your friends."

"Yeah, see you," Briar said.

Chapter 5

It was midnight and Briar still hadn't changed from her cinched-up gown. But there she lay in bed, eyes fixed on the brown-ringed ceiling. It was crazy. There were no such thing as walking wolves, and she knew it. But she couldn't erase the image of those fierce amber eyes, and those sharp teeth like ivory knives coming for her. *How could they exist? Simple. They don't.*

But then she remembered the weird podcast with the gaunt elderly woman. *It's dangerous,* she said. She called Briar by name. *Dangerous?* Briar wondered but only for a second. It was just too crazy. Neither of these things existed; they were evidence of her runaway imagination.

As she lay there, straining to doze, the dark muffled silence of the basement was disrupted by noises of shuffling shoes and kicked boxes. They seemed to come from the closet. *What?* Briar sat up, and she froze. Her mind became clear and taut, as sharp as the silence that now saturated the bedroom.

What noise? There was no noise. There were no wolves or any other creatures. There was no podcast calling her name. And totally no noise. Her gut twisted and told a different story. It was one that she wasn't sure would end well.

She was about to ease back onto her squeaky mattress, when the entire closet door thumped heavily. *For shit's sake, now that was a noise.* Briar caught her breath and heard heart throbs in her ears. "Dax?" she whispered, but no one answered. "Dax, you little creep. Very funny."

Briar wasn't sure which was worse, a response, or none. She clenched the edge of the mattress and eased herself off. She kept her eyes on the closet door as it slowly groaned open on ruined hinges.

"Dax?"

Nothing. The very air was dead. Her breathing stopped.

A white-gloved hand appeared from behind the door and gripped its edge.

Briar rolled her eyes. "By the way, your little ghost in the closet routine isn't really working—but the gloves are very *Breakfast at Tiffany's*." Still, whoever it was didn't respond. Briar began to feel sick with fear.

She bounded off the bed, sprinted to a far wall and snapped on the light. She grabbed a baseball bat propped up on a wall. "I see you," she shouted, "get out of there."

Like a coiled spring, a tall man leapt out from the closet. He was tall, thin and had a short, cropped beard. He wore a shimmering bustled ball-gown that glittered in the harsh overhead light. The strapless dress left his dark wooly chest rather exposed. "Briar Blackwood—is it really you? Am I dreaming?" the man asked. He straightened up and then stared at her.

Seemingly unaware of his height, he nearly grazed the crown of his vertical powdered wig against the low paint-peeled ceiling. He had a curious look in his stare. His eyes beamed clear and bright. But there was another world behind that clarity. It was a world of secrets, mysteries and things that wished to remain unseen.

Briar could feel the rise of the familiar, strange, burning sensation in the pit of her stomach. She gripped the bat tightly and cocked it back.

"Oh dear," the man said. His voice had the deep tone of a stringed bass. "A ball gown, yet again" he said. He looked down at his outfit, but seemed rather blasé about it. "That makes thrice this week." He sighed heavily and reached up to discover the powdered wig. He scowled darkly. "This is absolutely ridiculous. Glamorous, yes, but ridiculous."

Briar swooshed the bat to warn him. "Get back. I mean it."

"I know how this must seem. But try to stay calm." He tapered his voice to a whisper, but his resonance still hummed in her chest. He put a white-gloved finger to his lips. She opened her mouth to shout. But before she could issue a single sound, he speedily drew shapes—all geometric forms—in the air with his hand, finishing with a finger pointed toward her throat. That was when Briar felt something inside tighten. She grabbed at her neck with one hand and tried to shriek, but nothing came.

Her screams silenced, the man took a casual step toward her. But having little practice walking in high heels, he tilted to one side and steadied himself on a nearby table. "I'm so terribly sorry," he said. "If anyone knew that I used mute-magic on Briar of the Black Woods... You won't mention this, will you?"

She stared with her mouth open, still trying to speak, and the baseball bat to which she clung drooped toward the floor.

"Well, of course you can't say anything just yet. But when you can, please don't."

Briar tried to force another sound, but her face just reddened and her neck tightened further. It felt like a Chinese finger trap for her voice.

"Straining makes things worse," he said. "Now come with me. Spies are everywhere, and they've finally found you."

He tottered across the basement toward Briar. She flattened herself like a board against the wall, taking a stranglehold on the bat again. "I'm sorry," said the man, "but didn't you get our message? We saw you watching through your device."

As soon as he walked close enough, she raised the bat and swung at him. But he made another quick gesture with his white satin hand, and the baseball bat exploded into a flurry of white streamers and confetti that fluttered against his lacey ruffles like the first flakes of winter.

"Briar, please. Weren't the wolves enough for you?" he said. He brushed the mess away. Briar stood agog at the explosion of confetti all around her, but the word "wolves" seemed to penetrate her stupefaction. Briar mouthed something. And the man, exasperated, touched her throat. "Only if you promise not to scream." She nodded. He flicked his finger, as though he was turning on a light switch, and suddenly she could speak.

"Please don't hurt me," Briar said. She felt out of breath as her throat eased out of its cramp.

"Hurt you! Don't be ridiculous. I am here to save you." He turned toward an old cracked hanging mirror and adjusted his beauty mark. He teetered back toward the closet, like someone walking a tightrope, and he balanced himself against the wall. "Now, if you value your life, you will get into that closet with me!"

He opened the door and unsteadily lurched inward, doing his best to get his fluffed-up petticoats to cooperate. Briar rushed up and slammed the door behind him. There was a chair sitting beneath the window, and she jammed it between the knob and the floor, to brace the door shut.

Right on cue, the door at the top of the steps angrily scraped open, wood against wood, and Briar heard the unmistakable, unapologetic footsteps of Megan, Marnie, and Matilda, Briar's foster mother, clambering down.

Matilda was a beefy woman with broad, rounded ape-like shoulders. She was a former prison guard who tried to offset her machismo with bottle-blonde puffy hair, a French manicure, and deep makeup layers. She stood between her two daughters with mannish hands set defiantly on her hips.

Briar tried to wipe the astonishment from her face at seeing Megan and Marnie both wearing fuzzy slippers and awful matching pink crocheted bathrobes. Briar had never seen the girls after dusk, and knowing what lengths they took to assure a cultivated daytime look, she was taken aback by their atrocious get-ups.

"Oh Jeez," Briar said. She wasn't sure if she should feel relieved or astounded.

She started across the room, but Matilda held up a hand. "Stop right there."

"What? Stop? No you don't understand—" Briar cut her words short. She glanced over her shoulder at the closet. She knew they wouldn't believe her.

"Dear God. Here we go again," Megan said.

Matilda flashed her sloppily mascaraed eyes. "Now that's not quite fair, Megan." She crossed her arms so that they balanced atop her preposterously enormous bosom. "Let's give Briar a chance to explain."

Briar swallowed hard. "There was—something down here. I was scared. You didn't hear anything?"

"Well, that's just sad," said Megan.

"Pitiful, really," Marnie added. She was distracted with texting.

Matilda ignored Megan and narrowed her eyes at Briar. "Something? Down here?" She advanced on Briar, looking left and right. "And just what did you see?"

Marnie chimed in, bored as ever. "Maybe it was her queer-bait friend."

Matilda got red-faced. "We don't talk like that. This is a Christian home. We pray for all sinners here, whether they're gay, Jewish, or of Latin descent."

"Mother, that was so divinely inspired," Megan said.

"Thank you, darling. Now what the hell is going on down here?"

Briar knew she was screwed no matter what she said now. "There was a man in the closet," she finally blurted out. Sounding crazy was easier than she thought.

"Oh, then it definitely wasn't Dax," Marnie said. She was still glued to her phone. "He's been out of the closet since he could toddle."

Matilda paraded across the basement, fists clenched, trains of yellow chiffon fluttering around her rump. "A man you say?" She pounded on the closet door. "Who's in there? Come out!" But there was no answer.

"I'll tell you what's in there, mother," said Megan. "Briar's desperate cry for help. You know the rumors. For all we know she conjured up a demon."

Matilda yanked away the chair wedged beneath the doorknob and jerked the closet door open. But it was empty, except for Briar's few black outfits hanging lifelessly above some jumbled shoes.

Megan shook her head. "It just breaks the Baby Jesus' heart."

Staring into the emptiness, Briar felt a cold panic that started in her stomach. "I don't understand…"

Megan inserted herself again. "There's something more mother. I just didn't want to upset you. But, at school today, Briar stood on stage in front of everyone and spoke in tongues. I was so frightened."

Marnie picked her teeth. "Yeah me too."

"A sign of the Beast," Matilda blurted. Then she threw a hammy arm around Briar's shoulder. "But we mustn't give up on Christ's lost lamb."

"I pray every night for her soul," said Megan.

"It's true. She's down on her knees a lot!" Marnie added.

Megan glared.

Matilda then noticed Briar's phone on the bed. "What is *this*?" She snapped up the phone in her sweaty fist.

Briar's heart dropped into her stomach. "I don't know. There's so much junk in this basement—maybe it belongs to one of you?"

Matilda powered it up and scanned the logs. "Well, what a coincidence. Whoever owns this phone also calls a so-called boy named Dax." Her face tightened and her caked makeup flaked. "Who is paying for this phone Briar? Is it drugs? The Lord hates liars, and drug addicts, and cell phone users."

Marnie shoved her own phone into her robe.

"I—I…" Briar dared not say.

"We've tried mother—you've tried. There's no shame in calling Mrs. Poplar to put an end to all of this."

Matilda stuffed the phone between her bosoms. "Are you crazy? What do you think will happen when Mrs. Poplar gets involved?"

Megan tried to look angelic. "Well, I suppose she'll find Briar a more suitable placement."

"And just where do you think the check comes from every month for your salon trips and your...enhancements?" Matilda snapped. "No. We must help poor Briar in her hour of need. It's time to pray like never before. Girls, go bring down the kneelers and light the votives. We shall hold a night-long vigil to expunge the demons from this household."

Marnie shoved Megan. "She's talking about you."

Matilda snarled at Briar. "As for Miss Blackwood, you'd better pray with us that I don't change my mind."

Briar suspected she'd never change her mind, as long as the support checks kept coming, which meant that Matilda didn't have to go to work.

"Come along girls," Matilda yelled over her shoulder. "We need to find the heavy crucifix."

They were stopped in their tracks when three sharp knocks sounded from inside the closet.

Chapter 6

All four of them stood holding their breath, staring in disbelief at the paint-crackled closet door.

It knocked from the inside again.

"This better not be one of your tricks, you little worm." Matilda lathered up on her words. "Go open it up," she ordered Briar. But really, she was afraid to do it herself.

Briar edged toward the door, reached for the knob, but then hesitated. "It was probably mice. I've heard them before."

"Open-the-door." Matilda barked like a drill sergeant. But before Briar could do anything, the door swung open. Inside was Mrs. Poplar, dressed in the most outlandish fashion imaginable. She was short and round, with the lumps and crevices of middle age, and she wore a hip-hugging gray fishtail skirt with brass buttons that swept down one side to the floor. Her white blouse was a cascade of lace, and she sported an oversized hat with iridescent peacock plumage that bounced in all directions. A brass monocle with three telescopic lenses was fitted over her left eye.

"What in the world?" Mrs. Poplar asked. She adjusted the lenses of her monocle and ogled the Saulks.

Briar and her foster family stood awash in breathless astonishment, gawking at the tiny closet, barely big enough for Briar's clothes, stunned at the improbability of it all.

Mrs. Poplar stepped into the room and shut the door with a back kick from her button-down shoes. "I've been knocking for some time now. Were you going to let me wait on the front porch all night?"

"Front porch—" Matilda was disoriented, trying to understand the outlandish situation. "Mrs. Poplar, you're in Briar's basement closet. However—did you find your way there?" She approached Mrs. Poplar who abruptly turned aside and began inspecting the basement, twisting her monocle left and right, while scribbling on a clipboard she held tight to her breast.

"Are you questioning me, Mrs. Saulk?" Poplar asked. "You know, if you expect an explanation for everything in life, you'll be sadly disappointed."

She sized Matilda up and scribbled a short note.

"There's only one word to describe your behavior Mrs. Saulk—and that word is rude," Poplar said. "That is, the word is not itself rude—and yet, it is."

"What?" Matilda asked. She slowly backed away from the strange woman who was rummaging around and taking notes. "Girls," she said quietly, "why don't you go upstairs and—make a phone call, hmm?"

Dull as ever, it took Marnie a few moments to finally understand. "Oh right. Gotcha."

She poked her sister's side and they slunk up the steps. Suddenly the door at the top crashed open with great force, embedding itself into the wall. The girls screamed in stereo. A slim shadowed figure stood in the doorframe. A flash of lightning illuminated her silhouette. The surprise knocked the girls off balance, causing them to jumble together down the steps.

"Looks like the storm has finally arrived," Poplar said. "In any event, I brought along my supervisor from the Department of Children's Services, Mrs. Myrtle. I hope you don't mind."

"Mind?!" Matilda said. "Lady, are you nuts? What is going on here?"

The woman atop the stairs took dignified, starchy strides down. Mrs. Myrtle was unusually tall, gaunt, and severe. She too wore clothing that looked as though it was from another era. Then it clicked for Briar. The neck-high pearl-buttoned shirt and red waistcoat, miniscule glasses sitting on the end of her nose, the tiny black top hat perched upon her pulled back gray hair—it was the woman she saw on her handheld device this afternoon.

"Good evening, Mrs. Saulk," Myrtle said. She pursed her

crinkled lips as though smelling something sour and she petted a burnt orange fox stole that she had clasped around her shoulders.

"This is an outrage!" Matilda simmered. "You can't just invade my home. Where are your credentials?"

"*My* credentials?" Myrtle peered over her spectacles. "And just where are *your* credentials? How am I to know you are who you say you are?"

"What?" Matilda looked as though she had something vile in her mouth. "I haven't—what?"

Ignoring Matilda, Myrtle spoke directly to Poplar. "Is this the creature into whose charge we have left our Miss Blackwood?"

"Hey, nut bag! I'm not deaf. You can talk to me directly," Matilda said. "If you don't mind—"

"Oh, dear. It speaks," Myrtle said. She developed a lingering sneer. "I don't mind at all," she remarked. She sauntered past Matilda with a posture as straight and true as freshly milled lumber. She tried to force a social smile, but it looked more like someone smelling urine. Then it morphed into a look of outright revulsion while eyeing Briar's shabby furnishings.

"You are aware, Mrs. Saulk, that you've signed a county contract that we may inspect the premises at any time. Well, any time happens to be now. Congratulations."

"This is the middle of the night. You can't barge in here!"

"It is exactly nine forty-five, Mrs. Saulk. If it was the middle of the night it would be precisely midnight. In fact, the word midnight explains itself in plain English. Do you not speak English, Mrs. Saulk?" Myrtle stood nose to nose with Matilda. "Therefore, Mrs. Saulk, it is *not* the middle of the night, nor anywhere near such time. Are we quite clear on that point?"

Matilda found herself confused and backing away from Myrtle, toward the closet, when it erupted for a second time. The door burst off its hinges and knocked Matilda flat beneath, onto the pitted cement floor.

A man wearing a full suit of armor strode out. He lifted a lengthy sword and pierced the water-stained ceiling. "I am here to save you," he said. Muffled by his helmet, he sounded as though he was speaking through two tin cans and a string.

The girls screeched and clung to one another.

He began grumbling. "This makes four times this month in this ridiculous attire." He tugged the sword free, and it released a shower of plaster that pinged off the steel suit.

"Get off me!" Matilda shouted from beneath the door.

He lifted the helmet's slatted faceplate to see who was speaking. Briar could see it was the same bearded man who appeared to her earlier.

"Oh, sorry about the door," he said. He stepped off, removed it from Matilda and leaned it into the doorframe. Briar tried to suppress a laugh.

Megan and Marnie, trying not to look too flipped out, edged up the basement steps together. It didn't bother them one bit to leave Matilda behind. But before they could reach them, the door atop the stairs dislodged from the wall and slammed shut with such force that it nearly split. Megan charged up and threw herself against it grunting, prying it with her chipping fingernails.

"Let us out!" she shouted. Finally she broke down in tears while hanging onto the immovable knob.

Mrs. Myrtle positioned her spectacles and grimaced at the pair. "Really," she said. Then to Matilda, "Are these hysterical beasts your spawn?"

"How dare you come into my house and speak to me like that!" Matilda huffed while heaving herself to a stand.

Myrtle whispered to Poplar, " —like a beached whale."

"A beached—what did you just call me?" Matilda clenched her fists.

"Oh fuss," Poplar said. She petted the fox stole. "You were busy hoisting yourself using the least amount of grace possible.

It's a wonder you could hear anything while performing such a momentous task."

"I can hear you perfectly well, Mrs. Myrtle. Now—"

Myrtle smiled primly, "Good. Then perhaps you'll hear it when I say that I shall report what is happening in your home to the police authorities, to child protective agents, and to the Internal Revenue Service. I am certain that the criminal maltreatment of a foster child and the misappropriation of her support funds would be of interest to them."

"Oh quite so," Poplar chimed in cheerily.

The girls screamed and pointed at Poplar, who was in a corner of the basement now, busy eating the remains of a rat. Blood ran down Poplar's chin and she shrugged, holding the final third of the carcass by its fleshy tail. She pulled a crisp white doily from her velvet drawstring handbag, wrapped the rat within, and placed it away. "Portion control," she said patting her girth and smiling daintily. Briar could see a rat claw still stuck between her front teeth.

"Sensible of you," Myrtle agreed.

Matilda's face drooped like a saggy mattress and she slapped her hands together in prayer. "Lord, what fiends hast thou cast upon my home?"

"Do you think she knows Lord Toad of the Swamps?" Poplar whispered loudly. She wiped her bloody chin with her lacey sleeve.

"My dear woman," Myrtle explained, "Lord Toad has been indisposed for some time now."

Matilda looked positively sick.

"Oh yes," Myrtle continued. "He was imprisoned. Caught poaching magic beans, I'm afraid."

"Dear, you've gotten things mixed again," Poplar corrected. "You're thinking of that pumpkin eater."

"Oh yes, that's right, Peter." Myrtle said. "Spousal abuse. Put her in a pumpkin shell. And there he kept her. Just dreadful."

Matilda wasn't certain if she was angry or confused. "I am speaking of our Lord and Savior Jesus Christ."

"Good Goose," Myrtle said. "The poor creature speaks in gibberish. Are you quite ill, madam?"

"Perhaps she doesn't wish to soil her reputation by association with Toad," the knight suggested.

"Never fear Mrs. Saulk, your secret will remain safe among us," Poplar said reassuringly. "Goblins know you could be hanged for the mere mention of his name."

"Hanged? What?" Matilda said. "Now see here—"

"No. *You* will see here," Myrtle said. She ran her gloved finger across Briar's dresser and flicked away a heaping crumble of crud. "I will be kind enough to overlook your association with Lord Toad. But I will not tolerate the dungeon imprisonment of this poor child."

"Dungeon! This is a perfectly suitable dwelling for a foster child, considering the meager stipend I receive each month. There are sufficient supplies and amenities for her here."

"Is that so?" the knight asked.

"Yes, that's so, Oil-Can. You three have illegally invaded my home. I don't know how you did it, but in any event, you have insulted me and my family, and you've battered me with a door. There's grounds enough for all three of you to be arrested." She removed Briar's cell phone from between her bosoms and showed it to Myrtle with an angry smile. She started to dial the police when Megan stopped her with a sudden thrill in her voice.

"Mother, I get what's going on here now. They're the reason why Briar has—you know—weird powers. They're all witches. Admit it. You're witches."

"Witches!" Myrtle was positively scandalized. She held her hand aloft and made a beckoning gesture. Briar's phone slipped from between Matilda's fingers, soared across the room, and snapped into Myrtle's grasp. "Utterly preposterous."

Matilda clasped her hands over her open mouth. Unable to

scream, she just squeaked.

"Now then," Myrtle said, "are you finished with your babbling? Fine then. We shall be taking our leave with young Briar now. She will return after some time—how long I dare not say, for the tasks ahead are epic. Meanwhile, since you find these quarters so suitable, you shall dwell among them yourselves."

"Oh hell no," Megan said. Finding sudden courage, she puffed up and stood chest to chest with Myrtle. "Are you freaks high or something? You're not leaving with anyone. Briar stays. And as soon as we get the chance, we're calling the cops."

Marnie shouted, "Yeah, take that to your coven meeting!"

"My, my," Myrtle said. "Aren't we the brave little pickpockets? Well, let me tell you—from one freak to another— that you should take care to whom you are speaking."

"Oh, I can see that I'm speaking to some dried up old tea bag, who's nothing more than a busybody with a degree," Megan said. She slapped a high five with Marnie and they hooted.

With a placid demeanor, Myrtle removed a small golden wand, no bigger than her pinkie, which was tucked like a tissue into her starchy cuff. It pinged open on several springy hinges to the length of her forearm, and she pointed it at Megan. "Hickory," she said. Then she pointed the wand at Marnie. "Dickory." Finally pointing it at Matilda, she said, "Doc."

"What is she saying?" Matilda asked. She sounded like she was going to burst out into laughter.

"Sister, no!" Poplar covered her eyes.

"I said, hickory, dickory, doc." Again she pointed the wand at each of them.

Megan started busting up. "Are you kidding with this nursery rhyme bullshit? What—are you going to tell us a bedtime story and tuck us in?"

Myrtle squinted with an unforgiving expression, and with that, her wand glowed. "Goggles," she announced. Then she produced a pair of brass and leather goggles in her empty hand, which she held up to her eyes. A bright silver comet swelled up from the end and shot upward, flattening against the ceiling and spreading out.

The house groaned, the basement shuddered, and the room went black. Once the shaking stopped, an eerie cobalt glow filled the room. Suddenly it was as if a violent cyclone had burst into the basement. Posters and picture frames ripped from the walls, Briar's furnishings arose and joined the swirling tornado that gyrated from floor to ceiling. The Saulks screamed in unison as the spinning heap lurched forward, sucking in all three of them.

Megan, Marnie, and Matilda's shrieks suddenly halted altogether while the tornado shrank, leaving the furnishings exactly as they were. The gusts stopped. The pictures re-attached themselves. Order returned. But Megan, Marnie, and Matilda were nowhere to be found.

At least Briar thought so until she spotted three white mice, standing on their hind legs, tottering unsteadily out from behind a splintery pile of broken picture frames. Each of them wore a tiny pair of dark glasses and tapped around with a miniature white cane. They bumped into each other as they staggered into a nearby split at the base of the wall.

Chapter 7

"That was certainly awkward," Myrtle said. She slipped the wand back up her sleeve.

"Sister," Poplar said irritably. "Your temper!"

"Oh pish-tosh," Myrtle replied. "They'll be back to their revolting selves in short order—and none the wiser."

The knight nodded as he strode to the closet door. "She's right. *Squelch* never recall real magical acts. And besides, dillywig magic doesn't hold for long where the squelch live."

Myrtle's face dropped like a Shar Pei. "We do not refer to *commons* as *squelch*. With language like that, one might wonder about your allegiances."

The knight laughed. "Oh Myrtle, squelch don't care what we call them." He winked at Briar and smiled broadly like he'd just told a great joke. "Besides, she isn't squelch, is she? She's one of us."

Briar stood with her back leveled against wall with eyes fixed upon the strange intruders. "Mrs. Poplar, what—what's going on here? This is definitely the weirdest social worker visit I've ever had."

Poplar came to Briar's side and took her cold, pale hand. "I know it's a bit much to take in," she said. Then she ogled Briar with her telescopic monocle.

"Poor thing's never seen an alteration," Myrtle said to the knight who just nodded. "But you did get my message on your device, did you not? And Ash—he told you that it was no longer safe, did he not?"

Ash, the knight, was busy fitting the closet door into its frame. "I told her," he said. "It still isn't safe—not yet—nor ever, I would guess." He pointed his sword at the door. The sword glowed and the hinges reattached with a red-hot sizzle. "But, I told you that people just shut down when I show up in that damned ball-gown."

"No!" Myrtle cried. "Not the one with the diamond shoes and the tiara again?"

He nodded.

"Your favorite, Poplar," she said. "And you missed it."

Ash shook his head. "That was a fine way to meet Briar for the first time."

Poplar shrugged. "Still, it's better than if you had arrived as the geisha—"

Briar shook her head. "I'm sorry, I'm not following any of this. I stopped following once phones started flying, a big blue tornado spun through my room, and people started popping in and out of my closet like it was a freakin' carnival fun house."

Poplar took Briar by the elbow. "Come sit down, Briar, you're overwrought." Then Poplar told Myrtle, "It's her first time seeing an alteration."

"So I've heard." Myrtle seemed unamused.

"Let go of me," Briar snapped. She backed away from Poplar and edged toward the closet. "Yeah, and it's safe to say it's my first time with weirdo home-invading kidnappers. Good call, Poplar—or whatever the hell your real name is."

"I blame myself for this ignorance," Myrtle said. "Look at the poor thing. From the Blackwood clan and she doesn't even know how a proper door works." She looked away with glistening eyes.

"You see? This is what happens when you leave commons to raise a child like Briar," Ash said. He pounded with his steel boots over to the hole in the split baseboard, bent down on his shrill knee-plates, and searched for the Saulks. "They better get out of there before they change back, or this could get messy."

Myrtle pursed her lips. "I don't recall forcing them into the wall. Besides, I presume that's where most vermin live. I suppose they were only living out their deeper nature." She looked away with her chin aloft.

Briar shook her head. "Excuse me. I'm still trying to catch up here. Just how did any of you get in here through that closet?"

Poplar smiled. "I walked mostly. Although, I may have tip-toed once I got closer to the door."

"Hey, Straightjacket, you can't just walk through walls. We're in a basement—you know, like, underground," Briar said. She opened the closet door and peered in.

"Oh yes, underground, close to the roots of that magnificent apple tree in the front yard." Poplar clapped the fingertips of her lace gloves together. "She was quite fortunate in that regard." She nodded with Myrtle.

Briar began shouting. "You're full of shit. Now stop lying and give me some answers."

Just then the fox fur around Myrtle's neck lifted its head and spoke. "This is absurd. Miss Ingrate is ignorant, insulting, and has quite the potty-mouth."

Briar screamed. "What the hell?"

The fox hopped off Myrtle's shoulders, scurried to Briar and squinted at her with one eye. After a few moments he said, "Nope. She isn't the right one, anyway. Now come on. Let's all get out of here before Orpion's spies find us."

"Don't pay any attention to Sherman," Poplar said to Briar. "Just show him the key and he'll know what's what."

"The key?" Briar was staring at the talking fox, and could barely process what was happening.

"Yes, dear, the one around your neck. Show Sherman so he'll shut that chicken-poaching trap of his," Poplar said.

Briar followed Poplar's request, reached for the chain and pulled the key up from the front of her dress. She regarded it, tracing the black iron curls and floral design at its head with her gaze, turning its smooth barrel between her thumb and forefinger. Poplar had often told her that it was the last remnant of her birth mother, whose whereabouts were unknown. Briar went nowhere without it.

"That's not the key," the fox said. "It's supposed to be gold. I remember these things."

Briar felt as though the walls were closing in on her. *This shit is off-the-chain crazy.* And yet, there was something disturbingly familiar about it all. She started to back away from them, and inadvertently stepped through the closet doorway. Once that happened, she disappeared.

Myrtle raised her eyebrows. "Well how do you like that?" she said. "The child left without as much as a goodbye."

Briar suddenly found herself in a dim, red-carpeted hallway lit by flickering candles set in dusty gold brackets. "What the—?" she whispered. She turned around looking for the door through which she passed, and her heart paused.

Though the light was dim and unsteady, she saw that she stood within an impossibly long corridor lined with white doors of all shapes and sizes. Thousands of lustrous doors with gleaming brass knobs crowded the walls and even the ceiling. Some doors were small and round. Perhaps only a thimble could fit through them. Others were tall and square, and they reached as high as the ceiling would allow. The doors were stacked atop one another and jammed together tightly, making a ladder necessary to reach the highest of them.

She could be lost forever in these halls with bisecting corridors, all of which seemed to infinitely stretch out.

"Hello?" she called out. But the corridor was hushed, except for a tick-tock sound coming from somewhere nearby.

She tiptoed toward the first intersection not far from where she stood. Her every footstep creaked on the warped old floorboards beneath the carpet. Once she arrived, she only found another hall crammed with doors on either side and above her.

This hallway, however, was shorter, maybe the length of several parked cars, she estimated. A tall grandfather clock was wedged into the end of the hall. Not that Briar had much experience with old clocks, but this was unlike any she had ever seen. To begin with, it was at least two times the height of a full-grown man. Then, instead of the normal faceplate, from what she could see, the thing had three concentric dials crisscrossed with sixteen strange markings. She wanted a better look, so she stepped into the second, bisecting hall.

This one was tighter than the first. If she were to walk straight on, her shoulders would brush both walls. And, in fact she brushed a shoulder along an ancient tapestry she hadn't noticed hanging above a row of knee-high doors. It was probably a trick of the light, but it seemed to her that the faintly stitched roses in the graying background bowed aside.

Briar stood back as far as she could and studied the entire length of the weaving. It was stitched with crosshatched illustrations from a children's storybook, with images of cottages, creatures, and faded landscapes. Gnarled oaks and oversized flowers loomed over a yellow two-story dwelling with gingerbread trim. It looked just like the Saulks' home. Her heart dipped and she felt a fog of confusion rolling through her mind.

Toward the top of the musty old hanging was a red-cloaked figure that held a mirror in its hands. And a spinning wheel, with drips of red stitched in as though it were dripping blood from its spindle, was positioned near a gloomy palace. A dark cloud was carefully woven in the distance and was shaped like an ominous hooded figure that seemed to hold the whole tapestry between its clawed hands.

Hidden along the border of the decaying mural, amid scrollwork of vines and leaves, were short wiry creatures with pointed caps and sharp claws. Each one clamped a colorful jewel between its teeth. There were other images as well, hideous, monstrous things, or so it seemed to Briar. But they were too worn by time for her to fully make them out. She smoothed her fingertips along the stitching of a jewel-eating creature. The fabric felt brittle and easily torn. She felt her muscles seize when the woven creature suddenly recoiled from her hand and skittered across the tapestry to hide inside a distant cave.

Briar stumbled backward against the opposing wall, a doorknob jammed into her spine. Not taking her eyes off the moving cross-stitched images, she side-shuffled a few steps until she bumped into the clock. Its pendulum suddenly developed a panicked tempo and it click-clacked madly from side to side. Its various chimes then clamored together as though screaming at her. Then she saw clearly that instead of two hands, like a normal clock, this one had many hands pointing in every direction. One of the hands stood straight out, pointing directly at Briar as though accusing her of some unknown crime.

She covered her mouth with a gasp and barreled back to the other end of the dark hall. She began grabbing feverishly at doorknobs, but they all held fast. Briar's throat tightened and her knees could have crumbled like ruined sandcastles. The whole scene was so bizarre that she wasn't certain that any of this was really happening.

She closed her eyes and held them shut for a moment. Things might change, just as they would in a dream—if indeed this were one. She shook her head vigorously with her eyes still shut. Then she blinked and looked again down the corridor, expecting the vision to be different now. But every detail remained in its exact, vivid, inexplicable form.

She looked to her right, and in the dancing candle shadows, she noticed clear light seeping around the edges of another closed, paint-crackled door. She took a couple of hushed-toe steps toward what she hoped might be a way out, when another door opened. From it burst Ash, Poplar and Myrtle.

"Stay where you are!" Poplar shouted.

The sight of the three coming down the corridor toward her was enough to send Briar on a sprint to the door framed in light.

"Where is she going?" Poplar asked. Her face was screwed up into a question mark.

"Child, stay away from that room," Myrtle commanded.

Briar twisted the doorknob and, salvation, it was unlocked. She swerved herself around the door, slammed it shut, and pressed her body up against it. She felt a key in the door's lock. She twisted it until it clicked, and then she tested the door, making sure it could hold up against rat-eating crazed weirdos.

Just above her shoulder something struck the door with such fury that it left a hand-sized gouge. She whirled around toward her attacker, only to face a fluffy brown sparrow the size of a grizzly bear. The bird cheeped loudly and stabbed again with its pointy brown beak.

Briar moved her torso just in time and the bird pecked into the door again. Wood chips and splinters flew in all directions and the door rattled on its hinges. The bird hopped closer toward her on its spindly talons and cocked its head to get a better look. It chirped shrilly, and Briar covered her ears. The bird hopped backward, preparing to strike once more.

Chapter 8

"Sing to it," Poplar yelled from the other side of the door.

Briar reached for the key in the door, but the sparrow made another deafening chirp and bore down on her hand with its snapping beak. Briar jerked her hand away as fast as she could, but the bird was faster, snapped at her sweatshirt sleeve, and snipped it cleanly through. Briar fell backward and landed on her backside.

Myrtle pounded on the door and shouted to Briar, "Child, listen to me. You must sing to the bird! Do it now."

Briar kept her eye on the sparrow while stretching her hand once more for the protruding key. The bird struck again, but this time it clipped the key in its beak. With a speedy head movement, it tossed the key over its back. It landed with a metallic chime at a distant spot on the floor.

Briar scrambled on hands and knees away from the creature. It did not attack again but inspected her movements keenly with its jewel black eyes. This gave Briar a second or two to notice her surroundings. The room was of unfinished wood; nails the size of telephone poles were stuck through the walls into the room at various points. In a far corner, behind the sparrow, stood a downy collection of feathers, strings and twigs, all fashioned into a colossal nest. Next to the nest was a gaping hole in the far wall. It looked like a perfectly engineered round hollow, large enough to walk though. She didn't want to rile the bird any further by wandering close to the nest, but she could see the glimmer of starlight just outside the round cut out.

Then she heard voices again. "I don't think she can hear us," Poplar said fretfully from the other side of the door.

"Are you singing?" Myrtle asked. She sounded like a doting nana monitoring her charge's toileting. "If so, you're awfully quiet about it."

Briar crawled slowly toward the key, trying not to provoke the bird. "No, I am not singing. I'm a little busy at the moment."

"What does she mean, busy?" Myrtle burbled with a frown in her voice. "Child, do not busy yourself much. You need to get away from the bird."

"Really? You think?" Briar said.

Briar finally reached the key, snapped it up in her hand and crawled at a careful, creeping pace back to the door. Once she was within beak-striking distance, she sat below the bird's-eye level, and scooted toward the lock. She reached up with the key, maintaining eye contact with the sparrow, and she felt for the keyhole. The bird puffed its feathers, smoothed them again, then hopped forward like a wind-up tin toy. It towered over Briar, chirped and twisted its head to one side so that it see where on her body it should strike next.

Without warning, the knight's sword bored through the door above Briar's head, showering her with paint chips and wood splinters. It missed the bird, which then hopped back and cheeped so loudly it threatened to pierce Briar's eardrums. Suddenly the door swung open, and Myrtle and Poplar rushed past the armed knight to stand face-to-beak with the sparrow.

"Peeps! You naughty imp!" Poplar exclaimed.

Myrtle weighed in. "We've told you before. No eating the guests!" She made a shooing gesture with her hands. Then with an elegant flourish, breadcrumbs appeared in Myrtle's palm.

The sparrow cheeped, making them all cover their ears. "I told you, Poplar, we should have kept her as an *outdoor* bird. If we must share our residence, then she must at minimum follow the rules." Myrtle tossed the breadcrumbs toward the stack of twig and string in the far corner. Then, claws scratching the floor, Peeps bounded over to nibble and poke at her snack.

Briar sat, eyes like moons, fingering the clean hole snipped through her sweatshirt, trying to fathom everything that had occurred. Poplar and Myrtle hurried and helped her to stand while Ash jiggled and labored to free the sword.

"Poor dear," Poplar said. "You have to understand, it's Peeps' first time as an expectant mother." She fussed over the splinters and oddments on Briar's hoodie. Once Briar got her bearings, she looked across to Peeps' rough-hewn snuggery. She could see the domes of three brown and white speckled eggs peeking out from the top of the nest. Peeps finished her crumbs, then fluttered atop her eggs. The windblast from her wings filled the air with particles of straw and loose, soft down.

"Come now, Briar," Myrtle said. She raised her chin with an air of propriety. "We've spent enough time with diversions. You have much to learn and little time to learn it. If you would please follow me to the parlor."

Myrtle stepped to the door that Ash had closed to get leverage enough to pull his sword free. He stepped aside and when Myrtle opened it again, the hallway on the other side was gone. In its place was a timeworn parlor.

Briar could not formulate words coherently enough to express her complete bewilderment, so she stood, immovable.

Poplar took Briar by the arm and escorted her into the room. "Look at the poor darling," she said to Myrtle. "Probably can't make heads or tails of the diddles and daddles around here."

"What happened to the hallway," Briar asked. "Where did it go?"

"One door, one use," Myrtle said. "That's the first thing you'll need to remember." She smiled primly and stroked the fox clasped around her shoulders. It started to snore. "Well that wasn't so hard now was it?" she said. "Only about seventy thousand more things to learn and we'll be on our way."

Myrtle sat on an oversized couch covered in tapestry cloth, with her bony ankles crossed. She pulled the gold wand from her sleeve and twitched her wrist; the wand extended, climbing in zigs and zags and pings and twangs until it reached her face. The last arm of the wand then opened to a pair of spectacles that magnified her eyes to several times their normal size.

The room was busily decorated with an unplanned collection of strange antique objects, and faded, yet opulent furniture with wood framing that curved in luxurious, rhythmic art nouveau tangles at the arms and feet. She saw several crystal spheres on three-legged claws grouped together on a Spanish shawl-draped table. They had books of every sort with strange markings upon their crusted and disintegrating bindings stacked in piles upon floors and tables. On top of the book stacks, as well as scattered about in every stray nook, were potted plants of the strangest, most unidentifiable variety.

Long, woody roots and herb bundles lay tied with crudely made string on chopping boards wreathed with beeswax candles. It looked to Briar that the chopping boards had deep red stains engrained in them: like remnants of blood that they had unsuccessfully tried to scrub away. The room smelt like both a musty library and brewing herbal tea.

Poplar brought Briar to sit in a wooden chair carved with winged creatures as the chair's arms, and bird's talons for feet.

Sherman snorted awake and spat out a fur ball. "What is *she* doing here?" he asked. He lifted his head and didn't bother moving from where he lay. "I told you, this fatuous buffoon is not the one!"

Poplar's expression became dark and she walked toward Sherman with a hungry look. "I've already dined on a rat today, Sherman," she said. "And a fox seems to me very much like a plumper rat. So don't tempt me…"

The fox bounced down to Myrtle's knee and sat with its pointed ears tucked back and its tail curled. His eyes were fixed and wide. "You wouldn't dare," he said. But he didn't sound convinced. Rather than fight, he curled up into a ball of red fluff at the center of Myrtle's lap and flicked his tail at Poplar.

Poplar turned to Briar. "I apologize, dear, for the state of our home. Still, it's better than living in an old shoe. That is, unless you had so many children, you didn't know what to do..."

Briar looked like someone who had been zapped a few times with a stun gun. She wasn't following conversations or conventions any longer. "Can someone explain what the hell is going on?"

Ash marched into the room from a swinging door to the side of the parlor. He was now clad in a long, shabby gray-fur overcoat, knitted scarf, and snowshoes that looked like oversized tennis rackets. Briar could see his face fully now. He had ruddy cheeks, and around his eyes and his brow he showed the lines of his years. His salt and pepper hair was a curly shoulder length and it matched well his short-cropped beard.

He paraded awkwardly across the room, snowshoes sounding against the wood floor. Then he plopped heavily down on the couch setting a small flurry of snowflakes airborne. "First thing we need to do is fix that salt-mouth of hers," he said. He nudged Myrtle mischievously, but she was not amused.

"I don't think any of us were prepared for this—this virtual fount of vulgarity," she agreed. She pruned her lips, looking like she was swallowing a tack.

"Indeed not," Sherman added, though muffled by his tail fur.

"Who *are* you people?" Briar asked.

"You people?!" Poplar exclaimed. "Oh Myrtle, she doesn't even recognize us!"

"Well, how could she?" Myrtle snapped back.

"That's true." Poplar smiled. "She was only a babe in our arms. Look how she's grown! Except for her blackened cheeks, lips, hair, clothes, and metal thrust through her face, she is the Goose's image of her mother!"

"Is that so?" Myrtle asked. "We shall have to see about that."

"How do you know anything about my mother?" Briar asked.

Poplar sidled up to Briar and snatched her by the elbow, entwining their arms together. "*Knew*, dear. We *knew* your mother, once upon a time. You were just a wee thing. But she's been gone for a very long time." She shook her head and her eyes filled with tears.

"What do you mean—gone?" Briar asked. She stood from her seat and her throat almost choked out the final words.

"Please sit, dear," said Poplar. "This must be a shock. Why don't you drink a cup of my special tea? It'll calm your nerves."

Briar sat stiffly on the edge of the chair. "No, I don't want— What? Are you out of your mind, lady? I'm not stupid enough to touch your voodoo-witchcraft crap! The next thing I know, I'll be lying in a bathtub filled with ice, hand-stitched with dental floss across my back, while you're selling one of my kidneys on the internet. No thanks."

"Oh," Poplar said. "Well, my first choice was chamomile."

Briar looked around the room at the collection of oddballs. "If you know something about my mother, then I want you to tell me."

Myrtle shot Poplar a look of warning. Poplar tightened her lips and tried to dab her eyes inconspicuously with a lace hankie she had tucked into her bosom for just such an occasion. She snuffled a little and said, "Yes, well, dear, perhaps later."

"No," Briar drawled, shaking her head. "There won't be any later. This is just as I thought. You don't know anything about my mother. You're just a bunch of lunatics who get their jollies tricking and kidnapping kids." Briar felt a wave of defiance build within her, gathering the strength of an intensifying fire. She stood up and shouted, "You fucking freak-asses better let me leave or I'll—!" Briar felt like there would be some conse-quence—as delusional as it may have seemed. She couldn't fill in the final blank because she wasn't sure just what exactly would occur. But somehow, at the very bottom of her reasoning, without ever having thought out a plan, she knew she was right. Something would happen. Something big.

Myrtle's eyes widened during the uncomfortable silence that followed. She raised her spectacles again and this time inspected

Briar like a laboratory specimen. "Oh dear," she said. Sherman popped up to her shoulders and sat ogling her. "Do you see what I mean?" Sherman asked. After letting off steam, Briar felt a little stupid. She sat back down.

Then Myrtle said to Poplar, "Indeed. We may have made a mistake with *this one*, but we must be certain."

"But she has the key," Poplar said. "I've followed her every move for almost sixteen years now—just like you wanted me to do. However can you believe that this is the wrong girl?"

"The omens," Myrtle said. She sat back down. "The damned old seers have muddled things before. Rapunzel hasn't predicted anything accurately with that old cracked mirror of hers for centuries now."

"Well, seeing isn't an exact science..." Poplar said. She came close to Briar, as though inspecting her face. "Besides, the child's eyes—are they not familiar to you?"

"Oh my God, you psychos really are nuts. You're gonna kill me—and then take my eyes to sell. Just let me go and I promise I won't tell anyone," Briar pleaded.

Myrtle flicked her wrist and the spectacles turned into a solid wand again. With it, she made several quick angular gestures and suddenly Briar's chair came to life. The clawed arms of the chair sprang free and wrapped around Briar, forcing her to sit. Briar screamed and struggled, but to no end.

"Kill you!" Myrtle had a dangerous chuckle. "You have not yet even come near to the taste of death, child." Myrtle's face morphed; it became darker and sallow. Her eyes looked sunken and from the dark pits, there glowed a silvery blue light. Her teeth became sharp, jagged razors, like a shark's teeth. "Believe me," Myrtle continued, "you will know it when the Great Conclusion is truly upon you, sucking the last wisp of air from your lungs, bathing you in the darkness from which none return."

Briar stopped struggling in the grip of the chair and caught her breath. Even Sherman bounced away from of Myrtle's shoulder, tail tucked and backing into a far corner. Myrtle suddenly realized that she had lost composure and she cut her words short. She shifted her demeanor and her old prim looks returned. She gave a curt, unnatural smile, probably the first Briar had seen. She stiffened and turned away. "You will be glad to know that this is not that moment."

Briar bit down on the idea that she had seen too much, tasting it bitterly. She dared say nothing, but it seemed clear that they might never really let her go.

"If she must turn back, she must choose it now," Poplar said. But she sounded like a child who was required to return a puppy to the pound.

"Indeed," Myrtle said. She walked to a window and looked out into the night. The chair that held Briar changed back to its old form. Its arms and legs freeing her. She stood up, rubbing her sore arms, and backed toward the door.

Myrtle was still turned away from Briar when she spoke—now slowly, calmly, as if there was nothing left to lose. "Yes we knew your mother. She came from a humble birth, but she had a high and noble rebirth."

"Oh yes," Poplar said. "Quite the noble rebirth. It happened spontaneously—well, like they all do—when she turned sixteen. You know, one day you're shoveling the fireplace ashes, the next you're riding in a coach to the king's ball."

Briar held the key in her fingers and found courage again to speak. "This. What does it open?"

Myrtle shrugged. "How should we know? All we can tell you is that it was once your mother's." She turned back around to face Briar. "And now it is yours."

Poplar scurried close to Briar and fussed with her hair. "Oh, my dear, your mother was such a beautiful woman; a woman of high rank and influence, and beloved—she was so beloved. You came along sometime after she was already well into her power, which is why the seers all believe that your mother's same power may have, well, transferred to you."

Myrtle then spoke, her words like icicles. "Sister, say no more. She must choose by her own wit and her own knowing. You'll only confuse the situation. And time has run out."

"Don't be so certain, Myrtle," Ash said. His voice was deep and resonant, sudden and halting. The words carried weight. "After all, she knows nothing of us—of our world. I'd wager that a girl plucked from her home would more likely choose from fear than she would because of some humbug omen that she's never even heard about. We hadn't thought this through before we barged into her life. And now, though I'll admit her eyes are familiar, it seems that nothing less than a test would be in order before we could know with certainty."

"A test!" Poplar seemed to perk up now. She patted Briar's hands and Briar pulled away.

"No. I'm not doing any tests," Briar said. She backed up toward the parlor door. "I'm outta here."

She bolted through the door and clomped down the narrow hallway past the towering clock, which practically went into tick-tock convulsions. The stitched flowers in the tapestry bowed in her wake. She grabbed indiscriminately at doorknobs as she rushed down the hall, but each was locked.

Finally one miraculously swung open. Not caring if there was another giant bird, or a singing crocodile on the other side, she flung herself through and slammed the door shut.

Chapter 9

Briar pressed her back to the door and huffed, then doubled over, dizzy and nauseous. It was several minutes before she could stand without feeling as though she might topple over or spew all over herself.

When she could focus on her surroundings, she found that she was standing in a somber stone chamber. A bassinet covered in cobwebs stood at the far end of the room, standing across a gray expanse of interlocking flagstone blocks.

A swag of purple velvet pulled back with a tasseled rope hung solemnly against a wall from a high bracket that was placed at least three stories above her head. Behind the drapery, she saw part of a tall slim window of deep jewel-tone purple and lavender stained glass. But there was nothing else in the chamber except a short object, the size of a tricycle, covered with a sheet near the window.

She checked the door and found that it could not lock from the inside. She felt heat forming in her stomach and she wanted to scream to do something other than hide behind the door in some weird chamber.

But she was beginning to think she might be safe. They would never know into which of the million doors she had wandered. She released the knob and took a step back. She waited and waited, but still, no one tried the door. When it seemed like she wasn't being followed, she ambled across the room to the crumbling bassinet. It stood below long dramatic swags of threadbare cloth hung like decaying boat sails from the grand ceiling.

It seemed to Briar that the cradle was once magnificent—for a child of royalty she supposed. Scrolls of elaborately entwined carved wood looked like vines surrounding the top of the cradle. And into the headboard, there was a dragon gracefully whittled and trimmed with gold leaf that was now rubbed off in places and disintegrated.

As she had suspected, the cradle was empty. Thick webs covered the strewn bed sheets and flecks of something white and powdery speckled the bedding. Her eyes were drawn to the floor where she noticed more of the fine powder smudged and scattered by shoe and—could it be?—canine paw prints.

Daring not to disturb this arrangement, she backed away toward the sheet-covered object near the window. She couldn't understand why the bassinet was left to deteriorate, while some other object in the room was carefully protected.

First she kicked it lightly with her boot just in case something living was unseen beneath the cloth. But this only served to pull a portion of the cloth away to reveal what looked like an old spoked bicycle wheel—if, that is, bicycles were made of wood.

Not wanting to touch anything with her hands, she used her boot to pull aside the rest of the cloth. It was an old spinning wheel. Although it looked antique, it also seemed to be well cared for; it was oiled and gleaming as though in regular use. It had a shapely grooved and spoked wheel that looked like the captain's wheel of a pirate ship. A fattened spool of gray wool was perched prominently on the device and wrapped about a slim, gleaming spike.

She also spotted a crudely hewn doll tied with black cord to the horizontal flat board of the spinning wheel. It was made from brown sackcloth, dressed in a poorly sewn, cinched-up, Victorian gown and calf-high boots. Two large Xs were sewn in the place of the doll's eyes; the mouth was sutured with coarse zigzag stitches and stuffed with something dried, green and noxious smelling. The herbal stuffing protruded between the rudimentary stitches. Long black yarn hair hung limply around its cheeks.

Briar would have been alarmed by her appalling lookalike poppet, but the glinting spindle of the spinning wheel immediately absorbed her full attention. She was overcome by an urge to feel its sharpness, to even feel it pierce her skin, and see blood run from her finger. Her mind emptied of all other thought, so mesmerized was she by the spinning wheel and its intoxicating spindle. Oddly alert and focused, she stretched her hand out, craving the prick of steel much like she had felt before with her piercings of ear, tongue, and brow, the sharp satisfaction once metal lanced flesh. And now, wonderfully, deliciously, she would feel it again. It was just within reach.

The door behind her burst open, just as her finger hovered above the spindle. Two wolf creatures, like those that had attacked Leon's car, stood on their hind feet staring with their muzzles open. They both wore strapping thick, black leather and shining metal armor, spiked rivets gleaming at their shoulders, and they carried long spears.

"Stop!" One of the creatures growled in a canine perversion of a human voice. Its growl-words sounded sickening to Briar. She faced the two abominations with an indrawn breath, yet their grotesqueness, their ferocity, did not derail the unrelenting incli-nation to prick her hand—to even pierce her whole body through with the spike. But she had to address this interruption.

The two wolfguard rushed upon her, spears forward, gray fur on their hunched backs bristled. The second wolf's amber eyes widened in recognition and he stopped mid-stride. He tried to form words, but was not as successful as his comrade. His utterings were simple whining and animal grunts. He grabbed his fellow guard by the shoulder. They dropped their spears and lay with their bellies low to the floor, ears tucked back, as though in fear of Briar. They looked down, averting their gaze from her. "For-give." The growl-voiced wolf tried to form the words in its tartared, fangy mouth.

Briar stood, pulled by both fear and an ungovernable longing for the spindle. The wolves had spears, but they would not satisfy like the prick from a spindle of a spinning wheel. She had to touch it.

The whining wolf dared a quick glance from where he lay, then suspiciously eyed Briar. "Not *her*," he rasped. His version of a mock human voice was eerier than the first wolf's. Then he crouched as though he might spring to her throat. He curled his lips and bore his sharp teeth.

Perhaps he wanted to touch the spindle too, Briar thought. But it belonged to her now. She felt a surge of ferocity, like a protecting lioness.

"Get out," she heard herself say in a commanding whisper. The growling wolf narrowed his yellow-slitted eyes and dove forward. Briar put her arms out to protect the spinning wheel. The wolf that was left cowering on the ground, suddenly growled wildly and leapt at the first wolf, sinking his teeth savagely into his side.

The two wolves brawled, barking, growling angrily at one another. Finally the whining wolf caught the first one by the throat and clamped down. His muzzle became drenched with blood as he pinned the first wolf to the floor. The pinned wolf cried and wildly attempted to get free, his limbs helplessly flailing. But eventually he became still and his tongue lolled from his open mouth.

"Get out!" Briar's imperious energy filled the chamber. The victorious wolf, huffing in the cold chamber air, bared his fangs again. He looked away from Briar, almost deferentially. He bit the dead wolf by his blood-drenched pelt and carried his slack carcass from the chamber.

Briar followed the creature to the door and once it was gone, she slammed the door shut. She turned back now to the spinning wheel and outstretched her shaking hand. *It's mine*, she thought, stepping slowly, allowing the moment to linger before she savored the sharp bite. Not knowing any longer who or where she was, Briar inched forward. Just one more step—

"Stop!" Briar heard a resonant voice from behind her. A rope swooped around her waist. Quick as a striking rattlesnake, she felt herself jerked away from the spinning wheel and she fell on her backside to the floor. She squirmed to free herself, but the lasso only tightened.

"Leave me alone. Let me go! It's mine!" she shouted as she struggled to her feet to face the man who was holding her captive.

There at the far end of the room, holding the end of the rope, was Ash dressed now as a cowboy. "There's nothing in this place for you, Briar. Nothing that you want."

"I found the spinning wheel. It belongs to me," Briar protested as Ash pulled her away.

"This was a trap," Ash said. "One touch of that spindle and you would have been infected with the sleepdeath."

"I don't care! I don't...I..." Briar couldn't finish. She felt conflicted, dizzy, disoriented. Ash noticed that the key on Briar's necklace was outside her outfit. He flicked it with a finger until it made contact with the delicate skin at her throat. At once Briar felt as though a haze was lifting. She began to realize how strangely she was behaving. It felt as though she were waking from a deep sleep, a distorted dream.

"What happened?" she asked. "How did you get here?"

"I got here the same way you did," Ash said. Then he pulled Briar close enough to untie her. "You were under the influence of something very dark and powerful. And we would have lost you forever had you touched that spindle."

"What do you mean?" Briar looked over her shoulder at the spinning wheel standing near the window, contrasting so simply with its surroundings: wood, stone, metal. It seemed so small and unimportant. "It was—it was poisoned?"

Ash began untying her and he helped her to stand. "It was more than poisoned," he said. His face was now long, his eyes filled with an understanding tempered by some unspoken pain. "Your arrival in these Realms has been anticipated from a time before remembering."

"What are you talking about?"

"Many await you, Briar. But to some who hold power, you are a threat. And the only protection you have right now is that *trinket*," he said. He eyed the iron key pendant.

She touched it with one hand. "This thing?" she asked.

"Yes, that thing, as you call it, isn't simply a necklace. It is a *trinket*, a link to power and protection. It is the only thing as potent as the dark magic on that spinning wheel."

Briar held the key in one hand and silently regarded it.

"Myrtle, Poplar and I forged it in this very chamber against great odds and at great peril."

"Look, I don't want—wait, what I mean is that I *never* wanted any part of this—whatever all of this is with your trinkets and spinning wheels and freaked-out wolves—"

"I know that this may all be difficult to believe, raised by commons as you were. But to ignore or to believe that this is some sort of delusion is a dangerous mistake." He looked at the floor, tipping up the brim of his cowboy hat with a leather-gloved hand.

For the first time, Briar had no response.

"Terrible things, unspeakable things will happen to innocent lives should you pretend that this world does not exist. Very real beings, as real as your mother, are at stake."

"What do you know about my mother—?"

"I know that my people—no, *your* people—die every day at the hands of a dangerous tyrant."

Briar had sensed it from an early age. Her mother was never missing, as she had been led to believe. As hard as it was for Briar to hear this said aloud, she had known it all along in her heart. Briar couldn't remember anything about her mother. Not her face, her smell, her touch. Nothing. And for Ash—this peculiar man who felt more like a dream than anything else—to confirm what she suspected seemed cruel and unfair.

"What?" Briar's voice was almost a whisper, but she shook

shaking her reddening face. "How dare you drag my mother into this! You don't know anything about her!"

Ash looked down again and waited for Briar's pain, her fury, to subside before he spoke. "I know that she loved you very much, and she would have wanted you to do what was right."

"How do you know that?" Briar fought back tears. "Anyway, I can't. This is too much for me. I'm just some random high school kid. I'm not whoever it is you think I am. It's just a big mistake," Briar said. She hoped that she was right.

"Yes. A mistake," Ash said. He nodded sadly. "Have you looked in the bassinet?" he asked her. He tipped his head to one side, gesturing toward the cradle.

"What?"

"Beneath cobwebs, the headboard. Have you seen it?" Ash looked up from the floor and nodded toward the bassinet.

Briar's heart thumped louder and harder than it ever had before. "No," she said. She felt like something was stabbing her in the gut. Then she stood and paced the stone floor to the dust-covered crib. She pierced the thick webbing, pulling it apart. And there, chiseled into the headboard below the dragon carving, painted with crumbling blood-red paint, was her name.

Briar reeled back and covered her mouth with a hand. "How can this be?" she asked, but not to Ash. "I was raised by my—my foster mother, Matilda." Briar finally backed up to the wall and slid down to a crouch. She covered her face with her hands.

Ash approached and lightly placed a hand on her shoulder. "We hid you where the Lady Orpion would never find you. It was our only hope to save you, to save the people of our Realms."

"Don't lay this on me," Briar snapped. She shook off his hand. "*My people* are at home. My foster mother, her girls, my friend— and for the first time ever I have a boy that just might be interested in me. Those are *my people*—not a bunch of weirdos doing fantasy role-playing games. Don't you have some kind of convention to get to?"

Ash stood watching her, but didn't move. Briar looked up and he locked his crystal blue eyes with hers. "I understand," he said. "You do not know this world or its people. And I should know that hoping and waiting are fools' games." He looked down at the floor. "As are holding fast to the tongue-waggings of old wives and soothsayers."

He leaned against the stone wall next to Briar. Exhaling quietly, deliberately, he shut his eyes tight with unmasked pain. "There is but one thing more for you to see."

He took Briar by the hand. Looking up at him with pleading eyes, she stood. Together they walked to the chamber door and Ash opened it. There, on the other side, was Briar's basement bedroom.

She gaped at the unexpected scene. "But how?"

Ash shook his head. "It matters no more. If I cannot spare the lives of all, I can at least save one." He gestured for Briar to enter.

Briar stepped to the doorframe, but something gnawed at her and made her turn back to Ash. "Please forgive me," she said. "I just—I can't. Whatever is happening for you—that life, your world isn't for me. I'm sorry. I can't be who you want me to be."

Ash nodded formally. "Better for you to have lived your life freely, than to have been bound, as others, to a life not of their own design," he said.

Briar didn't understand, but she managed a flicker of a smile.

"Do me one last favor," Ash said. Briar's smile faded. "Always wear that trinket. It must touch the skin. And none but you should see it."

Briar nodded and clasped the key to her chest.

"Goodbye, Briar of the Black Woods," Ash said. He made a motion with one hand and the closet door swung shut.

Briar wanted to say goodbye, but once she was on the bedroom side of the door, it swiftly shut. She reached for the knob, thinking to perhaps open it again. But she just stood there with her hand extended. She felt a wave of sadness for something unnamable lost. Instead of re-opening the door, she backed away into the safe, familiar darkness.

Chapter 10

Who am I?

It might be a little late to be asking the question now. Right? Still, I go over it again and again, especially since that crazy night. I know the answer. Deep inside I know it. But I'm afraid to admit it to myself. I'm afraid because it means my whole life is a lie. So I go around and around, whittling it in different ways. But I always come up with the same answer. I've been playing at being Briar the foster child—the abandoned—the unloved. I'm an impersonation of some in-your-face outsider. I'm not made up of my past, or my thoughts or my feelings—no.

Who am I?

It's so clear to me now. I don't exist at all—and I never did. I am not. And at the same time, I am. I am Briar of the fricken' Black Woods.

Dressed in flowing Renaissance-era robes of crushed red velvet, Briar stood in the shadowed wings of her school auditorium.

"Big night, huh?" Dax asked. He was standing behind her.

"Oh," said Briar. She looked out on the empty stage, but her mind seemed much further away. "Yeah." She flipped through the pages of the script, giving them one last glance.

"I don't get it," Dax said. "You've been moping around for six weeks now. If you need something to cry about, let's talk about my love life."

"I know, I know," Briar said. She rocked her head as though shaking off a bad dream. "I don't know what's wrong with me. I guess I'm confused." She shifted uncomfortably, rustling the pleated folds of her heavy gown.

"Really," Dax snorted. "Well, that's because your script is upside down." He turned around the small booklet in her hands. "Hey look, it's opening night! You've never done anything like this. And remember, before any of this you and I were nobodies.

Worse than nobodies—we were laughed-at nobodies. But look at you now: You're playing opposite Leon Squire in the school play. Leon Squire! You even kiss him in one scene. We're the next best thing to being one of those Lucky Kids. Have you practiced the kiss? Tell me you've practiced the kiss." Dax smiled mischievously.

"He's dressed like an ass when we kiss, Dax." Briar looked like she was chewing sauerkraut.

He looked at Briar's outfit. "Well, so is everyone else. Don't let that stop you."

"No, you don't understand," Briar said. "He's wearing a donkey's head when we kiss. It's just a stage kiss—it's fake. So it doesn't count. Besides, it's painfully obvious that he's not into me."

"What are you talking about?" Dax said. He was shaping Briar's perky breasts to look a bit plumper in her gown. "He's crazy about you."

"Dax. He's dating my foster sister. The only one he's crazy about is her. And frankly, anyone who voluntarily socializes with Megan is just plain crazy, if you ask me."

Right in that moment, Leon emerged from behind a curtain, came up from behind Briar and grabbed her by the shoulders. "There's my girl," he said. He was wearing his usual broad, sideways smile.

"Hey, Leon," Briar said with a smile she hoped was hidden.

"How's the best Titania since the invention of Shakespeare?" he asked. Dax crinkled his brow and gave Leon the once-over. He was wearing his own Renaissance garb of black velvet with a rivet-studded black bodice complete with puffed-out shoulders and puffy short pants.

"Nice tights," Dax said.

"Thanks. I think they make me look fat. Don't you?" Dax laughed and put a hand on Leon's shoulder. "Wow, someone's been hittin' the gym."

"Down boy," Briar said to Dax.

"What? It's merely an observation."

"Down boy."

They all laughed.

"Ready for our opening?" Leon asked Briar.

"I suppose," Briar said.

"You look…" He paused to consider his words carefully after taking a step back and inspecting Briar's gown. She could feel his eyes on her, following the curve of her velvety silhouette. "Incredible." He sounded surprised by his declaration.

And it was true. Briar was hardly recognizable now that she had removed her usual Goth black lipstick and eyeliner. Now that she wasn't able to retreat behind her mantle of grunge boots and tattered Victorian garb, she looked delicate, elfin, refined. Her skin was milky, and her cheeks had the slightest blush. Her lips were a watercolor pink and she pulled her raven hair up into a sleek ballerina's bun. Her piercings even seemed less noticeable now. But Briar felt naked, even vulnerable without her usual outfit that armored her against the dangers of the teenage world. And Leon staring at her in this way, with a goofy grin on his face, made her more self-conscious than ever.

"Thanks," Briar said. She knew he wanted her to say something back, to acknowledge that she understood that he might have thought of her as more than a buddy. But she was never going to embarrass herself again; she made a vow the day that they sat in his car together, not to mention the issue with Megan being his girlfriend. Briar would rather not awaken that demon. Best to handle this with a one-liner, she thought. And with a raised eyebrow she said, "Nice tights."

"I can't argue with that," Leon said. But he didn't laugh, or say anything more. Instead, his eyes trailed her beauty once more and it made her blush.

Then from the shadows of the stage, Megan appeared, smiling cruelly. "Well, handsome, what are you doing here in the dark?"

She sauntered out from behind a faux iron garden gate ornamented with plastic vines and bright yellow roses at the center of the stage. "Oh, I'm sorry. Was this a private conversation?"

"Yeah, private. Ha! Love it," Marnie said. She was following Megan like a shadow, nose in her phone.

"Shut up, Marnie," Megan said.

"Oh hey, Megan," Leon said. "We were just having a little pep-talk before the show."

Dax whispered to Briar, "Did she have a freakin' homing device surgically implanted in him, or what?"

Megan slinked up to Leon and wrapped her arms around his neck like two pythons ready for lunch. "I wouldn't want my little Bottom to tire out before the play," she said. She embraced him and placed her chin on his shoulder.

"Excuse me?" Dax blurted.

"That's the name of his character in the play. It's Bottom," Briar said from the side of her mouth.

"I wouldn't advertise that," Dax said.

Over Leon's shoulder, Megan glared at Briar and Dax. Then she turned her attention back to Leon. "I brought you a little opening night gift," she said. Leon laughed uncomfortably.

"Marnie!" Megan snapped like a gruff dog owner. Obediently, Marnie produced a red rose. Megan grabbed it and sniffed it before handing it to Leon along with a protracted kiss that was aimed at making Briar and Dax feel as though they were inconveniences. "Promise you'll think of me when you have your unfortunate, awkward moment with Briar."

Leon took the rose. "Who's the best girlfriend ever?"

Dax couldn't contain himself. "Just about anyone but her."

Megan ignored Dax. "Let's go over your lines one more time," she said. "Practice makes perfect." She escorted Leon through the trees, across the stage. Once Leon was safely out of earshot, Megan stepped back into the dim light where Briar and Dax could see her. "Break a leg," she said with a taunting lilt.

"Uh, thank you?" Dax looked disgusted.

"And if that isn't convenient," Megan added, "break something else." Then she turned with a hair flip and disappeared into the black curtains.

"Yeah. Catch you on the flippity-flip," Dax shouted back. Then to Briar he snorted, "That girl's got game. Creepy as shit—but game."

This exchange with Megan and Marnie could have thrown Briar off completely. Instead she plunged herself into the play. Once it began, she lost all track of her life with Megan and Marnie. For now, she was only Titania, Queen of the Fairies. Just as at her audition, Briar spoke her lines as if she had eerily transformed into her character. Dax sat in the front row beaming at his friend and her brilliant, if not anomalous talent.

Before Briar knew it, the time had come for her stage kiss with Leon. As Titania, she lay asleep amid a bed of plastic stage flowers. Leon as Bottom began to sing.

As Briar roused herself from her pretended rest, she said, "What angel wakes me from my flowery bed?" She looked at Leon, now shirtless, but donkey-headed. The light exaggerated his broad, clean musculature—his rippling abdominals and his barber-pole thick biceps. Briar found it distracting. "Gentle mortal, sing again…" she went on a bit mechanically. Her mind darted as they neared the kiss. At first she thought about the other kids at school, and how they would see her differently from now on. But that was a distraction from her fear. Sure it was a stage kiss, but it held meaning for her—and maybe it did for Leon too. "Mine ear is enamored…"

Her heart beat faster, her stomach knotted. She locked eyes with Leon through his mask and felt queasy. "Thy fair virtue's force doth move me to say, to swear, I love thee."

Leon smiled beneath his mask. Before the kiss, Titania called forth her fairies: "Peaseblossom! Cobweb! Moth! and

Mustardseed!"

But instead of the actresses playing their parts, an unexpected dark-robed figure, face—shadowed by the deep folds of a hood—entered through the garden gate. The figure stood next to Leon, who didn't seem to notice anything unusual.

The intruder pulled back the hood to reveal a young woman with thick blue dreadlocks. She wore strange gear-covered goggles, and there were strange dark shapes tattooed above and below her eyes. Her shoes were black with white spats that buttoned up to her knees, and she was fitted in a body-hugging corset. She gazed at the floor for a moment, and mouthed some words, looking like a perverse nun irreverently reciting a prayer. Then she fastened her dark empty eyes on Briar. Her goggles made a strange hissing noise as gears clicked causing the lenses to mechanically refocus.

The intruder pulled her dark red lips into a sickening grin while reaching to her side. Briar noticed the steely musculature of the woman's arms as she reached across her body, and how the boned bodice fit snugly to her tight, athletic physique.

Briar turned her eyes to the audience and noticed that no one was reacting to any of this. The only apparent oddity was Briar, who seemed to have stalled with her lines.

The intruder produced a short sharp instrument, like a thick needle, and with it she unexpectedly jabbed Leon's side. Briar waited for Leon to react, but he barely noticed. Then the woman produced a silver hand mirror with green jewels along its border and across its back. A small trickle of blood oozed from Leon's wound. The woman dabbed it with a finger, then licked it clean. She turned the mirror to reflect Leon. A stream of tiny silvery lights sparkled around his body. In an instant, he shrank to the floor, and his clothes collapsed into a heap. From them, a frog hopped out. The woman stuffed the transformed Leon into her cloak.

The audience gasped and applauded what appeared to be a

theatrical special effect. Briar froze with fear and confusion. She watched as the woman re-hooded herself and strode at a measured pace to the iron gate, vanishing through it with Leon.

Chapter 11

Briar stood onstage alone, fear stabbing her. There was only one thing to do, and she felt she had little time in which it could be accomplished. Even though other characters entered the stage and continued with the play, Briar bounded from the set and grabbed at Dax's wool scarf as he sat in front row. "Let's go," she said. There was a force in her voice.

"Oh, good lady," Dax said. He turned toward the audience in an awkward attempt to save the play. "Dost thou not need to return to thy players?"

Briar gripped Dax's scarf tighter. "Now," she said. Then she yanked Dax out of his seat.

"Jesus Christ, m'lady," Dax said.

The two of them picked up momentum through the center aisle and burst through the double doors into the shadows of the car-lined street.

"O.M. to the G., Briar. Have you lost your mind?" Dax asked. He pulled Briar's iron grip from his scarf and he rubbed his neck to get the feeling back. "Jeez, have you been working your biceps with Leon or something?"

Briar was about to attempt an explanation when she heard a noise like long fingernails tapping and clicking on cement. Briar looked away from Dax, focusing on the sound.

"Helloooo?" Dax sang waving a hand in front of Briar's eyes as if waking a hypnosis subject.

Not again, she thought. "Did you hear that?" Briar asked.

Dax looked left and right, shifting his eyes rapidly with are-you-kidding-me eyes. Then he spoke to Briar as though she was an un-medicated psychiatric patient. "Were you struck in the head with a dodge-ball? What in the hell are you doing? You've just left in the middle of your play!"

Briar heard growling. She saw a dark shape with luminous

amber eyes hiding in the shadows at the auditorium doors. She pulled Dax down and they fell behind one of the parked cars—hands first, onto the street. "Stay low," she commanded, and peeked up just enough to scan the area.

"I was going to say you're losing it. But now I see you've completely lost it," Dax said.

The creature stepped out from the shadows—it was one of the walking wolves Briar had seen before, with its long hand-like paws, sharp dripping fangs, and its crazed, hungry eyes. "Are these things fucking tracking my every move?" Briar mumbled.

Her thoughts became sketchy and unfocused; her breath was shallow and rapid. Then her stomach churned with heat that spread like liquid fire throughout her body. She would have panicked with such a feeling, but the heat-energy seemed to block out all fear. Briar's focus became acute and her vision sharpened. She reached up and tried the door of the car behind which they hid, but it was locked.

"Where did you park your car?" Briar asked.

"Uh, crazy much? I'll tell you right after you tell me what you think you're doing."

"Dax, we are in danger. Well, actually, *I'm* in danger, and you're just in harm's way. Sorry."

"What are you talking about?"

The wolf stepped one of its scraggly limbs down the school steps toward them, as though hungrily hunting, not wanting to disturb its prey. It squinted its furious eyes and saliva dribbled in long strands from its jaws.

"I know you can't see what I'm seeing, but believe me, Dax, we need to get into your car *right now*."

Dax sensed a desperation in Briar's voice that he had never heard before. He knew that whatever this episode was—even if she was having a mental breakdown—it wasn't the time to debate. Better to just get her home and hash this out later.

"This way," he said, though he didn't want to encourage any

of this.

"On three," Briar whispered. She counted on her fingers and then, holding hands, they darted away from the parked car and ran across the street to the gated school lot.

The wolf leapt on all fours, and bulleted toward them with a vicious, gravely growl. Briar yanked Dax's hand and pulled him through the chain link fence, crashed the gate closed, and fumbling for the chain and lock. The wolf slammed into the gate and tried to fit its snout through the links to bite off Briar's hand. But she managed to lock the padlock and pull her hands clear. She grabbed Dax's hand and dragged him deep into the lot. Then she pulled him to a crouch between two tightly parked cars.

The wolf yanked at the chain link with its knife-edged teeth, rattling it, wrenching it apart. Once it tore a hole big enough, it squirmed through and into the lot. Then it jumped and landed, claws first, onto the roof of one of the nearby cars, buckling the roof under its weight. Long claw marks ripped up the car's paint where the creature skidded to a stop.

"What was that—?" Dax stood up, gawking at the wrecked car. He turned on his cell phone to video record, but Briar slapped the phone away and dragged him down again.

"We have to be very still," she whispered. She felt a battle waging inside her—one side felt like melted gum on steaming pavement, the other felt an almost animal-like sense to survive— maybe even to destroy. She had never felt this other side before, but she could sense it all coming from that heat-energy coursing through her body. But it wasn't clear which side would win.

She peeked low through a car window and watched the wolf sniff the air, trying to get the scent of its prey. Then it bayed with a thirst for blood. She knew they must have thrown the creature off, making it both confused and angry. It snarled, and then with a shriek of its nails on metal, the beast sprang away. It hopped from one car roof to another, crumpling hoods until it left Briar's view.

Hearing each car buckling beneath some unseen force, Dax sank low to the ground. "I didn't sign up for this bullshit," he said.

Briar grabbed his arm. "Shut the hell up, Dax. Just tell me where you parked your car. I can't see it."

The reality of danger finally occurred to him and he couldn't find a way to form words. He began hyperventilating. Briar shook him, repeating her command. Finally he whispered, "It's over there." He pointed toward the cruddy old white convertible parked about six cars away from where they hid.

Briar needed Dax to focus. Just one wrong move could lead to ripped out throats. She held him by the shoulders and made serious eye contact. "Give me your keys—very quietly," she murmured.

Dax nodded. His eyes were clear and focused now. He drew the keys from his pocket and they made a small tinkling noise. In response, another car bounced and scraped as the wolf jumped atop, sniffing and grunting. Briar pulled Dax low and signaled for him to follow her beneath the car. Dax handed the keys to her and together they wriggled on their bellies across the asphalt beneath the cars.

Before crossing to the next vehicle, Briar looked around for paws. Then they'd scurry beneath the next car, and the next. It was slow going, and strenuous, as they snaked along. But eventually, Briar saw the notched footboard of Dax's car. They crouched low and Briar eased the key into the lock.

"Rush past me and get into the passenger seat," Briar said almost silently. Dax nodded and then flexed his neck as he curled himself into position. Then she pulled on the door handle and it opened with a mechanical clink. She swung the door as wide as she could, and Dax scrambled across the seats. Briar jumped in and slammed the door.

"Lock 'em," she said. Her voice was like steel girders.

"The doors don't lock anymore," Dax replied.

"Hey, Garden of Eden, bite the apple already and get your damn doors fixed."

Briar fiddled with the keys in the ignition. The engine turned once and then stalled. Dax looked around, still seeing nothing that could cause such damage. But he held the door handle in a vice grip.

The wolf landed with a thud on the hood of the car just in front of them. Dax only saw the car rocking by some unseen force, but Briar saw the wolf balancing itself on its shaggy, knotted limbs. "Get down!" Briar said and they both slid down as low as they could.

The wolf stood, its teeth glistening with rage. It cranked its head back with a mournful call to the moon, announcing the end. It flexed its hand-like paws, extending its sharp, black claws and it stepped across to Dax's hood. The old vehicle rocked on its corroded shocks. Dax held his breath, but that slight inhalation was enough to signal their presence.

The wolf lowered its ears and slammed its front paw against the car windshield while snapping its jaws and making wild, ferocious sounds. It gripped with its black claws and the glass cracked and punctured, showering Briar and Dax with sharp little crumbs. The creature battered the windshield again, this time breaking through. Glass sprayed inward like tiny chunks of ice, and Dax let loose a full-bodied shout. Now the wolf knew they were there. It reached its pointed claws in through the broken glass, flailed at the dashboard and tore out deep gouges. Then it fitted its muzzle in and tried to bite whatever it could.

Briar sat up and twisted the key in the ignition. The engine turned and the car rumbled with a roar that rivaled the wolf's own. Looking down for the gearshift, Briar placed the car in drive, and she stomped on the gas pedal. The car lurched forward and rammed the car in front of them, sending the wolf skidding over the other vehicle's hood. It whined, then slid down between the two bumpers and lay on the ground, stunned.

Briar then slammed the car into reverse and hammered her foot on the gas again. Then once more she shifted into drive as she clobbered the gas pedal. The car lurched forward. By then, the injured wolf was trying to stand. But before it had a chance to rise completely, the car smacked into it, squishing it between the two bumpers. Dax's car hood crumpled like a paper cup, and there was a hiss like pressured steam escaping. Briar watched— Dax still saw nothing—but the creature evaporated into a black cloud that blended into the black paint of the car in front of them.

Briar was not about to wait to see if anything further could happen. The engine still rumbled with its tinny, yanking gyrations, so she thrust it into reverse. Going backwards, the vehicle boomed through the chain link fence onto the street. The undercarriage scraped against the pavement, and sent sparks flying. Briar floored the gas pedal and steered, looking over her shoulder. "These things travel in pairs," she warned.

"What things?" Dax asked. His voice was strangled and he gritted his teeth, preparing to fight, if it came to that.

The car rocked as something heavy landed on the roof, and began tearing the fabric up. "Holy shit," Dax yelled as something he could not see pierced through the cloth roof with four small holes. Briar watched the black, hairy digits twisting around until they hooked onto the cab ceiling and began to pull, as if trying to open a can of sardines. "Kick the ceiling," Briar shouted. Dax hit the lever to make the seat drop back and he began bashing his shoes into the holes. The wolf on the roof screamed wildly and Briar watched as two of its claws pulled out. The bloody things dropped between Dax's legs.

Then the car conked out. Briar twisted the key in the ignition, but the starter only clicked.

With the car no longer in motion, the creature persevered with a frenzied panting. It ripped and pulled with its remaining claws until it succeeded in gouging a hole big enough to fit its fangy muzzle though. The beast snapped at whatever it could.

Dax could see the fabric tearing and ferociously shaking. "Try the car again," he shouted.

"Dax watch out!" Briar screamed. But it was too late. The wolf sank its teeth deeply into Dax's scarf and it pulled it out through the hole, strangling Dax. The wolf began to shake its head, as though killing small prey caught by the throat. Dax stiffened against the attack and tugged back on the scarf enough to open his airway.

"Oh my God! Start, you fucking car!" Briar yowled and slammed her fists against the steering wheel.

With that, her hands began to tingle and then two blue flames engulfed them. Briar gasped. She felt her heart make an indecisive tremble. But it subsided when she realized that the flames only tingled a little, and didn't burn. Instinctively, she reached up to the wolf's muzzle with one of the blue-flames.

"What—is—that?" Dax choked one word at a time through gritted teeth. I don't know!" Briar yelled back as the undulating blue thing suddenly detached. Tiny bolts of electrical current ran up Dax's scarf and she heard something sizzle. It suddenly smelled like overcooked meat.

The creature let out an ear-piercing shriek as it flipped onto the street. It was badly singed and much of its exposed flesh hung rubbery from where it had fallen away from its face, leaving half of its skull visible and bloody. It hobbled away from the car and down the empty street, screeching in a high-pitched wail through the blackness.

"Dax! Holy shit!" she shouted. But Dax couldn't hear her. He was twisted into ball, coughing and drinking in air. "Dax are you all right?"

Briar didn't dare take time to turn the car around. She drove it backward all the way home, hoping that no other wolves could follow.

Chapter 12

Briar chugged Dax's car up to her driveway and backed in while scanning the street for more danger. As soon as she turned the car off, it fizzled and sighed, as though it were exhaling its last gasp. Dax remained silent. He stared out the window, flexing his jaw. He had long since taken off the scarf and his neck was boiled-ham red.

"Dax, everything's going to be okay," she said. She tried to sound reassuring, but she wasn't sure at all. Briar tried to take his hand, but he sharply stared at her as though she were the invisible thing that choked him. "You told me wolves. I thought it was a joke." He yanked his hands away and turned to look around for more of *them*. "I have no idea what we need to do now. But we can't stay here." He reached to explore the shredded opening in the roof.

"Dax—you have to trust me now," she replied. It was more than a little surprising to Briar that she could sound as authoritative as she did. But then again, she had never found herself in such circumstances. She smoothed his hair and he refocused his eyes. "First things first."

Briar grasped the key pendant dangling from her neck. It was protection, or so Ash said. She didn't know what to believe anymore. But she had no choice but to trust in the impossible. "We have to go—together." She pushed open the squeaky car door with her foot. "Go?" he asked. He braced himself against his door at first, but knew they couldn't stay safe with the door open. He gave a short nod—at least giving the form that he understood, but his wild eyes told another story. He grabbed the door handle. "On three," he said. They counted down together and then rushed out from the car to the front porch.

Briar shoved open the front door and together they spilled in. Then they scrambled to slam and bolt it behind them.

"Well, well," Matilda said, uncrossing her fuzzy-slippered feet and tossing aside a double-layer box of chocolates. She was sitting just beyond in the living room, watching old television re-runs, her puffy, coiffed hair wrapped in sheets of toilet paper. "Look who's decided to grace us." Her words slurred together; when she stood, she lost her balance, sloshing the contents of her glass. She never noticed that it dribbled down to the shag carpet. Matilda sized up Briar's costume. "It's Lady Godiva. Or—who are you, anyway?"

Briar ignored her, shored Dax up around the waist, and headed for the basement. "You just wait there—just a minute, your royal heinie," Matilda growled. Then she took a hearty gulp.

"Leave us alone," Briar fumed.

"What did you just say to me?" Matilda asked. She moved to block Briar's way. "You're no stage diva. You're nothing! And it will be a cold day in hell before I let you bring some renegade cast member from *Brokeback Mountain* to your bedroom. This is a goddamned Christian home."

Briar stopped and glared at her for a moment. She pushed Dax aside and marched past Matilda into the kitchen.

"There goes our little money maker," Matilda said. She had a lopsided grin. "Oh, pardon me. That's not politically correct." She pressed a shushing finger to her lips and slurped from her glass. "She's our cash cow. Better?" Matilda asked. "Haven't paid rent in ten years." Then she yelled over her shoulder to the kitchen. "Cash cow! Moo!"

She lost her balance and her glass tumbled to the floor. "Ooh, how impolite," she said. She went to fill another glass. "You're a whiskey man, right?" she asked Dax.

Briar emerged from the kitchen with a mousetrap in her hand.

"What's that?" Matilda asked, her upper lip curling. "What have you got…there?"

Briar held the trap out and snapped its spring-coiled

mechanism in Matilda's face.

She squealed and fell backward into the marshmallow koosh of her overstuffed armchair. She cowered, huddled into a heap of decorative pillows, and twitched her nose.

"That ought to take care of her for a while," Briar said. She grabbed Dax by the hand and together they clomped down the decaying wooden steps to the basement, making sure to lock the door behind them.

She sat Dax on her bed, then ran to the closet door shouting, "Help!" But once she swiveled it open, rather than seeing the strange, endless, candlelit hallways, the white doors or the parlor, it was only her usual limp black outfits hanging there. She closed the door and ran to the basement window. She could see the birdhouse hanging from the apple tree, and she waved her arms frantically, hoping someone inside could see. But there was no dim flicker of light this time. "Myrtle! Poplar! Peeps— anyone!"

They were probably gone now, Briar realized. They had watched over her. But she turned them away and they probably left for good—wherever it was they were going.

Then Briar realized it was only days away from her sixteenth birthday. *What had they called the thing people believed about her? Omens?* Even if it still felt like a serious lapse in judgment for her to entertain these ideas, it was clear that other people—beings— whatever knew her, and wanted her—one way or another. Her vulnerability was complete—and it was all her fault. She knew nothing really of spells, werewolves or curses—just what little she had picked from dusty volumes in the used bookshop. And she really only read those to help develop a style-statement. Staying where she was, in her depressing-if-not-familiar world, meant that she was now hunted and completely defenseless.

A primal, gut-level panic began to spread through her whole body. It felt like she'd never catch a full breath again, and every- thing took on a spinning, dream-like quality. She ran back to Dax, grabbed him by the arms and dragged him toward the closet. "What are you doing?" he asked.

Briar let him go and then shouted to the air. "If you're there— if you're real—I need you now." It felt like she was in quicksand. Her struggles just took her deeper.

Dax raised his voice. "Just stop it now. You're acting crazy. We've had enough for one night."

She turned to face the closet again. Ash told her that the key— the trinket—needed to touch her skin. It seemed so silly to do. But there was nothing left but to try the ridiculous. She clutched it in one hand and closed her eyes. "Please," she whispered. "Someone help me." She reached for the door, but before she could touch the knob it turned by itself. Then it slowly creaked open.

The world behind the door was there, but it was changed. The long candlelit halls were gone. All that she could see in the murk of darkness were giant nails, stuck through splintered wood walls. The place was deserted. "Hello?" she called out. She didn't want to step into that place again for fear of not knowing how to return. But she had little choice. "Help! Someone please!" The only sound was some airy rustling.

She grabbed Dax by the arms. "Trust me. This is our only safety now." He looked at her with his impassive chiseled face. Then he peered into the closet and saw the dank room extending behind it. "What—?" he asked. "How long has this empty old room been here?" His eyes widened and his face slackened in wonder.

She took him by the hands. "We have to keep moving, Dax." He nodded and they entered the closet-passage. Once through, the door closed by itself, shutting them in complete darkness. Briar heard the airy rustling again, this time it sounded like it was a little bit closer. It took time for Briar to adjust her vision in the dark. But soon she could distinguish a few blacker shapes within the deep blackness.

"Hello?" She called out louder than before.

The strange noise started again; it sounded like great bees buzzing about her ears, or a swarm of humming birds trembling their wings, but just out of Briar's reach. This time the sound came from a different spot in the room. Then it happened again somewhere else.

"Dax, where's your phone?" He fished in his front pocket while Briar called out, "Who is that? Poplar? Myrtle? Ash?" He handed her the phone, then she fumbled with it, and turned the screen to light the way. The glow was enough to see perhaps a foot or two ahead. That's when she saw something brown flicker in an instant from her view. It seemed to go up toward the ceiling. But when she pointed the phone's light upward, nothing was there.

Dax took the phone, scrolled through the screen, turned on a flashlight app, and illuminated a bit more of the area with its small, mean glare. Briar felt something pull at her dress and she whirled around. Dax shone the light down and there, only as high as Briar's waist, was Peeps' chick. It looked at Briar tilting its head, then it preened the small new feathers on one of its wings. The chick suddenly burst into a storm of frantic wing beats and disappeared from view.

"Jesus—did you see that?" Dax threw the tiny beam of light around the room some more.

Then more wing beats started from another part of the room, and Briar remembered that Peeps had three eggs. Dax tried to shine the light toward the sound, but before he could do so, something sharp struck one of Briar's ears. She doubled over, wincing, groaning, grabbing at the wound, feeling her fingers getting wet with blood. Dax dropped the phone to help her, but she never felt his touch. She couldn't hear if any of the chicks were close by, as the ringing that now played in her ears deafened any other sound.

"Help!" she shouted again to the air.

She reached for Dax, but couldn't feel his arms. He was right there, she thought. "Dax?" She picked up the phone, pointed the small beam around, and found the corner of the birdhouse where Peeps built her nest. There she saw two of the chicks, their curious black shining eyes watching something other than the light shining in their direction—which seemed odd to Briar.

Then she felt a great windy vortex. Feathers and straw filled the room and she had to cover her eyes to keep the airborne grit out.

"Help me," she heard Dax say. His voice seemed far off and small.

She shone the light toward the pile of sticks and feathers again, only to find Peeps perched on the edge of her nest, holding Dax up by his shirt collar and dangling him above her babies. The chicks opened their beaks and began to cry sharply.

"Dax!" Briar shouted. Her ear felt singed and it amplified as she shouted. She grabbed at the pulpy mess and it suddenly occurred to her that Peeps might have clipped it off.

Peeps turned her head at an angle toward Briar, suddenly swinging Dax out of the nest.

"Peeps no!" Briar screamed. "Drop him."

But Peeps didn't seem to understand or perhaps she thought of Briar as one more morsel of food. Then Briar remembered how to stop the sparrow's attacks.

"Hush little baby, don't say a word..." Briar began to sing. Her voice cracked and the tune was thready, but she went on. "Momma's gonna buy you a mocking bird." By now Peeps seemed to forget her task. She turned her head, swinging Dax out of the nest again. "And if that mocking bird don't sing—" Peeps dropped Dax and he slouched to the floor. "—Mama's gonna buy you a diamond ring." Briar signaled to Dax to get away. He crawled as fast as he could on all fours away from the deadly nest.

Briar couldn't remember any more of the song. The chicks

started screeching again and this seemed to awaken Peeps from her trance-like fascination. She flitted down from the nest, scratching the floor as she bounced toward Briar, cheeping as shrilly as ever. Briar turned on the phone's internet browser to quickly look up the lyrics, but Peeps charged forward. Soon she was upon Briar, and pinned her back against a wall with one of her sharp talons.

Chapter 13

Peeps opened her beak to snip across Briar's throat when the door behind Briar opened, bathing Peep's birdhouse with a glaring illumination. Briar fell backward onto the gleaming parlor floor planks, right between Poplar and Ash. In the commotion the enormous sparrow fluttered away. She landed on her brood and voiced an angry objection with a few sharp chirps.

Briar lay on the floor, covered in stray straw and loose down.

"I heard her sing that time," Poplar said.

"I thought one of us gave her the gift of song," Ash complained. "That was just awful."

Myrtle spotted Dax on hands and knees at the far side of the birdhouse, and she clicked along in her sturdy heels to examine him. He knelt nearby, his face was pale green and his eyes were fixed like a melted doll. Myrtle held her glasses up to scrutinize the boy. "What in the Goose's name is *this* about?"

"Oh dear!" Poplar scurried and fussed over Dax, helping him to stand.

Sherman was draped around Myrtle's shoulders as always, and she petted him. He lifted his head and saw Briar. "Well, well, if it isn't Miss Ingrate. Come scurrying back to shelter like one of the Three Piggies, have you? Well you're too late," the fox said. Then to Ash he said, "Make them go away. We have serious matters—and none of them concern *her*." He jumped from Myrtle's shoulders to an oversized wingback chair. He tucked his nose beneath his tail and ignored her by pretending to sleep.

Myrtle strode like a stork back into the parlor, stepping over Briar who was still sitting in stunned amazement. Myrtle posed against a locked bookcase, folded her arms across her chest and drew her ruby lipsticked lips tightly together. "So, you've brought...a friend."

"It's not like I had a choice," Briar said. She stood up and brushed off loose feathers and straw. "He and I were attacked. I had to bring him with me for safety."

"Attacked!" Poplar said. She was already walking with Dax tottering him toward the antique couch. Poplar already began fussing with his hair and wiping smudges from his face. "He needs a little of my special tea," Poplar said.

"Chamomile, right?" Briar asked.

"Oh don't be silly," Poplar clucked. "This calls for the Wolfsbane, Poison Sumac, or maybe even Dragon's Blood. Poor thing's nearly out of his mind with fear. Oh—" Poplar stopped her rambling and thought for a moment. "Unless, of course, he's just out of his mind in general. What's his name dear?"

"Dax," said Briar.

Poplar suddenly brightened. "I know what will help!" She suddenly slapped Dax's face.

"How was that supposed to help him?" Briar asked.

"Oh don't be silly," Poplar said. "That was just for me."

Dax blinked a few times and then began to rub his jaw where Poplar had smacked him.

Myrtle marched over to Briar with her librarian's posture. "We haven't a moment to lose."

Briar erupted in a flurry of raw emotion now that there were no more immediate dangers. "I think—I think we're too late." She thought of Leon and realized that all of this was happening because of her. There was nowhere to hide her feelings, and she began to cry. "The attack—it was out of control."

"What do you mean?" Myrtle asked, the lines beneath her eyes deepening.

"They got him. Whoever you thought was after me took a friend of mine. Someone changed him into a frog and vanished. Then two wolves—" She couldn't finish. Leon was gone and there would be no getting him back.

Ash, now dressed as a Japanese geisha, with a white silk kimono and wooden sandals, rushed to Myrtle's side. "The Lady

Orpion's work." He straightened the chopsticks stuck in a V-formation in his black hair bun, which looked outrageous in contrast to his short-cropped beard.

Myrtle hesitated. "A worthy guess, Ash. But how can we be sure? You know as well as I that those who would profit from either success or failure of the child are legion." Then she turned her attention back to Briar. "How was it done?"

It took Briar a moment to choke down the pain and return to the present moment. "What do you mean?" she asked.

Myrtle simmered, but contained it. "I mean how was the boy altered?"

"A cloaked woman—blue hair—tattoos on her face. She had this totally pimped-out hand mirror. She stuck him in the side—my friend Leon—and took his blood. And then he just—changed."

Myrtle and Ash nodded to each other. Ash snapped open a small painted fan and whooshed himself with it.

"Indeed. The speculum. Blood magic." Myrtle's eyes slowly tracked back and forth. She turned tautly and paced. "This is quite serious. There are three days remaining before your sixteenth birthday, and our protections wane with the setting of each sun." She reached out to trace the outline of Briar's key. The key responded by glowing bright blue. Then it faded, like a burning fire poker doused with water. "And when the sun sets on the third day, nothing will stand between you and the Lady Orpion."

"Who is this Lady Orpion? What the hell does she want from me? What did I ever do?" At the mere mention of Orpion's name, Briar's heart throbbed as though she were dangling from a cliff. Her breath became unsteady, and she had to consciously work to regain control.

"There are those who believe that you alone can champion the Realms," Ash interjected, flashing his shadowed eyes at Myrtle. "The Lady Orpion sees you as a direct threat to her throne, to her power."

"The Realms?"

"Our home," Myrtle said. "Your true home, Briar."

"Oh yes, dear," Poplar sang. "Born in our cottage in the Squirrel's Province, you were. We hid you ourselves here, among the commons, when you were just a day or two old. Do you remember how sweet she was?" she asked Myrtle, clucking. "Always putting that key in her mouth!"

Briar realized that once again she had put the key pendant in her mouth without thinking. She let it fall out.

"Lady Orpion vowed to find and destroy you, so we sealed off the gateways between the Realms and the commons ourselves," Poplar continued. "That way no Realmsmen or common could ever cross between them."

"...Nor find you." Myrtle finished Poplar's thought. "But sixteen years have almost passed. Our protections run thin. Interested parties have begun their own quests to fulfill one omen or another."

"Omen?" Briar asked, looking alarmed.

"Many have waited for your return," Poplar said, nodding assuredly.

Myrtle raised her hand above her head making a quick geometric shape with a finger. In turn, the bookcase behind her unlocked with a loud clink and the doors opened wide. "The thing of omens is that details change from one seer to the next."

"Sister," Poplar said. She took on a singsong voice like a school teacher instructing. "Circumstances change. Omens must change with circumstances." Myrtle raised a single eyebrow and sucked her lips together as though tasting a lemon. Then Poplar said, "Always had her doubts about old Rapunzel and her visions, she has."

"Rapunzel?" Briar asked looking into the faces of Poplar, Myrtle, and Ash. "Wait a minute—you mean, like the fairytale character, *Rapunzel*?"

Sherman made his way to Myrtle from his sleeping place on the old plush wingback chair. He hopped to her shoulder and wrapped himself around. "Why do commons insist on calling dillywigs by that distasteful name?" he asked. "It's absolutely degrading. And coming from Miss Ingrate, it's even worse."

Briar looked confused.

"We're dillywigs. Not *fawyries*, you absurd pretender!" Sherman shouted.

Poplar snapped back. "Don't you have a chicken coop to raid somewhere?"

Sherman just snuffed and looked the other way. "That, madam, is a stereotype that goes unappreciated by me."

Myrtle looked down at the floor. The only sound in the room was the pop and crackle from a burning log in the fireplace.

"Well, tell the girl, sister," Poplar insisted. "She must know what she must—"

"Enough of this dithering!" Sherman flashed his tiny white fangs. "Either you tell the girl this instant, or I will." Briar searched the faces of Poplar, Myrtle and Ash. The three of them eyed one another, but remained silent. Then, without waiting for a response Sherman blurted it out. "Very well. You are Briar of the Black Woods, fated to the Tale of Briar Blackwood and the Grim Sleepdeath. There! Was that so difficult?"

"Sherman, so help me, I'll have a herd of huntsmen with bugles and bloodhounds after you!" scolded Poplar.

Sherman curled up around Myrtle's neck with a smile that showed his pointy front teeth. "Well, I don't know about you, but I feel much better," he said. Then he bit his own tail to form the usual fluffy loop around Myrtle's shoulders.

"Grim Sleepdeath? What is he talking about?" Briar asked.

"Oh—details, details," Myrtle said. She made a gesture with her hands like shooing flies from a picnic. She stammered for a moment, seeming to chew each word over in her mind before saying anything further. "Well—it involves a curse, a spindle of a spinning wheel, and, well—I think the rest is self-explanatory. It's all in your Tale—"

Watching Briar's open mouth and bugged eyes, Poplar intervened. "Sister," she said, "you're scaring the poor thing." She turned to Briar and took her hands. "It's not a real death, dear. We softened it as best we could with enchantments." She looked down at Briar's pendant. "You'll just enter a kind of, well, sleep, for a long time." Then she smiled as if what she just said made everything better.

"Are you fucking kidding me?" Briar asked.

"Oh—there's that potty mouth again," Myrtle said.

"So, you're telling me that it's already fated that I'll die from some sleepdeath when I turn sixteen?"

"Not die, dear," Poplar said again softly. "Just sleep. For a long, long time."

"How long? A day or two?"

Sherman perked up, "Longer."

"What, like a week?" Dax asked.

"Longer," Sherman tittered.

"*How* long?"

"I've heard the sleepdeath can last for a hundred years, maybe more," Sherman said unable to suppress his glee.

Briar sat down on one of the ornate chairs and put her hands to her mouth. Everyone remained solemn faced, mute, staring at the ground. Briar recalled her experience in the stone chamber, and her awful, uncontrollable obsession with the spinning wheel she found there. She realized just how close she came to pricking her finger. She looked at Ash with wide eyes. He subtly put the fan across his ruby bow-lips and almost imperceptibly shook his head.

"Wait a minute. Are you telling me that I am—I can't even say it. It's too outrageous." She laughed out loud. "That I am the sleeping beauty?"

"Beauty might be a bit of a stretch," Sherman sassed.

"Sherman!" Poplar thundered. "How would you like to be a piñata at a hyperactive child's birthday party?"

"Humph!" Sherman pouted, and scampered down from Myrtle's shoulder. "I was only trying to lighten the mood." He trotted into the kitchen, his nails clicking irritably against the floor.

"Yes," Myrtle said, crossing the room to sit on the proper edge of the couch. She smiled weakly, straightening her red skirt and touching the small top hat that seemed to defy the laws of gravity sitting at the impossible angle on her head. "Commons often refer to this Tale in that fanciful way," she began after clearing her throat. "They know it only from dream and distant memory; our worlds have been separated from times before our own. The Tales are never true as remembered by commons. But most important for you to know, Briar, is that the Tales are our fate. Yours and ours; none can escape."

"There are rumors, though," Poplar interrupted. "Rebels, *talebreakers*, they call them."

Myrtle turned pointedly to Poplar. "Sister, I think it may be time for tea." Poplar smiled broadly, clapped her lace-gloved hands and scurried into the kitchen. As usual, Poplar got pots and pans clattering behind the swinging door.

Myrtle arose and sat straight-backed next to Briar. "Your friend Leon was altered and stolen only to draw you into the Realms—away from our protection. True, the Lady Orpion may have him, but others with designs of their own may have him as well. There's no real way to know. But one thing is for certain: you or your friend would fetch a price at market."

"I don't like the sound of this," Dax said. To Briar he said, "What have we gotten into?"

"*We*? I am not exactly thrilled that you've been dragged into our little situation," Myrtle said with a precise clip in her tone. She poised her hands upon her lap and her pearl-button cuffs glistened in the firelight. "Yet, here you are." She drew her lips into an annoyed smile, and then her face fell.

Briar stood up and then sat beside Dax. She took one of his hands and leveled her gaze to meet his. "We can't leave Leon there—in those Realms, wherever he is." Then Briar asked Myrtle, "How can we bring him back?"

"There are two things, for now anyway," Myrtle said. She traced some triangles and squares in the air with one hand. Suddenly, one of the bookcase's built-in drawers snapped and clinked as a dozen or more internal locks released. A drawer at the center of the cabinet, big enough to hold a large book, opened. From it flew a leather-bound volume the size of a dictionary. It soared across the room like a bee into Myrtle's hands.

Ash spoke up, heat in his pancake-white face. "You can't send the girl into the Realms. It's too dangerous. She has no skill. Not yet, anyway. How will she survive, Myrtle?" It sounded to Briar as though this conversation had occurred many times before.

"If she stays here, the boy's fate is sealed," Myrtle said without looking at Ash. She thumbed through the pages of her book. "—As is hers. If she finds the boy and the book before three days, she can return to our safety."

Myrtle's usual, sensible approach never sat well with Ash. He was visibly shaking in his kimono. "She cannot find the book. *We* cannot find it, ourselves. What madness is this?"

"What book?" Briar asked.

"There is a certain compendium that was once in our possession," Myrtle said like an old mother reading a child's story. "*The Book of Cinder and Blight.*"

"Sounds like a real page-turner," Briar said. "What kind of a book is it?"

"A book of dark things. Wicked, vile things," Myrtle said.

"Why would you want it then?" Dax interjected.

"I think I liked this boy better when he was scared out of his wits," Myrtle said. "We need it—*you* need it because within the

Book of Cinder and Blight is the antidote for your Leon." Myrtle placed a hand on a page of the tome in her lap. "In our possession, Orpion cannot use it for her own ends."

"This is suicide," Ash insisted.

Myrtle made a motion, midair, with her index finger and thumb that mimicked sewing with a needle and thread. Ash fell back into his chair, grabbing at his mouth. When he moved his hands, Briar saw that his mouth was now sewn shut with zig-zagging sutures. Briar gasped; Dax looked like he might vomit.

"Well, what say you, Briar of the Black Woods, champion of the Realms?" Myrtle asked with a penetrating stare and an air of anticipatory triumph.

Briar turned to Dax, a strange look in her eyes. From that look, Dax understood that life as they knew it up to now had come to an end. There were things that must be done now—matters of life and death.

"I can't go back, Dax," Briar said. "Not to that place. Not to that life." Dax could not answer.

He shook his head and bit a lip. "But think about it, Briar. What can you do about magic? What can you do about plots that have been hatching for who-knows-how-long? And so what if you go to wherever they're suggesting? Don't you think someone is waiting for you to follow the trail to Leon? You'll step right into their trap."

Briar shook her head. "As screwed up as this sounds, Dax, if I don't do something—if I don't act now, they'll just find me and finish me off anyway. We've already got wolves creeping out of every corner. I either do something, or I just wait around to be killed."

"She is correct," Myrtle said. "Magic is the only way to stop the forces at play now. She may not know much of magic yet, but she soon will. And a master of it she shall become."

Dax looked into Briar's face and saw a fire of determination burning. He knew that Briar would likely do this alone, if need be. But she shouldn't. Now was the time to stand by her side and see her to safety. Things would be different, he knew it. But there didn't seem to be another way. He took Briar's hands and nodded with a smile.

"I always liked this boy," Myrtle said.

Briar turned to Myrtle with a daring smile. "So tell me more about this book."

Chapter 14

"Perhaps Ash has a point," Sherman piped up as he entered from the kitchen. He shimmied like a squirrel to stand on the arm of a couch and he clutched it with his claws, his wild bush of a tail went straight. "This girl has the magical ability of gravel. And even that's an insult to gravel," he huffed.

Myrtle raised her eyebrows. "That is exactly why you shall accompany young Briar and her friend."

Sherman's eyes seemed to grow to twice their size. "What?" he asked. "You can't be serious."

"Oh, I am quite serious, Sherman," Myrtle replied. She stood carrying the old leather-bound book in both hands. Then she turned to Briar and Dax to explain. "You see, before Sherman came to live here with us, he was quite the accomplished enchanter. Novices from every shire and province sought his instruction."

"I see where this is headed." Sherman intervened. "And it shall not work. I am not going with Queen Emo and her foppish satyr back to the dangers of the Realms. No thank you."

Dax looked at Briar. "Nothing gets past that fox. He nailed you, all right."

Poplar ignored Sherman and chimed into what Myrtle had said, "Sherman instructed the greats: Ashputtel, Little Red Cap, Fundevogel, Hansel and Gretel— Recites most of the spell books by heart, he does."

Sherman turned up his nose. "As tempting as the offer may be to help Little Miss Ingrate go on this marvelous and existential journey to find the meaning of life, I am telling you once and for all that she is not the girl we seek, nor shall I accompany such a rank amateur."

Myrtle pivoted around on her sensible button-spattered heels. "You can and you *shall* go, Sherman," she said. Then with a touch of heat, she added, "You know as well as I that the Realms have been sealed off. No Realmsmen may cross the boundary without immediate incineration. But a fox—a fox can cross through."

"Ah, well, whose idea was it to use the Char-Char Charm?" Sherman asked with a told-you-so tone. "Certainly not mine. Now it won't fade until the girl turns sixteen."

"Don't worry," Briar said. She marched over to Myrtle and Poplar. Sherman decided to take over Myrtle's pre-warmed seat and he curled up in a smug little ball. Briar continued, "Dax and I will do just fine. I'm not sure we could learn anything from him anyway. Besides, I think I've picked up a thing or two just by watching the two of you. Look—" Briar flicked her fingers at a nearby candelabra, but nothing happened. She tried again, this time moving her hands and hips in gyrating hip-hop moves, finishing by pointing her hands at Sherman. All the while, Sherman watched with his white-trimmed muzzle agape, and he flattened himself as soon as she pointed her hands in his direction.

Then he puffed out his fur and gave a short growl. "This is beyond ridiculous. You're not even using your trinket. It's a world gone mad."

"Who needs a trinket?" said Briar, "I know what I'm doing. Step aside, fur coat." Then she began flicking her fingers at other things in the room.

Sherman dove behind his chair and Briar could only see the soft white tufts from his ears. "Someone stop that lunatic before she hurts someone—or turns herself into a flaming gecko," Sherman shouted.

Dax said, "I'm with the fuzzy little dog, Briar. That's not even a decent pop-and-lock."

Myrtle watched with the ends of her ruby lips curled up into a crafty smile. "That's marvelous raw talent."

"Oh yes," Poplar replied as she emerged from the kitchen. "Can you show me that last move, dear?" She tried to imitate, but nearly ripped her hip-hugging skirt.

Myrtle nodded. "Yes. I can see it—a whole new trend in magic. Soon we'll all be doing this. I'm starting to understand that perhaps the Omens were right after all—"

Sherman peeked from behind the couch. "You call that talent? Those aren't magical passes. They're just rubbish."

"I don't know—" Myrtle said.

Sherman's face drooped like a stuffed animal that had its cotton batting extracted. He wriggled up Myrtle's body, curling up around her neck. "Not another word about it. I know I shall regret it, but I shall take on this extreme-makeover. If I can teach this nose-ringed slacker to cast even one decent enchantment, it shall be among my greatest accomplishments."

"If you say so," Myrtle said.

"Now, I suggest we all get a good night's sleep." Sherman gazed at Briar with his fierce gold-flecked eyes. "I dare say that your feeble mind will need rest, if you are to learn anything in such a short time."

Myrtle placed her thumb and forefinger on an illustration in the old book she carried. The image stuck to her fingers and she lifted it off the page. She stood and held it in front of her eyes. "Goggles," she warned the others. Myrtle reached up a sleeve and found her brass goggles with her free hand. Briar helped her to strap them on while Ash and Poplar put on their own. "Shield your eyes," Myrtle said over her shoulder to Briar and Dax.

"These were to be your quarters at Blackwood Manor," Myrtle murmured. Briar peeked through her fingers at what looked like a holographic transparency of a room. "That was before the Lady Orpion burned the place to the ground." Myrtle sighed heavily. "No sense in wasting a picture of the place, at any rate." Then she stretched the image with her finger and thumb. The image glowed brightly and remained suspended in midair while she set the book down. Then she stretched the image more with her hands, stretching it out here and there, like taffy, until what once looked like a small transparency became a three-dimensional room in which they were all standing.

Once the blinding glow of her magic faded, Dax uncovered his eyes and looked around in wild wonder of how any of this could be possible. "There's no emoticon that expresses how I feel right now," he said. Briar took his hand and they stood with their faces looking like deflated balloons.

The room had a vaulted ceiling, at least two stories high, with thick arched wooden supports. A queen bed was leveled against the wall closest to the bedroom door and deep blue velvet swags draped around its ornately sculpted redwood frame. A carved Gothic armoire stood opposite the bed. Bats, gnarled ogres, cyclops, and wolves were seamlessly intertwined in a macabre dance that stretched across the face of the wardrobe. Breaking up the carving were two full-length mirrors, inset into the doors.

Bizarre portraits framed in ornate rococo gold neatly adorned the soaring red satin-lined walls. In one depiction, a white cat dressed in dark robes and a judge's powdered wig stared out with steely blue eyes. In another, a pale ominously smiling woman stood within a dark misty forest. Her long curling orange hair flowed down her body, covering her otherwise bare breasts; a long red-hooded cape hung loosely on her shoulders. Each painting was more peculiar than the next: a goose sitting cross-legged on a plush antique throne, a goggle-eyed marionette with a trickle of blood seeping from its wooden mouth, and a black-cloaked figure whose face could not be seen, standing beneath storm clouds over grasslands that stretched out to the distant horizon.

Myrtle and Ash left the room to get blankets and Poplar stayed behind. "That's the Blackwood gallery, dear," she said. Briar watched Poplar's dreamy smile while gazing up at the portrait of the red-haired woman. "Brings back memories," she said. Then her expression changed and was laden with some unseen weight. "Some of them are oddly disturbing, but they're memories nonetheless." Then she made a quick intricate design with her fingers and a feather duster popped into her hands amid a flurry of sparks. She began dusting objects in the room with the wrong end of the duster. "It's like the old rodent-free days." She patted her stomach and looked away, as though hiding some emotion.

Briar and Dax looked at the odd pictures and shot each other puzzled looks.

"You mean you didn't always eat—you know—?" Briar asked.

"Eat what?" Dax asked. "You mean—? Okay that's just a hair ball waiting to happen."

"Heavens no—who would ever *choose* to eat such things?" Poplar said. She clutched the feather duster to her chest. "Insects perhaps, but not rats. And Ash, always changing from one look to the next. And poor Myrtle—" Poplar put a hand to her doughy cheek. "She got the worst of it—" Her voice cracked. She turned away and busied herself with dusting, not saying anything more about what had happened.

Briar and Dax exchanged glances, but neither decided to press Poplar for more. Instead, they ambled across elaborately woven rugs, touching the glittering array of treasures and oddities scattered here and there, including a floor-to-ceiling library, and an arched window that looked out to a starry sky.

While passing by the mirror in the armoire, a ghostly image caught Briar's eye. In the reflection of the room, off to one side and behind her, stood a creature—or perhaps it was a tiny man— Briar couldn't be sure. A little thing it was, indeed—no bigger than a human hand. He had golden skin that looked leathery and scuffed, and the tiniest deep black eyes. He was wearing a red and gold cap with fringe and feathers that he removed with one of his clawed, gangling hands. Then he smiled broadly, showing hundreds of golden toothpick-sized splinter-sharp teeth. "Findery me," it said in a whispering rasp. Briar turned around, expecting to see the little gargoyle behind her, but it was not there. When she turned back to the mirror, it had vanished.

"Did you see that?" Briar asked.

"What, dear?" Poplar asked, still preoccupied with her thoughts, and still fussing with the room.

"In the mirror. I saw some—I don't know—a creature. It was wearing a weird hat." Briar turned and looked around the room again. "I thought I saw it. And when I turned around, it was gone."

Poplar clutched her heart. "Sister," she exclaimed. "The mirror."

"Ash!" Myrtle shouted as she clip-clopped at a brisk pace down the hall. She entered the room with an armload of blankets. Poplar pointed to the mirrored armoire. Myrtle rushed over and covered it with blankets. "How did you overlook the speculum?" Myrtle shouted to Ash as he entered the room.

"With all the excitement, I guess none of us really noticed it," he said. He clapped his fan closed and helped Myrtle to cover every inch of mirror.

"Should the Lady see us—the consequences!" Myrtle said.

Ash clapped the fan shut and slapped it twice on the palm of his free hand. Then he made a quick mid-air star with his hand. "Cover your eyes," he said. Then twinkling sparks floated lazily from between his palms and covered the armoire. The light specks multiplied until the entire thing was illuminated.

Briar felt the heat of his magic, and at the peak of its brightness, the specks detached and drifted back to Ash's palms leaving no trace of the armoire behind. He snapped open the fan, as though he had barely exerted himself, and busied himself with fanning again. Briar and Dax uncovered their eyes and blinked at each other.

"Did you see anything in that mirror?" Myrtle asked. She sounded positively ill.

Briar shook her head. "I think it was just my imagination."

Poplar glanced at Myrtle with a worried expression.

"You needn't concern yourself with anything here. There are indeed shadows and memories of shadows in this place," Myrtle said. "But shadows and memories have no substance. They'll never harm, unless you beckon to them and linger in their presence. And in this place, after all, they are nothing but ink, in a picture, in a book."

It sounded convincing enough. But Briar could hear the sense of worry clutching behind their soothing words.

"Tomorrow morning your journey begins, so sleep soundly." Myrtle took Poplar by the elbow and ushered her out the door.

"Sleep well," Poplar said, wiggling her fingers goodbye. Ash followed behind, but lingered in the doorway for a moment. He seemed to be pondering something.

"Is there a bathroom around here?" Dax asked him.

"Just down the hall, seventy-seven doors to your left," he replied.

Dax looked like his face might slide right off. But he marched from the room, determined. Briar listened to Dax count each door aloud, until his voice finally faded in the distance.

Ash watched Dax traipse down the hall with his dark-lined geisha's eyes, and when he was far enough away, he turned back to Briar. He closed the door with care not to make a sound, and leaned his back against it. Briar noticed drips of sweat on his forehead and his eyes shifting left and right.

"I could lose my head for this." His voice trembled a bit. "Know that there are stories within stories, young Briar." He looked up at the Blackwood gallery, and nodded at the strange portraits.

Briar remained silent, but found it odd that Ash would choose to tell her this separate from Myrtle and Poplar. She wondered if perhaps he could read her thoughts, and then she wondered if maybe all three of them could do so.

"Trust no one," he said. "The wheels that turn are immense

and a thousand-grooved."

"What do you mean?" Briar asked.

Ash seemed not to hear her, but stayed true to his task of warning. "Do not tarry long in the Realms. The longer you stay, the more there will be forgetting."

"Forgetting?" Briar could feel her pulse rising. "Forgetting of what?"

Ash reached into his kimono and pulled out a shiny black stone. He handed it to Briar and said, "Keep this with you at all times." It felt smooth and cool in her hand. Then she noticed a strange design etched onto the top that looked like a sixteen-pointed star wreathed by twining dragons.

"Won't Sherman teach me to use the trinket?" she asked.

"There are some sorceries that go beyond trinkets," he said. Then he clenched his red-bowed lips. "Even masters have their limits."

Briar heard Myrtle call from beyond the door. "Ash, come along."

"Keep it with you. Keep it hidden," he said. Then he darted away.

Chapter 15

Briar slept fitfully that night. She dreamed that she was wandering down the flickering candlelit halls of the birdhouse. She wore a long, stiff gown. White, maybe, gold perhaps, and of a heavy brocade, it was certainly something from another age. She held a candelabrum as she passed by the locked hallway doors, and she thought she heard muffled cries from behind them. A distinct voice gasping or whispering said something like "save us," amid the general murmur of hundreds, perhaps thousands of other voices.

Then the chaotic din sharpened and distinct voices took prominence. It was as if she was able to hear all of them at once with the bracing clarity of a cold spring. They were calling her name, some of them spoke in a strange, throaty language. Over and over the voices tumbled across her like cold ocean waves, begging and pleading with her.

She tried a door, but it was locked. Then she tried another and another. Far into the distance, she saw a dark shadow float into a particularly tall doorway. In a blink, Briar found herself facing it, reaching for the knob. It turned without resistance. But just before she pushed it open to see what might lie beyond, she paused, hearing the whir of a spinning wheel and a woman's dark laughter.

She awakened with a gasp and sat upright. It was already morning and the sun shone in bright golden ribbons through the arched window. It didn't matter that the room felt cheery; Briar found herself tamping down a growing sense of foreboding. She looked up, and the gallery of odd paintings loomed overhead, seeming almost to leer at her.

"Well, look who's decided to join the living," Dax said. He came through the door with a silver tray piled with scones, black currant jam, butter, and steaming tea. "Sleep okay? Oh, wait what am I talking about? You're the sleeping beauty—you should be giving seminars or some shit like that."

Briar rubbed her head and then tucked her long black hair behind her ears. "Yeah, well I guess a wicked queen with a poisonous prick would know. Are you just getting back from the bathroom?"

"Ooh snap, Your Majesty. Let's put it this way—considering the crazy-ass shit in your life, I think it'll be easier if I just invest in some adult diapers—" He rolled his eyes. "Anyway. When I got back, you were already out. I couldn't wake you for anything. It was creepy."

Dax plopped the tray on the bed. "I tried to kiss you to see if that might work its magic. But alas—"

Briar wrinkled her nose. "That's the story of my life."

Briar grabbed at a scone and stuffed her mouth. "Oh my God, Dax," she said. Her mouth was still full. "Have you tried these? They're fantastic."

"I'm still not used to this magic shit," Dax said. "Poplar just wiggled her fingers and buh-bam! This whole tray appeared. At least she didn't give us anything she found in one of her mouse-traps." Dax split one scone open and let some butter melt between the halves. He slathered one half with the black currant jam and bit. "Hello lover. Will you marry me?" he asked the scone. The two laughed together and it felt good to laugh again after going through so much.

Myrtle knocked on the doorframe and entered. "Good morning," she sang. Poplar and Myrtle entered dressed in their usual, biddy attire. Sherman was wrapped around Myrtle's shoulders as always. Ash then straggled into the room, now dressed in a Renaissance hunter's garb. He had a leather strap across his green fitted vest, black velvet short pants, and a black cloak.

"I trust you've rested well," he said. He focused his gaze on Briar, then his eyes flicked quickly to Myrtle and Poplar on each of his sides.

"Yeah, sure," Briar said.

"Well, that makes one of us," Sherman said. "Honestly, this whole idea simply exhausts me."

Briar threw her thigh-high stockings over the side of the bed and was shocked to see them. Before going to bed, she had slipped out of her theater costume. But magically, she was back in her usual cinched up black Victorian dress. Her black hoodie and grunge boots were neatly placed on a trunk at the foot of the bed. Briar was amused at how comfortable she had become with these kinds of magical changes.

"I hope you don't mind, dearie," Poplar said. "I just thought you should dress comfortably for the road."

Dax sat looking like a deflated bounce house. "I did not see that coming," he said.

Before Briar stood, she checked a pocket at her hip. She had slipped Ash's protective stone into the dress pocket, but it was now there in her Victorian gown. She felt her neck for the key pendant.

"It is time to say goodbye," Myrtle said.

Poplar began blubbering into a lace handkerchief. "We've only gotten to know her," she said. "And now she's off."

Rapidly whirling her hands in a clockwise manner, Myrtle made a design that was as intricate as fine lace. Amid sparkling lights, a revolting black widow spider, the size of a Chihuahua appeared between her hands. "Mittens will help," she said. The spider dropped to the floor with a dry papery sound and it approached Dax, clicking its legs along the floor.

"What the fuck?" he said, backing away.

"Mittens is perfectly harmless. She has been the family locksmith for generations," Myrtle said. "True, she has sucked the life out of a victim or two. But not since little Miss Muffet, right, Mittens?" She reached down and stroked the hideous thing's back and it hunched up in pleasure. Then it clicked around and made a high-pitched screech.

"So what are we supposed to do?" Briar asked.

"Oh, this is useless!" Sherman snapped. "She's never used a locksmith before."

Poplar stepped around the bed with Briar's shoes and hoodie. "Don't worry about Sherman. He knows to be on his best behavior while you're away—or he'll make a lovely winter muff for some common in Nepal." Once Briar decked herself in her garb, Poplar ushered her to the infinite, candlelit halls. Dax hurried behind them and Mittens scuttled close on his heels. "I need a really big can of Raid right now," he said while eyeing the repulsive arachnid.

Myrtle urged Briar on. "All you have to do is pick a door," she said. "Mittens will do the rest."

"With our luck, she'll pick the door that leads straight to Lady Orpion's chambers," Sherman said.

Ash then entered the hallway and he gave Briar an encouraging nod. "It's your first real magical act," he said. "Take the trinket off, but leave it on its chain. Let it dangle before you, close your eyes and just breathe. You must rescue the boy and find the book—so hold these two knowings in mind."

Briar looked back at Dax, who smiled but shrugged his shoulders. Briar closed her eyes and drew a deep breath. She imagined Leon, and a vision of him in a cage flashed like a sudden strobe in her mind. Suddenly she felt a pull from the key on the necklace. She opened her eyes and saw she was standing before a small round door that only reached as high as her knees. She saw the key, defying gravity, outstretching on the chain, pointing toward the little door.

She looked back to tell the others, but saw that they were all standing a long distance away. It was strange how she had wandered so far, when it felt as though she had only taken a step. Mittens was lying in front of the door and made another small cry as if to acknowledge her selection.

Without having to say more, Mittens crawled up the wall and stuck two of his long black legs into the keyhole. The mechanisms inside the lock made a metallic tinkling noise. Then the spider took on a strange luminescence until it became translucent. Like a wisp of smoke, he floated into the door lock. Once he was inside, the door illuminated and also became translucent.

Briar shaded her eyes but looked through her fingers. Through the door she saw a series of cruddy boots standing on a wooden floor. Then there was a distinct sound of a latch unlocking. The little door solidified again and then it opened wide.

Dax, Sherman, and the others ambled down the long hallway. They arrived out of breath. "Very well then, Briar," Myrtle said in a tone as bracing as crisp, tart apples. "Listen to Sherman. Follow your intuition, and speed your journey."

Dax spoke up. "Uh, won't our friends notice that we're gone?"

"What friends?" Briar asked.

"I stand corrected," Dax said.

"In one world they will know your presence; in the other, you are already forgotten," Ash said. He gave Briar a brief but meaningful gaze, and she recalled what he had said about forgetting.

"I wish I'd done this before my last math test," Dax replied.

Myrtle straightened her neck and leveled her chin so that it rested on her high collar. "A word of warning, Briar," she said.

"Uh, hello? You're warning me *now*?"

"Whatever you do, never open the *Book of Cinder and Blight* or read from its pages. That would be—an unfortunate situation."

Briar nodded, and then Myrtle pulled her close with her black gloves. At first Briar thought it might be another part of her instruction, but realized it was not Myrtle's characteristic business-as-usual, but an offering of affection. Briar realized in that moment, that that might be how it feels to be cared for—

maybe even loved. Myrtle stiffened up again and dusted off invisible specks from her red suit.

"Oh, how could I forget?" Poplar said. She reached into her drawstring bag and handed Briar the cell phone. "You never know when you may need this." Briar took the phone with a wide grin. Poplar too embraced Briar and began sobbing. Then she threw her arms around Dax.

"Are we all done now?" Sherman asked. "I'd like to get this over with so I can see where Miss Ingrate has landed us."

Poplar stood back and snuffled.

Sherman sat up on his hind legs for a moment, then without saying more, he darted through the door, disappearing on the other side. Myrtle gave another nod of encouragement.

"Briar has the trinket, so hold hands to pass through the door safely," she said.

So Briar and Dax knelt down and crawled through the doorway, while awkwardly holding hands. Before they knew it, they were scrabbling on the pitch-stained floor of a smoky old tavern. Briar stood upright immediately, and almost knocked her head on one of the ceiling's low-hanging wood beams. She brushed off her knees and helped Dax to stand.

Sherman was already seated at the bar, leaning forward into a tankard of something that smelled like rotting death. But she had a hard time seeing him clearly, as the room was enveloped in a haze of burning tobacco, and woody herbs. There was a filthy finger-smudged door just a few paces away behind where Briar stood.

"Don't speak," Sherman said in a hushed voice. He turned his head slightly, glancing—just for a flash—at a hulking, warty old woman who was seated at the end of the bar. Under his breath Sherman ordered the two of them to sit. Briar grabbed Dax by the arm, and together they found stools next to Sherman.

"Where are we?" Dax asked from the side of his mouth.

"The Horn and Hold Tavern," Sherman said. He showed a bit

of fang from the side of his soft red muzzle as he spoke.

A man tending the bar had black scaled skin, the color and texture of a rattlesnake. He stared at Briar and Dax for a moment with his neon green eyes. "What'll it be?" he asked. A slim forked tongue flicked out from between his green lips as he spoke.

"Whatever she's having," Briar said, jerking her head toward the warty woman. Sherman shook his head, disgusted, and he placed his snout into the tankard before him.

"Two squished beetles it is, then," the bartender said. He began grabbing at a container full of shiny black insects from behind the bar with his two sets of arms. Briar watched with a woozy expression as the man placed several handfuls into a mortar and with his free hands, began to pulverize them into a gooey mess.

The room was a stage for the strange. A group of ghosts dressed in shrouding hoods played a card game at the far end of the room. Wisps of spectral smoke from their phantom stogies arose and disappeared. A hairy winged bat-like creature played the harpsichord near a wooden staircase. Several disfigured witches in black conical hats stood in a group near the keyboard player. They wore tattered, old-fashioned under-garments, and thigh-high stockings. They tried to look enticing to the various male patrons.

"Here," the bartender grumbled. He slammed down two tankards. Briar refused to look, but when Dax spied several beetle legs dangling from the rim of the mug, his lips quivered with nausea. The Bartender wiped a mug with his several hands and a filthy rag. "That'll be six Forge for the lot of ya'."

"My dear sir," Sherman began. "Forge is the currency of the Lady Orpion and the kingdom Scarlocke."

"Yeah, so?"

"I beg your pardon, but surely that is not the currency of the entire Realm."

The bartender laughed and poked a bear that was snoring, his head laid on the bar top. "This joker thinks Forge is only Orpion's money. Ha!" He turned to Sherman. "Mister, I don't know where you've been, but Forge is all there is, see?" Then turning back to Briar, he slammed one of his four hands onto the counter. "Like I said, that'll be six of 'em." Briar looked at Sherman who hunched and buried his face in his mug. The bartender moved in closer and leaned his four arms on the bar in front of Briar and Dax. "Hey! We got moochers here?" He began to crack his knuckles and clench his black scaly fists.

The door at the back of the bar burst open, and in marched a dozen troopers. They were oversized wolves outfitted with masked helmets and inky leather breastplates, just like the two that Briar had seen in the spinning wheel room. Each soldier carried a spear as long as he was tall.

The bartender backed up and pressed himself against the ornate framed mirror behind him. He watched the troopers file in, and a bead of sweat formed on his brow. The wolfguard paraded in unison, a well-drilled militia. They knocked over a witch and the others of her kind squealed and leapt aside. One slid off the harpsichord and landed with her rickety high heels thrown in the air. Another pretended to use her broom to sweep the floor in a corner. The ghosts playing cards glanced over their shoulders at the commotion and then evaporated. Their playing cards scattered and their phantom cigars puffed out of sight.

The wolfguard created a formation around the hunched old woman at the end of the bar who was bent over into her drink. Sherman hopped off the barstool and backed toward the door. Briar and Dax followed him, backing slowly.

A wolf in the lead of the pack spoke. "Baba Yaga?" he asked. Briar was taken aback by the clarity of his speech. The other wolves she had seen before could barely form words in their muzzles.

The old woman was droopy eyed and toothless. "Who wants to know?" she asked. She downed another gulp from her tankard.

The wolfguard all raised their spears and pointed them at her in unison. The lead guard unrolled a scroll of yellowing parchment. "You are hereby charged by Scarlocke, with the act of talebreaking."

Baba Yaga spoke with a carnival fortuneteller's accent. "Now, what you going on about?" she asked. She turned her body only partially toward her accusers. Briar could see her crepe-lidded eyes that seemed to be holding a secret. She nervously touched a gold ring that dangled from her nostrils with her stubby, gnarled fingers. "I never broken Tale in my life," she insisted. "Live by the Book, I do, just as Great Lady tells us. Live by Grand Design."

The guard read from a scroll. "On or about the full moons, you were seen foraging in Dankally Woods near known portals."

"I don't know nothing about por-tals. I swear." The woman turned to face her accusers fully now. "I swear. I am grand-mother." Her body was at least three or four times the mass of any soldier and grotesquely misshapen. Briar could see fear and pleading in her eyes, beyond the hairy facial tumors and lopsided lumps.

"You are hereby the property of Scarlocke."

"Property! What you saying? I told you: I don't know nothing. You make mistake. I am old woman. Grandmother—" The hag stood from her stool and towered above the wolves. She gave a benevolent smile and reached to pat the head soldier's paw.

He gave a short howl. In unison, the others jabbed their sliver-tipped spears through Baba Yaga. Her eyes blinked and her mouth opened as though she wanted to gasp. But she did not breathe. Instead, she staggered back a step, blood surging from the many spears that filled her. Then she leaned on the bar, looking at her pierced body. "I don't know...nothing," she tried to say. But blood filled her throat clogging the words. She opened her mouth and heaved like a fish pulled from a stream, gasping for air. Glancing up at Sherman, she slumped to the floor.

The bear at the bar roused from his stupor for a minute. "Huh?" he asked. Then he sank back into unconsciousness.

The lead soldier motioned to a comrade and through the door several of them rolled a short wooden barrel that was bound together with black-stained ropes. The contents seeped black and red through the decaying planks and stank of putrid bodies. Soldiers then uncorked animal skin flasks they had fitted to their belts, and held them to Baba Yaga's wounds, collecting her blood. When a guard filled his flask he emptied it into the barrel opening. They rolled her on the floor, stomping on her limbs and her stomach with their boots, trying to juice every drop they could.

The head soldier looked up at Sherman, Briar and Dax. He sniffed the air. "Well, what's this, then," he said. He stood well above Briar, his wolf-body was massive, larger than any that Briar had seen before. He pawed at her hair and sniffed it. She couldn't see his entire face, but his gray muzzle jutted out from beneath the helmet. She almost choked on the stench of decomposing flesh from his mouth. "I've never seen you here before," he said.

Briar felt a trembling at her core. But she knew she must speak, sounding unafraid. "Really? I've never seen you either."

The soldier laughed to his buddies. "This one's got a bit of sauce." Then he sniffed at her neck.

A soldier with a high, rasping voice, not as well developed as the lead soldier came from behind. "Sir—a word with you."

"What? Do you know this creature?"

"Sir—please, a word with you—" The wolf sounded breathy and anxious, like someone pumped with adrenaline.

Briar recognized the voice. It was the wolf she saw in the spinning wheel chamber. The two soldiers whispered and Briar felt her tongue stick in the back of her throat. She touched the pocket with the stone Ash had given her, and she willed it to protect them, if that was even possible.

The head soldier laughed with a whining bark. "The Lady Orpion?! Here?" he asked. Then he paused and sniffed the air near Briar again. His laughter became snarl. "Or someone who says she's Orpion...a talebreaker."

Briar backed up against Dax. They joined hands and made a break for the door.

Chapter 16

Briar and Dax ran from the tavern. Without looking, without thinking, they stumbled out onto narrow, rain-slickened cobblestone lane. To the left, the street inclined toward a stark blocky mountain; to the right, it snaked down to a misty oak forest. The lane wound in lazy curves for long distances in either direction, with rickety buildings of wood and stone cobbled together, lined up for patronage. Market signage above somber black doors boasted the likes of butchers, bakers, and candlestick makers. The air was thick with the smell of onions, frying fat, and excrement.

"Now you've done it," Sherman shouted. He trotted in a crouched position, looking anxiously behind.

The head soldier followed slamming through the tavern door, breaking it off its upper hinges so that it hung at a sad angle. With his fangs bared, the wolfguard poised his spear at the fugitives. The bartender appeared in the doorway shaking his many fists. He shouted, "Didn't pay her tally neither. That one's a talebreaker *and* a moocher."

The spear flew and missed Briar by a hair, lancing the door behind her. Then she heard someone bolt it from the other side. She grabbed Dax's hand and together they took off down the road, splashing through the cobblestone puddles with their furious feet. Sherman scrambled at top speed behind them, and eventually passed them in his panic.

Briar heard the wolfguard, all of the soldiers pursuing, a stampede of heavy boots and gear sounding with wrath down the lane. But before long, she felt her limbs getting heavy and her lungs burning. She wished she hadn't cut gym class quite so often now. Dax was huffing too and he finally gave up, put his hands on his knees, and tried to catch a breath. Briar stopped with him, her lungs searing, gulping down air.

She looked up and saw villagers peering out from behind

shutters—some of them cautiously curious, others pale and shaken, wishing they hadn't seen anything. Any who saw or heard barred their shutters and doors. Briar just couldn't run further; her legs quaked, they felt loose and rubbery. If the wolfguard took her, then that was what had to happen because there was just no going forward.

The wolves indeed came upon them, fiercely baying and yowling, hungry for their blood. The head soldier was himself winded, but the fury in his face was unmatched. This was it, Briar realized. She shut her eyes expecting to feel the sharp point of a spear, when a great storm of thundering hooves came from around the bend. Briar opened her eyes and scarcely had time to act before the horses, and the carriage they towed, beat past her.

Dax stood staring, so Briar pushed him out of harm's way and dove, face down, after him. They both splatted, face first, into a mucky puddle formed where a large section of cobblestones had come loose from the road. Briar spit some of the sludge from her mouth and wiped her face with her sleeve, hoping whatever foulness she was tasting was just mud. Sherman skidded beside them, clutching to the rain-soaked stone with his claws. All three looked down the road where two black horses drew to a stop so suddenly that they almost overturned the dark, glossy carriage.

Briar saw what had happened: the wolfguard, who did not react as quickly as did Briar and Dax, inadvertently hurled his spear at the side of the carriage. The spear pierced a gold crest that was emblazoned upon the side panel.

Some of his soldiers were not quick enough to avert the carriage. Several were crushed by the wheels, their spines pulverized, or their skulls smashed apart. Luckier soldiers avoided the careening horses and packed together beneath a cobbler's sign, yapping in a wild, high-pitched chorus.

The driver, dressed in black cape and top hat as tall as a man's arm was long, struggled to control the reins. The horses whinnied and bucked but then came to a standstill. A small hand pulled back the swags of burgundy and gold fringe that curtained the inside carriage windows.

Two more top-hatted men in black capes, positioned outside at the rear of the carriage, stepped off and scrambled to open the elaborately ornamented door. One of them placed a cushioned stool upon the street, while the other clamped down on a gold handle and opened it. They both bowed.

Out from the shadows of the carriage stepped an enormous walking egg. His burgundy velvet breeches were contrasted by the blanched white of his distended shell. He had a crown like small golden flames with red jewels atop his smooth head.

Behind him trotted out a tiny figure, something akin to a man, but no bigger than a hand. Its skin was sagging, but shimmered like gold. Briar inhaled with the sharpness of a knife, remembering the little creature from the vision in the armoire mirror. Just as he appeared before, he wore a red and gold cap with trails of fringe and feathers. Around his neck was a leather collar cinched tightly, and from it led a strap that the egg held in his free hand.

The creature hopped up, defying gravity, from the carriage to the king's crown. He sat within it, holding the edges and peeking out with tiny, dull black eyes.

Meanwhile, on the far side of the carriage, Briar felt a tingling in her hands, and she raised one of them from the mud puddle. The worrisome blue flames had returned, cutting through the brown sludge and shimmering brightly. She stared at her hand, not knowing what to do.

The egg-king tottered through the street in his curl-toed shoes. The wolf who had thrown the spear stood opening his muzzle as though trying to find something to say, but he remained silent. Then, in deference, he removed his helmet and folded in half. "Your Majesty," he growled.

His helmet removed, Briar could see the wolf's whole face and she felt a twinge of sickness in seeing it. The creature had apparently been scarred in battle. The fur that once covered a side of his face was missing. She guessed it was likely singed away as the skin that remained was fire-pocked, blistered, and ill-mended. One of his amber eyes was scarred and glazed white; puckered black skin surrounded the blind eye.

The king was busy staring at the tangled carnage of the wolfguard that had been trampled by his carriage. He regarded the scattered carcasses like a disgruntled driver who unhappily discovered a flat tire. He spoke in a beefy boom. "What jurisdiction do you have in the kingdom of Murbra Faire?"

"Your Majesty, behind you is an imposter and a talebreaker," the head wolf said. Briar noticed that he never raised his solitary good eye to meet the king's.

The king chuckled heartily, slapping the back of one of his top-hatted coachmen. The coachman lurched forward from the blow and caught his hat before it tumbled to the street. "There are no talebreakers in this kingdom, good sir. But there do appear to be javelinists, to say the least." He tsked as one of his men worked the spear until it released from the side of his carriage with a horrible scraping grind.

The bartender was apparently still perturbed by the loss of Forge to his till. He had followed the soldiers and from behind the crowd he shouted, "She's also a moocher, don't forget that." And he made what appeared to be a rude gesture with his four scaly fists.

"Goodness," the king said. There was a tickle in his tone. "A talebreaker. An imposter. And a moocher. Who is this dangerous person?" The tiny golden creature in the king's crown covered its mouth in a pantomime of fear.

Sherman tried to stand on tired, shaking limbs when he suddenly caught sight of Briar's hands, which were completely engulfed in blue flames. Briar was just staring at them as though hypnotized, oblivious to anyone else who might be watching.

Briar hadn't noticed, but the king toddled around to the

opposite side of the carriage. Sherman jumped on Briar's hands, forcing her to dunk them deeply into the cover of mud. The pitiful sight of Briar and Dax face down in the thick gunk caused the king to wheeze with laughter.

Sherman stood on Briar's hands still and tried to act as though nothing unusual was happening. "Good day, Your Majesty." He bowed low and flicked his tail in Briar's face.

"Here's a tip," she said. "Try cleaning with a couple of moist towelettes before you bend over in someone's face."

Sherman continued as though she was not there. "These claims cannot be substantiated. These two young persons are within the domain of my charge and they have made no errors, save ignorance of our ways. Allow me to take them from this place and keep them as my wards, lest they be charged falsely again."

"Now who else would speak like that, save my old friend Sherman?" the king said. He kept clucking with amusement.

"Cole?" Sherman asked. Then he blinked. "Is it you?"

"Perhaps a bit rounder, but yes," the king said slapping his thin pointy knee and guffawing. "What the devils are you doing here, Sherman, with the likes of these vermin?" The king tilted his head in the direction of the bartender and the wolf, who abruptly stood upright with a snarl. The king seemed to be amused by his irritation.

By now, Briar no longer felt the tingling and she lifted a hand while no one was watching to see if the blue flames were gone. And they had. This was becoming increasingly alarming as they seemed to come and go of their own will. She realized that they might appear again at some more unfortunate moment, perhaps endangering them all. She decided then that she should keep track of any patterns in their coming or going.

"As you know, Your Majesty, I must from time to time educate a newling in our ways," Sherman said. He nodded toward Briar.

She stood up, shaking off water and road-slime from her

Victorian getup. Dax hadn't fared much better. The front of his shirt and jeans were soaked in brown muck. The sludge matted his hair and trickled down his cheeks.

The small golden creature jumped out of the king's crown and landed next to Briar weightlessly, sticking to the ground as though it had disembarked into glue. It was then Briar noticed that his tiny dull eyes were, in fact, empty eye sockets. Nonetheless, the vile thing seemed to know how to flick a glob of mud at Briar and Dax with accuracy. Then it hissed with laughter through a sharp-toothed grin.

"Tarfeather!" the king growled. "Be still!" The small jester slapped a second handful of mud he had collected onto the ground with a regretful pout.

"Tell me, Sherman, which of these filthy piglets is dillywig in your tutelage?" The king couldn't help his glee and he gave another small giggle. "Ooh, that reminds me. I'm famished," he said. He turned to one of his men. "Suckling pig! And speed it!" he shouted.

Tarfeather, mimicking the king, shook a sharp scolding finger at the footmen.

One of the cloaked men climbed up the back of the carriage. He opened a leather-bound trunk strapped to the back and proceeded to step down inside of it, disappearing completely. From the street, Briar and the others heard the sounds of pots and pans clanking around.

"It is the smaller of the two, with long black hair," Sherman said, to address the king's question.

"Ah," said the king, "Well she certainly looks a bit bruised up, now doesn't she? Her eyes look like a couple of ripe plums. And what are those pieces of metal suck through her skin? Who would commit such a crime on such a young beauty?"

Sherman coughed. "Yes, uh hum. Well, we're still trying to find that out."

The king's miniscule attention span was strained again and he interrupted Sherman. "It has been far too long, my friend. Come, stay with me and celebrate my son's engagement this night." He gestured at them to all enter the carriage.

"Your majesty, I couldn't," Sherman said. "We are here with specific instructions."

The tiny jester put his gristly golden hands on his hips and looked askance. "Nonsense! I'll not hear another word." The king kept laughing—at what Briar could not tell. Then he spoke to his servants. "Take this fox and his feculent young charges. Put old leather down to save the seats from their mud." Then he doubled over with choking laughter, as though he had told a great joke.

The king's attendants helped Briar, Dax, and Sherman into the magnificent carriage. The wolf, now dismissed and scorned before his comrades, once again bowed slightly. "Your Majesty, we have orders from Scarlocke to watch for a dillywig child of nearly sixteen years. I am afraid I must take these three into custody."

The king had already turned to step up into the carriage when the guard spoke. Annoyed, he turned to address the creature. "Your authority here is in question, sir—er, or dog. I'm not sure which. In any event, I suggest you take your troops back to your own Scarlocke where you may spear anything of the Lady Orpion's you like."

"Of course, Your Majesty," the wolf mumbled. He bowed again, but Briar noticed his barely contained snarl.

The king then tossed a small black velvet purse that clinked in the bartender's grasp. "I believe this will more than pay for a moocher's debt." This, of course, resulted in another small explosion of kingly laughter.

"And my soldiers?" the wolfguard asked. He turned his amber eyes to those fallen, pulverized into the cobblestone crevices.

"I should expect the others of his troop will learn to stay out of a busy street at rush hour."

The wolfguard said no more, but regarded the carriage with a look that told Briar he wasn't through with them yet.

Then, with nothing else to say, several footmen heaved the rotund king into the carriage. Tarfeather was happy to see that he could once again make use of that scoop of mud by flinging it at the wolf. Then he hopped into the coach.

With a crack of the whip they rumbled away with the clack of hoof beats on stone. Upward, upward they rose along the village streets, speeding toward the palace of Murbra Faire.

Chapter 17

After several tankards of some ale with a pungent under-arm stink, and a lunch of whole suckling pig, King Cole dozed and finally began to snore. With each turn of the carriage, the wobbly egg-king rolled left and right, back and forth. Dax, who sat beside him, had to press against him to keep him from shattering all over the floor. As the king never bothered to clean his shell after the oily meal, Dax found this to be a revolting task.

"Hey, Omelette," Dax said to Cole. "Ever hear of a washcloth? There's enough grease here to lube a truck."

The king kept snoozing.

Sherman rolled his eyes and turned back to face his window in silence.

Dax spoke to Briar. "I'm sorry, but I'm a little confused," he said. "Isn't the creepy talking egg supposed to be Humpty Dumpty or something?" Briar shrugged. Nothing was as she expected since meeting the dillywigs.

Tarfeather sat perched in the king's crown, surveying the newcomers with his dark eye sockets. Briar shifted uncomfortably beneath the strange gaze of the creature's blackened and shriveled eye holes.

After a long time in silence, Sherman spoke aloud, but in a dark whisper. "Some redeemer." He muttered to himself. "The girl almost gets us killed. The curses will never be undone."

Cole, burbled and then burped, but remained fast asleep.

"How was I supposed to know what I was doing when I choose that door?" Briar protested. She tried to keep this disagreement to a whisper, but hearing herself speak, she realized that she was sounding like a hissing snake.

"Myrtle told me to pick a door. I wouldn't know a wrong door from a right one, now would I? I thought we were going to the magical land of sleeping beauty—you know, like with spinning tea cups and soft pretzel vendors—not with murderous freaks who have horrifying skin conditions."

"Do you ever shut up?" Sherman said.

"It's in my nature to comment on the bizarre and the unusual," Briar said. "Case in point: a fox that's all talk and no action. I thought you were supposed to be some kind of grand-poobah-wizard-thing. Where were your effing powers when we needed them?"

Everyone sat in silence listening to the jangle of the coach. Finally Dax spoke up.

"You're forgetting that if it weren't for Briar, we wouldn't have run into the king who saved us—"

The king licked his lips with a wide white tongue and snorted with great effort.

Briar ignored Dax's support. Sherman had come to help them, and all he did was pretend he didn't know them in the bar. Why didn't he stop the wolfguard from touching her, sniffing her? She wiped her neck where the wolf had sniffed around. "And why did you accept this stupid invitation? Now we have one day less to find Leon and the book."

"Well, we wouldn't be here if we hadn't ended up in the Horn and Hold."

"You know what?" Briar snapped. "Why is it every time I see you, all I can think about is old-lady face powder and pearl earrings?"

Dax held up hands to both of them. "Sh, sh, shush, both of you!" Briar and Sherman quieted, but Briar knew she was right. The fox knew things—secrets—but he guarded them.

"Now," Dax said, "don't make me pull this car over."

Sherman sat, turned away, wrinkling his muzzle. Then after a long while he spoke. "Can you please explain to me why you never mentioned your Dragon Powers, Miss Ingrate?" He wouldn't look in her direction. Instead, he stared sullenly at the distant patchwork of landscape that sprawled below the steep mountain passes.

"My what?" Briar reached over to shore up the king on one particularly sharp curve.

"Those blue flames. Those are Dragon Powers—as if you'd know a Dragon Power from a nose piercing," Sherman said.

"Yeah? Well, you can have your shit-ass flames if you want them."

Sherman's eyes darkened. "No one here knows who or what you are." He whispered this—another secret, Briar supposed. "And I recommend that it stays that way. Seeing those flames would risk everything. And those who know what they are would assume that you were in league with the Lady Orpion. Either way, if we're caught, that would be the end for all of us."

"So what are Dragon Powers?" Dax asked. "Is she, like, going to grow wings and sharp teeth or something?"

"Perhaps you're amusing to other commons. But here, you're a nuisance. How could you ever expect to understand the rarity of Dragon Powers?"

Dax gave up trying to mediate some kind of truce. Let them snap at each other. He was out.

"It's a mystery to me how such power could find its way to most unlikely and—needless to say—undeserving of persons."

Briar couldn't agree more. Even if those flames were rare or special, she wanted nothing to do with them. True, they could make her a celeb on campus. But they could also be yet another reason for the kids to think she was weird.

Sherman looked as though he was thinking of something very serious. Opened his yap to speak, but then turned away. "These powers can be...replicated." Briar watched him closely. There would be Tales within Tales—she was told.

"Replicated?" Dax asked.

"To some degree. But trying to do so is a perversion of the Grand Design. It does irreparable harm." Sherman turned to see Dax staring with a dull, uncomprehending expression. "That's a bad thing," Sherman clarified. He sat brooding about this for a moment. "It produces dangerous, monstrous results."

"How does someone replicate a power you're born with?" Dax asked.

"Blood sorceries. Dark workings. The Book of Cinder and Blight." Briar could hear the weight in Sherman's words.

"Is that why the wolfguard collected the old woman's blood?" she asked.

Sherman did not answer. He looked away and stared dismally out at the overgrown black oak and fern forest that clung to the sides of the mountain.

King Cole wheezed and then mumbled a little. But he remained asleep, lolling back and forth on Dax, who was clearly beginning to tire of this messy situation.

"So I have to hide my hands?" Briar asked.

"For starters, yes. For now."

Sherman withdrew into silence, and in it, the sounds of the springy carriage hinges took on meaning.

Upward, into the low-hanging storm clouds, the king's carriage rose. It jangled along switchback cobblestone lanes that wound around a limestone outcropping that jutted suddenly from the landscape. Tufts of pink and orange wildflowers fit themselves neatly between rocks, breaking up the otherwise sandy-white scenery.

"What were you mumbling before about curses?" Briar asked.

"That is none of your affair," Sherman said. He kept his eyes on the land formations.

"You can't be serious. Poplar munches on rats whenever she can find them. Ash has some freaky fashion show going on. And Myrtle had something happen to her that Poplar said was the worst of them all—but she wouldn't tell me what. I'm starting to get tired of all these riddles."

"I repeat. They are none of your affair."

Briar had little patience left after her recent ordeal. "Oh yeah?

Well what if something like that happens to Dax and I? Huh? Don't you think you should warn us a little?"

"It isn't my job to warn you, Ingrate. I am only here to teach you, if that's even possible."

While the king continued to snore, now even louder, the others sat listening to the twanging of wheel springs straining beneath their collective weight, until one of the coachmen shouted out, "Wriggle!" That awakened the king with a loud snort.

Briar and Dax thought it a curious thing to shout, and they knew it must have been said with reason. They twisted their bodies to look out the small windows. Just ahead, Briar spied an iron bar gate as tall as several city busses stacked on end. The gate was topped with gold filigree and shimmering lions.

"Wriggle? Did he say wriggle?" asked the king in a haze. "Yes, why?" Sherman replied.

"Wriggle!" the king shouted.

In his fluster he tried to open a small pillbox that he extracted from a pocket in his billowy velvet pants. The pillbox opened too quickly in his eggshell-smooth hands and tiny black pills no bigger than poppy seeds scattered all over the juddering carriage floor.

"Oh dear. Oh my!" Cole said straining forward to collect the pills. But he rolled forward onto the floor and lolled between the other passengers. As he rambled back and forth between Dax and Briar he shouted, "Get those, Tarfeather, hurry."

Tarfeather had already jumped clear and before Cole could say more he was speeding along, his tiny claw fingers tweezing the flyspeck pills from beneath seats and in corners of the cab. "Quickly Tarfeather, one for each of us!"

The coachman atop the carriage counted off. "Five…four…three…"

Tarfeather moved so quickly that Briar saw little more than a trace of his tiny golden body moving from one to another in the cab, popping a pill in everyone's mouth.

"Swallow!" Cole crowed.

Briar didn't want to know what would happen if she didn't. She felt the tiny seed at the tip of her tongue and she swallowed it down.

"…two…one…wriggle!" the coachman exclaimed.

Briar watched from the window as they approached the gate, but the carriage didn't seem to be slowing down.

"What's happening?" Dax asked. "We're not stopping."

Just then, the horses and the coach went directly through the gate's iron bars. Briar watched as they sliced through the horses, the cab, and the seats they sat in, splitting Sherman and the king in half. She noticed that the bars had also severed one of her arms, which separated, but stayed aloft at shoulder height. Dax crammed himself tightly into a corner and managed to get through without being sliced. Once they passed through the gates, the severed body parts fit back neatly together as though nothing at all had happened.

"Someone needs an automatic gate opener," Dax said.

"Oh, I do find that bothersome," the king said.

Sherman helped the king back to his seat. He fitted the crown back on his head and then then rolled himself aright so that he could sit back in the center of the bench. Cole brushed off his trousers. "Too much sorcery for my taste. But—this is my life now."

Briar thought it was an odd thing to say, coming from someone who lived in a land of enchantments.

Tarfeather sighed, relived that was over. He grabbed the king's hand, which still clutched the empty pillbox, and he sprinkled the remaining recovered pills inside. With a single hop he landed back inside the king's crown and slumped down.

Dax blinked in disbelief again. "Don't you think you should just open the gate up before you try to go through it?"

"Of course," the king said huffily. "It isn't my idea that the gates remain forever locked."

"Your majesty," Sherman said. "I must remind you that we are here in the Realms with specific orders—"

"Oh, fiddlesticks, Sherman," King Cole groused. "Always fussing like an old maid." Then he laughed, suddenly feeling amused again. He paused with a heavy sigh, then added, "Besides, tonight at my son's engagement party I need at least one ally with whom I can speak freely. Be a good chap, won't you?"

Sherman sighed.

The carriage tottered, slowed its pace and came to a sudden halt. The force of the stop threw Briar and Sherman onto the king and Dax. Tarfeather hissed and bared his golden fangs.

"Please tell me he's not really a jester," Dax remarked. "Because, he's not exactly *Saturday Night Live* material—"

The cab doors opened simultaneously on both sides. More of the footmen, top hatted and white gloved, stood on either side of a long strip of burgundy and gold-fringed carpet.

Briar followed the long carpet with her eyes, and noticed that it stretched to a pair of enormous steepled doors. The palace was a vast and intricate structure. Many buildings crowded the complex with their verdigris copper roofs. Each of them was constructed of heavy sun-bleached stones, the same color as the rock outcropping on which the palace was erected. Briar realized that the central building had to be Cole's quarters; it was a plain square with two round turrets on either side that streaked up to the sky.

A man wearing a brown hooded robe of a rustic and granular weave, seemed to appear from nowhere. His eyes remained lowered, and his movements were minimal, subtle—just enough to step through gaps in the crowd of guards and find his way to the front. He bowed with his hands pressed to his abdomen and the king stepped down from the carriage.

Cole nodded, but was distracted. "Ah, Damarius," he said.

The robed man had a long carved staff strapped to his back and he used it right himself after his stiff bow. Then he strode alongside the king at a surprising clip as they made their way toward the towering doors.

The man acted as though he hadn't even seen or cared to notice Briar, Dax and Sherman who had to help themselves off the coach. They hurried along after Cole and Damarius. Briar especially wanted to keep pace to listen in on their discussion.

"The preparations for tonight's festivities have all been tended to, save one small incident," Damarius said. His eyes remained lowered and his face seemed long and tense. Once they were beneath the front steps, Damarius removed his hood and Briar saw that he was completely bald. He had electric blue tattoos in various bold patterns, swirls and sweeps across his entire head. When he turned enough for Briar to see, she noticed two triangles above his eyes, and two X marks below. These were the same markings as those of Leon's kidnapper. The X marks reminded her of the doll tied to the spinning wheel. Her heart seemed to rumble beyond her control, and she lost her breath, but she tried to seem incognizant.

The king fitted Tarfeather once again with his choking collar and leash before letting him down from his crown. He hopped along behind the king and Damarius like a golden flea with his metallic collar rattling like chainmail until, finally tired of the king's wide strides, he hopped into Damarius' open hood and hitched a ride.

"An incident? Not another," Cole grumbled. Briar thought he seemed like lost, petulant a child who had been forced to take the crown and make something of it, rather than a monarch who knew his place and acted from the certainty and gravity of his throne.

"It is best for you to see," Damarius said.

Briar, Dax, and Sherman jogged along the carpet to keep up with the men. They passed cloaked musicians who held fluted trumpets by their sides. And as the king passed they blasted a royal welcome salute. Cole yanked away a horn from the pucker of one trumpeter, bent it in half, and handed it back with a look of disgust. The other trumpeters stopped and looked at one another.

"Obviously not a music lover," Dax whispered.

Cole grumbled as he and Damarius hurried into the palace. "Ninnies. How much are these good-for-nothing street vagabonds paid?" he asked. Without waiting for a response, he answered his own question. "More than I care to afford. Damarius, I want you to disrobe them, empty their pockets, and throw them out onto the street—preferably far beyond the palace. Make sure that there is no further frivolity unless it is by my decree. Is that understood?"

Damarius bowed his head, and showed no sign of emotion.

Briar and the others followed with frantic steps, barely making it into the palace vestibule, as a dozen shirtless strongmen heaved from behind the immense doors, straining with their tree-trunk arms to close them. Several more arrived with an iron bar that heaved into slots across the door.

Cole addressed Sherman. "They know in these times our movements are to remain as hidden as possible. Why the blasted trumpets is a mystery."

Sherman scurried along to keep pace. "Forgive me, Your Majesty," he said. "Why exactly must you be so elusive?"

"The damnable Orpion." The king spoke in a whisper, but still his words carried across the emptiness of the hall. Briar and Dax, followed along to one side and glanced at each other. "Not much of a lady, if you ask me," the king continued. They rushed along another long runway of burgundy carpet.

Briar marveled at the high stone walls with hundreds of tiny square windows lined in rows extending far above their heads. Banners emblazoned with a crest depicting a gold lion and a green tree fluttered at the head of the drafty hall. The banners flanked a throne backed with the shields of soldiers who had given their lives—freely or otherwise—in service to the crown.

"My friend," the king continued, "perhaps in your leave you've not known that most of these Realms are commanded now from Scarlocke. The marriage of my son to Orpion's ward will seal the last of it. After that, the whole of our world will be in the hands of…I dare not say it. At least my son and I will be safe. It is indeed a perilous time that you have chosen to come from the shadows to do your business."

"You would wed your only son to the kingdom of Scarlocke?" Sherman asked.

"And why would I not? She has inflicted wars upon our kingdom to its furthest reaches and beyond. Drained us of land and gold," the king said. "A marriage between our kingdoms may ease the burden of innocents. If lives can be spared, then is it not a necessity?"

They finally reached a raised platform upon which the throne stood. Tarfeather hopped out of Damarius' hood and jumped alongside the king. He plopped down on a velvet cushion at the base of the throne.

Briar wondered how this creature, obviously intelligent, must feel about being treated like a cocker spaniel. Maybe that's why she saw him in the mirror—he wanted Briar to set him free. The king paid no attention to the small creature and almost stepped on him while fitting himself between the Throne's arms.

"Well, Damarius?" the king asked.

Tarfeather studied the king and then mimicked him.

Damarius bowed and stepped aside. He whispered to a nearby attendant who nodded and rushed away. Shortly thereafter, two more guards brought in a cage with seven other golden creatures that looked exactly like Tarfeather—save for the fact that they all had their eyes. Golden darting eyes, they were, with slits like that of a cat. The guards positioned themselves on either side of the cage, watching them carefully as though the tiny things were a great menace to the country and in need of maximum security.

"Dwarefs," Damarius said. He had a hard time disguising the loathing in his voice. The seven creatures were without clothes and they clung together, some clutching the cage bars and ogling the king as though they had never seen anything of his like before. "They were found along the eastern wall, gouging at the foundation stones."

Tarfeather tried to get up and approach the cage. But Cole yanked him back with the choke-chain. Tarfeather gagged and then obediently sat back down.

"We were hungry, Your Royalness," said one of the dwarefs. His voice was scratchy and sounded like rocks rubbing together. He spoke the truth, Briar realized, seeing his distended belly and counting the ribs in his chest beneath his faded golden skin.

Damarius struck the cage with his staff. "Shut up. You are not here to state your case."

Briar could feel the familiar tingling starting in her body while watching Damarius speak this way to the helpless creatures. She began to realize that if she could focus her attention to something else, her feelings would subside and this might keep the blue flames away.

"Let them speak Damarius," said the king. Damarius bowed and tried to collect himself. Such an obvious display of personal aversion was not befitting one of his position.

"No eatery for weeks, Royalness," the dwaref pleaded.

"And my palace was the only meal available?" the king chuckled.

"Your majesty," Damarius interjected, "all stones of worth, and of value to *them*, have been confiscated—to rebuild the royal coffers."

King Cole sat for a moment in weighty silence. "Yes, of course. Well then, Damarius, take them where they will cause no harm and set them free. One of them is enough use for one king." He glanced at Tarfeather, who had gotten up from his cushion again, and was standing quite close to the cage.

The jailed dwarefs smiled back at Tarfeather. Some tried reaching out to him through the bars. Tarfeather simply regarded them with his hollowed eyes, but did not reach back. It might mean another sharp yank at the neck. The dwaref that spoke seemed relieved at the king's pardon; he smiled with his horrifying pin-sharp teeth, and attempted an elaborate approximation of a courtly bow.

"I beg pardon, Majesty," Damarius said. His tone was humble, reverent. "But the mines beneath the Flowery Hill are in eternal need of strong diggers."

"Oh yes. Quite right," the king said distractedly. "But I have no time for such matters, Damarius. Our guests will be here any time now. Take them wherever you must, only leave me out of it."

Damarius once more whispered into a guard's ear, and the two positioned beside the cage lifted it and took it away. The seven dwarefs looked at each other, perplexed, the smiles in their eyes fading to panic. Tarfeather sat on the ground as though all strength had left him. He sat gazing without eyes at the space where the cage stood, touching the choking collar and leash around his neck.

"Shall I make preparations for three more guests?" Damarius asked, bowing toward Briar, Dax, and Sherman.

"Oh, Damarius. You're still here," the king said. "Take these young persons and their master to chambers of their own. Have them scrubbed properly and fit with clothing suitable for the occasion. Thereafter, they shall remain at Murbra Faire, until it no longer pleases me."

Sherman spoke up. "Cole, please, we must be on our way."

"That will be all!" King Cole boomed. And with a wave of his hand, several guards armed with drawn swords accompanied Briar, Dax, and Sherman down the long stone corridors, Damarius leading them with his head bowed.

Chapter 18

Damarius smiled like someone who had something dark brewing just below his neatly manicured exterior. "Well, then," he said. He strode ahead with his robes billowing impressively behind him. "On a little adventure, are we?"

Briar, Dax, and Sherman shuffled together between the flanking, spear-carrying soldiers. Sherman looked more worried than ever and this didn't help Briar feel any better about what was happening. "Sir, I neglected to introduce myself," Sherman finally said.

"Did you? I hadn't noticed," the king's advisor replied. Damarius finally decided that smiling was too much effort. And seeing that there was no king to witness his words or deeds, he suddenly seemed even darker and heavier than before—like the clouds that gather before a torrential rain.

"Yes, well, my name is Sherman Herbclaw, dillywig teacher of enchantments. Perhaps my name is familiar to you—?"

Damarius saw no need to turn, but kept his stride down the flickering torch-lit inner passageways. "The name is as unfamiliar to me as you will soon be with the light of the sun—"

"Yes—" Sherman went on nervously. "Well, you should know that my charges and I would not make suitable company for the king, his court, nor the night's festivities. We are simple folk from the Squirrel's Province—"

"Fascinating," Damarius tossed out.

"You wouldn't want to be responsible for marring His Majesty's' reputation—especially on such a joyous occasion, now would you?" Sherman tried.

Damarius stopped at an arched wooden door. He fitted an iron key into the lock and with a rusty clank, the door groaned open. "Don't be modest," he said. He widened a smile that looked like he had too many teeth. "The Lady Orpion and her entourage will welcome you all with open arms this evening. Of that I am sure."

Damarius' face fell like it was full of wet sand. His gazed at them with a cold, flat indifference. He signaled the guards, who then roughly shoved the lot of them into the chamber.

"Tonight shall be an event that none will soon forget," Damarius said. Then he slammed the door shut. Briar ran to it, but it was already locked.

Dax looked ill and incurable. "When the Lady Orpion sees you, she'll know who you are." Then he turned to Sherman. "I thought you were friends with Cole. Why is this happening?"

"I—I don't understand it myself," Sherman admitted.

"Oh God. I just want to throw that asshole egg against someone's front door," Dax said.

"There must be a way out," Sherman said. He inspected the high stone walls behind several of the faded tapestries for hidden openings.

In the center of the room was a bed fitted with sumptuous linens and thick, opulent pillows. The walls were higher than two men—one standing atop the others' shoulders, but they had no windows. They were, however, fitted with several small torches to give the room some vacillating light.

"Use magic," Briar said.

Dax joined in. "Yeah, what the hell, Sherman? You're supposed to be Mr. Hot-Shot *Lord of the Rings*. Well, it's time to pull a rabbit out of a hat and get us out of here."

Sherman continued searching the walls, but allowed a long silence to fill the room before he said anything. "Magic is rarely the answer we seek. It's to be reserved for more serious occasions." Sherman would say no more. Or perhaps he had run out of excuses.

Briar was in a state. She felt the choke of worry. "What could be more serious than this?" she asked.

Just then, they all heard sounds of stone scraping against

mortar. Briar backed up to the bed, watching as a small stone lifted, held up by a pair of thin golden hands with sharp claws. Tarfeather carefully peered in. Seeing no danger, he popped the stone aside and lifted his head in full view.

"Look what's behind door number three!" Tarfeather said. His words and voice perfectly mimicked a television game-show host. It seemed odd to Briar, since his fellow dwarefs spoke in choppy sentences with voices like sandpaper on granite.

Sherman looked a bit shocked too, which told Briar that even he thought it outrageous.

"Help is on the way—right when you need it most," Tarfeather said. This time sounding like a chipper woman from a commercial.

He hopped out of the small tunnel, then, as quick as water sizzling on a hot skillet, he hopped up onto the bed. He stood very close, looking up and down Briar's body with his empty eyes.

"Tarfeather!" Sherman said. "What are you doing? If someone finds you here we'll all be hanged."

"Why, just one tablet helps you to get to sleep and stay asleep longer," Tarfeather said, again like an advertiser. Then he gave his horrifying spikey smile as he pointed to the ceiling.

"Wait," Briar replied. She realized he was pointing to the chambers above them. "Is someone asleep?"

Tarfeather nodded.

She thought for a minute. It must be the king. How else would Tarfeather get away. "The king?"

The dwaref nodded again.

"Why did you come here?" she asked.

"You're in good hands—" he said, again like daytime TV.

"You mean you're here to help us?" Briar asked.

Tarfeather nodded yet again.

"Oh dear, where is my boyfriend—?" he said mimicking a scratchy 1960s movie.

"Hey, Creep Show, Leon's not my boyfriend."

Sherman said, "It sounds like he knows something. What is it?"

Tarfeather then announced, "A book is a child's best friend."

Dax caught on to Tarfeather's weird television snippet language. "How does he know about the book?"

"Don't be ridiculous," Sherman said. "We discussed Leon and the book in the carriage."

Tarfeather then held a shushing finger to his leathery lips and whispered, this time using his own scratchy voice. "Briar Blackwood helpery Tarfeather find ha'tua. Helpery get two eyes."

"Let's try that again in English." Briar said.

"Ha'tua is dwaref language for something like *spirit*—as if this creature had one," Sherman said. "Dwarefs believe that the spirit lives in the eyes."

"She's a bad, bad woman," the dwaref said like a vintage B-movie actress. Then back to his raspy voice, "Bad lady takery ha'tua. Puttery ha'tua in king food. Ha'tua gone king belly now. King makery Tarfeather doery bad things."

Dax looked striken. "He ate your eyes? Now that's taking an eating disorder to a whole new level."

Tarfeather nodded. "I can help ya', see?" He said just like an old time gangster. "Tarfeather helpery Briar Blackwood findery boy-friend."

"He's not my boyfriend!" Briar insisted.

"Findery book. Book givery Tarfeather new eyes, new ha'tua."

"This is extremely dangerous!" Sherman said. "We can't open that book, let alone use it to help some stray rock-eater get new eyes."

"If this nightmare from Elf-Street can help us, then we better accept, Sherman. I mean, what's the alternative?" Briar asked.

Sherman leapt on top of the bed and growled at Tarfeather. "May I remind you that we are here without anyone knowing who you are, Briar. How does *he* know you? I think this is a trap and that we should put an end to this by feeding me lunch." He stood nose to nose with the dwaref, who then began backing up against the pillows.

"He's got a point, I've got to hand him that," Dax said.

Taking off his cap of fringe and feathers, the dwaref looked even smaller. He shivered and drew back his gold pointed ears.

"Don't you threaten me, you no-good snake in the grass," the creature copied a trilling female vibrato. Then he spoke past Sherman to Briar in his own voice. "No trappery. Briar Blackwood girl from Three Omens. All dwaref knowery Three Omens from mines. No harmery to you. Believery me, Briar Blackwood. Tarfeather wantery eyes." Then switching back to a television announcer's voice, "—and it's absolutely free!" His lip quivered and then he broke down sobbing into his sharp, spindly fingers.

"Humbug!" Sherman huffed.

"Sherman, I think believe him," Briar said. She was watching Tarfeather carefully. There was something in his manner that Briar found innocent. After all, he seemed to be as much of a freak as she and Dax. Why shouldn't she cut the little guy a break? "He is risking too much by coming to us," she ventured. "All we have to do is say no and he will have to live the rest of his life as a pet at the end of a leash. And if the king or Lady Orpion ever found out that he came to us—well, you know better than I what would happen."

"Don't be naïve. He's nothing but lies," Sherman said. He turned to the dwaref again. "You seem to know so much about the boy. Where is he?"

Tarfeather wiped his cheeks and caught his breath. "Boy, oh boy!" The dwaref parroted a child actor. The he switched to the voice of a dramatic woman. "You mean he's coming tonight? Here? Why, how could I ever have visitors?"

"He's coming here to the palace?" Briar asked.

Tarfeather nodded timidly then said, "Bad Lady bringery him. Makery him frog. Trickery you. Boy like bait in trap."

"How do you know this, you vile, vomitus thing?" Sherman snarled, exposing his sharp canines.

"Tarfeather many stories listenery with king."

Dax looked sideways at Briar. "Okay, so he may not be a Berlitz graduate, but he gets his point across."

Briar sat down on the bed and looked at Sherman. "Before him we had nothing. And right now, something is better than nothing."

After a short silence, a polite knock at the door caused them all to jump. A woman from the hallway called out in a petite voice. "Madame? Monsieur?"

"Quick, hide!" Briar said. She swept Tarfeather up, and stuffed him behind two dusty pillows.

"Sorry. We didn't order room service," Briar said. She shrugged and placed a finger on her lips.

"Madame, I am to bring you to zee dressmaker," the woman said. From her tiny voice, Briar figured she would be no taller than Tarfeather. The door jiggled until the rusty lock clicked. She swung open the door and stood hulking in the hallway: big, hairy and too broad to enter the room.

She hunched over to peer in, and Briar was nauseated by the single eye she had at the center of her forehead. She held soft white towels folded over her arm. "Oh, madam and monsieur are zo pretty. Zo handsome." The cyclops grinned, exposing about six or seven rotten teeth. Then she stood upright again and reached in with an enormous hairy hand. "I zee you zere," she said in a singsong voice.

Briar signaled to Tarfeather to leave. He slipped down from the bed and into his floor hole. Before he placed the floor stone he whispered. "Disguisery, Briar Blackwood."

"What's that?" the cyclops asked.

"We're coming," Briar replied. The dwaref nodded and fitted

the stone down over his head.

Once the creature stopped flailing her arm through the doorway, Briar and Dax were able to step out into the corridor.

"Zere you are!" the cycolps squealed. She lifted them both under her arms, then she kicked the chamber door shut.

Sherman whispered to himself. "Be careful."

The evening's event was both elegant and odd. Creatures of all sorts dressed in white and gold, lace, satin, and silk danced in pairs atop the glowing, burnished marble floors. Wolves and knee-high gnomes with grubby hands and feet danced together while winged bird-men in tuxedos and curly powdered wigs played a sedate violin chamber dance.

But there were other creatures too, that confounded Briar. Some were as tall as basketball players with hairy backs and pendulous breasts. These lovelies held up the sides of their dresses with long-gloved hands and danced daintily with their waist-coated counterparts, which appeared to be tusked ogres. Meanwhile, gauzy pink-winged girls danced and flittered together above the floor around and around the ballroom. It was a better freak show than the nerds at Gluteus High, Briar had to admit.

Briar and Dax stood at the top of a curved marble staircase watching the scene below. Just as Tarfeather had suggested, they disguised themselves with sculpted powdered wigs and black masks tied in satin ribbon bows that covered their eyes and noses.

Briar could barely catch her breath. The brutish cyclops fitted her into a white silk bodice that was as stiff as formed steel. It drastically tapered to her waist, cinched her ribs, and squeezed like a grizzly. The Lady Orpion might already be within the crowd, she thought, hoping that if they could just spot her, they might be able to keep their distance. She strained to see across the vast, sparkling ballroom, but no one gave special deference to anyone else. So it might not be that a woman of great, dark power was yet among the crowd.

Dax stood beside Briar smoothing down his own overgrown golden attire—the shimmering vest layered beneath an equally glimmering waistcoat, the golden knickers and the black shoes each fitted with a puffy golden bow. With the added powdered wig, he looked a bit like a walking wedding cake. He snapped open a lace fan and whispered behind it, "Just act natural—"

An overgrown toad fancied up with a ribboned white wig and white gloves stood at the head of the staircase. He announced to the room, "The dillywig charges of Sherman Herbclaw." Making the announcement gave Briar a gurgle in her stomach that wouldn't stop. The frog gestured, and the two knew they had to descend the stairs. To Briar's relief, no one in the ballroom seemed to notice or care. They all continued dancing and laughing to the lilting violin that played lengthy, complex baroque loops.

Dax spotted Sherman and pointed him out to Briar. He was standing beside Cole and another broad-shouldered man with his back turned to the crowd. As Briar and Dax approached, Sherman's eyes grew wide with warning. "Good evening," he said with a tense, constricted voice.

"Ah, your charges have arrived—" Cole said with a merry chuckle. Briar realized that Cole's laughter was more from anxiety than it was from being tickled.

"They never left," Sherman replied. He gave Cole an uncomfortable sideways glance. Cole was busy nodding to guests and scarcely registered Sherman's comment.

Dax attempted a curtsy but midway through the move, he realized a bow might be more appropriate. Then he awkwardly stepped on one of Briar's shoes and almost fell over.

The man whose back was turned saw Dax almost fall, and he slipped his arms around his waist, righting him in his firm grip. He smiled with impossibly gleaming teeth. "My Lord, caution with your step," the brilliant youth said. Then he gave a slight bow.

"Ah hah," Dax said. For once he was at a loss for words, stunned by the young man's good looks.

King Cole seemed to become suddenly more present and he spoke, sounding a bit flustered. "Oh Great Goose, where are my manners? This is my son, Valrune." He nodded toward the young man with shoulder-length blond hair, tied back smoothly with a black ribbon. He had the steely looks and physique of an Olympian, Briar mused.

"Valrune, this is...oh what the devils are these two young person's names, Sherman? You never bothered to say," the king chided. Sherman opened his muzzle to speak, but no words came.

"The name's Dame Titania, good sir," Briar fibbed. She wasn't certain how she grabbed at the name so suddenly—nor how she was able to adopt a sound that mimicked their formalities. But she wasn't about to question any of it.

"And this is Lord Bottom," she gestured to Dax.

"Thank you, *Dame Titania*. I shan't soon forget this." Dax scowled.

Briar elbowed him and then whispered, "Perfect name for a wise-ass—"

The prince gave a slight bow. "Titania, Bottom, it is my pleasure." When he stood back up, he latched his gaze on Briar, only fleetingly. It was enough to cause Briar to feel heat in her cheeks and a sudden giddiness in her heart.

"I beg your pardon, Dame Titania," the prince said. He took Briar's hand and met her gaze more boldly. "Have we met before?"

Briar smiled, but then felt guilt layering in. She was here for someone else, not this stunning man who stood before her looking as sturdy and powerful as a groomed racing steed.

"No, but *we* might have," Dax interrupted.

Valrune laughed. "The Lord Bottom is amusing."

Dax whispered to Briar, "Okay. That's just rude."

A dance finally ended with rousing orchestral fanfare and everyone applauded sedately. The ensemble started the next tune. After the applause, Valrune took Briar's hand again. She cleared her voice with discomfort and held the mask close to her face. "Dame Titania, will you take this next dance with me?" Valrune asked. Without waiting for her answer, he swept her out to the floor.

"What does she have that I don't—besides killer breasts and a vajay-jay—" Dax said to himself. Then he sat on the nearby marble bench with a dark cloud over his head.

On the ballroom floor, Briar tried to beg out of the dance. "I'm afraid I don't know your kind of dances," she said. "Where I come from, we do it much differently."

"Really?" Valrune asked. He traced her form with his eyes and held his hand on her slim waist.

"Oh yes," Briar said. "There's the Macarena, The Chicken Dance—really there's just too many to name."

"I'd like to learn this Chicken Dance, Dame Titania. But for now, let me teach you the dance they are playing. I learned it as a boy and it brings fond memories. It would please me if you would dance it with me." He gleamed with pure, bright eyes, and she could feel herself getting lost in them.

Her heart felt like tied knots knowing that the answer she wanted to give Valrune was *yes*. She wanted to dance with him. She felt drawn to him as though he had a powerful gravitational force. And he was drawn to her too. She could see that. He said it in his unrelenting gaze, in the flex of his arms around her small waist.

Valrune taught her the dance. It was simple, direct, straight-forward, like he himself. A hop, clasped arms, a turn left and right. In a short time, they were looping in wide, unashamed, heartfelt circles around the dance floor. Other couples stopped in their wake to stare, to titter and gossip about the mysterious girl who had won the prince's attention.

"You learn quickly," Valrune said. He smiled with a hint of mischief in his eye.

"Yeah, well"—Briar stumbled on her words—"I grew up with cheerleaders."

"I don't know what cheerleaders is, but whatever it may be, the Tales bless it!" Valrune laughed. He spun her again, holding her more tightly.

Without warning, the music ceased and a few of the females tried to stifle their gasps. Briar and Valrune spun a few more times unaccompanied by the tune, completely unaware that the music had stopped. Briar first noticed when Dax, now standing along the sidelines, was gesturing frantically toward something with his fan. Briar slowed her body and Valrune responded. They came to a stop at the foot of the marble staircase and looked up its sweep.

The fancy toad at the top of the stairs announced the next guests with a theatrical roll of his tongue. "The Lady Orpion and her ward, Gelid."

From the top of the stairs marched several dozen of the wolfguard, dressed in their black uniforms and helmets that hid their eyes. They descended the stairs and formed ranks in two lines, facing one another. One wolf gave a yip and they drew their spears, clanking their tips to the floor to mark a path. The room seemed to dim a bit, and the temperature plunged.

Briar's heart felt like it dropped into her stomach and she checked her mask to make sure it covered as much of her face as it could.

Almost unnoticed, a woman in flowing black robes that hooded her face descended the stairs with steps so light and soundless that she seemed to be floating. She held her hands clasped modestly together, and the cowl of her sleeves draped at her hips. In a wide leather belt next to her hip was the hand-mirror that changed Leon. Its reflective face was turned inward, its green jeweled back exposed.

Next to the hooded woman was a younger maid, perhaps the same age as Briar. She had blue dreadlocks and tattoos marking her face like the king's advisor, Damarius. A translucent black veil draped over her head and across the front of her body. Like the Lady Orpion, this younger woman had an unassuming yet threatening presence all at once. Her eyes were lowered, her lips drawn into a painted bow. Between her hands she carried a small, black, domed cage. Inside of it was the frog-Leon. Through the pathway of swords, the Lady Orpion and her ward swooped with their black cloaks flapping, stopping when they reached Valrune and Briar.

They all stood facing one another for a moment in silence. The Lady Orpion raised her green, reptilian eyes and looked into Briar's face with a cold eminence. Her hair flowed in red ringlets like drips of fire against her pale, slim features. Although she was slight and coldly demure, she had an animalistic aura of dominance that sought and required submission.

Briar felt dread like none other before. There was no place for her to run or hide. She suddenly felt the familiar tingling in her hands that came just before the flames appeared. She thrust her hands behind her back, hoping nothing was seen. Then, with her heart thumping in her mouth, she feigned serenity and met Orpion's penetrating gaze.

King Cole rushed up. Sherman trotted by his side with a worried expression. "My dear Lady," the king crooned. "Welcome to Murbra Faire."

The Lady Orpion seemed not to hear the king, as she continued to hold her scrutinizing gaze on Briar who felt a cold wave of her rage wash over her and run through her like a frozen river.

Dax stood immobile along the sidelines, as though something invisible were physically restraining him.

It wasn't until Cole dared to lightly touch the Lady Orpion by her elbow that she acknowledged him with a faint smile. "Cole," she said with a practiced charm. "What a momentous occasion. Our two kingdoms—soon to be joined as one." He ushered her past Briar. But as she passed, the Lady turned again with a studying gaze.

"Yes. Indeed—" the king agreed. There was a reluctance in his voice that he could not suppress. He tried to change the subject hastily. "I know time has passed since you last met, but you remember my son, Valrune." The prince bowed out of protocol, but his resentment was notable.

"How charming," Orpion said with a smooth hypnotic tone. "And this is Gelid of the Shrines." The girl beneath the black veil looked up, her eyes like shards of midnight. But her face was exquisite. It was pale and refined with berry-red lips and rose-pink cheeks. She had no smile. But it was no wonder, Briar thought, as it seemed as though life itself had been drained from her.

Again the prince bowed mechanically, but his eyes kept returning to Briar.

The king joined Valrune and Gelid's hands together, hoping to cover for his son's tepid response. Then he spoke with a twittering, uneasy laugh. "I don't know about you, but I'm getting warm from all this heat. Perhaps these two lovebirds would enjoy a dance."

Orpion looked over Valrune and Briar. She noticed their physical proximity, the flush of their faces, the pulses at their throats. "It appears that the prince may have tired himself prematurely," she said. There was a clear fury growing behind her silky words.

Cole laughed with a fretful vibrato, hoping to deflect Orpion's account of Valrune's indifference. "Nonsense. He would like nothing better than a dance with his future bride."

Orpion came closer to Briar, who began to feel a stab, like

icicles piercing her stomach. She looked at the key necklace. "What an interesting charm you are wearing," Orpion said.

Briar found it difficult to speak. She cleared her throat. "Thank you."

Orpion drew her bony white hand forward to touch Briar's trinket. "What is your name, dear?"

Valrune could see Briar's face become paler by the second and he intervened. "This is Dame Titania, My Lady."

"A Dame?" Orpion asked, amused. "I don't seem to recall a family within the Realms with a girl-child having been appointed to that title. From where do you hail, *Dame* Titania?" she asked. Then she stroked her index finger down the length of Briar's key.

It felt to Briar as though a frozen knife was slicing into her chest. Her eyelids fluttered as she struggled to remain conscious.

Valrune watched in horror as Briar began to have small convulsions. He swallowed hard and spoke again. "She is from the Boundary of the Four Wizardries. She is a cousin and friend of the family—nothing more." He placed a hand on her back to help support her, should she faint.

King Cole watched his son and decided it better to remain silent than to contest the lie and bring the Lady's wrath upon them all.

Orpion then turned her attention to Valrune, raising a cold finger to reach his throat. With Orpion's finger gone from her chest, Briar wheezed for air and tried to remain standing.

"You know," Orpion said to Briar. But she held her gaze upon Valrune. "Once upon a time there was a girl-child, whose squelch mother entered these Realms, never to return home again. It was quite tragic, really, to hear how she begged and pleaded to see her infant daughter one last time."

Orpion was ready to place her cold black-nailed finger at the base of Valrune's throat but held it a fraction away. "And in the end…well, I suppose there is no need to rehash such gruesome details on a festive occasion."

Damarius slithered down the cold marble staircase accompanied by several forbidding creatures that looked like overgrown hairy gargoyles. They stood at shoulder height to Damarius and they drooled through their filthy underbites.

Each had eyes that were the color and clarity of mud, and grimy fingernails long and sharp like poisoned arrow tips. Orpion turned her head delicately to one shoulder, sensing their presence. "Your ladies in waiting," she said to Gelid. With that, Orpion stepped back, but seemed unable to keep her eyes from Valrune's beautiful dance partner.

The king was aghast at the creatures that drug their arms and grunted. "Damarius"—Cole croaked out the syllables of his name—"see if you can coax these two to dance." He chuckled a little, but ended it with uncomfortable silence.

Lady Orpion watched Briar like a snake following its prey. "Damarius," she said. "We are weary from travel." She gracefully enunciated each syllable. Briar held her hands behind her back, but they trembled with the energy built up by the flames.

"Of course, My Lady," Damarius said. "Your chambers have been prepared."

The king looked at Gelid holding the cage with the frog inside. "Yes, Damarius, please escort them to their quarters," he said. "And carry their pet, for Pumpkin's sake!"

Orpion gave Cole a stare that caused him to cramp inside. "This creature shall not be touched," she said. Her eyes flitted to the frog. She caressed the cage and strummed the bars with her polished black nails. Leon hopped as far away as he could get. With his sticky green back against the bars, he shivered.

Briar fought hyperventilation and tried to hold very still. She watched Leon's terror and wanted to let him know she was standing right there. She wanted to rip the cage out from Gelid's hands and run.

"Very well, My Lady," Damarius said. He solemnly lowered

his eyes. "Follow me." He stepped to Orpion's side and held up a forearm. She placed her thin, pale hand atop his and they glided like ice skaters past onlookers. Her wolfguard followed in formation behind her flowing black trains, filing past Cole, who watched with desperate, worried eyes. The last to leave were the hairy gargoyles, who slogged behind their mistress leaving trails of saliva.

When they had passed, Cole pushed himself between Valrune and Briar. He stood touching noses with his son. "This was to be your engagement party, Valrune! How could you dance with that girl—that stranger?"

Dax rushed up to Briar's side and tried to steady her.

Sherman spoke so quietly to Briar that she could barely hear it. "Keep your hands behind your back, and let us leave this place." Briar only acknowledged his statement with a flick of her eyes. They had to somehow get Leon from Orpion, not escape from Murbra Faire. Not now, anyway. No matter the cost, Briar was not about to leave without her friend.

Orpion continued her subdued stroll from the ballroom, people on either side bowing in her wake. Valrune responded to his father in a hushed tone. "I do not wish to be married to the ward of that monster!"

Red-faced, the king tried to remain hushed. "It is not for your own sake that you must do this. You are no longer a boy. And for the sake of your kingdom, you must bear a man's burden. Mark my words: in a week's time, you two shall be wed."

It was then that Briar heard gasps and mumbling from the crowd. She looked up to see that Lady Orpion had turned around with her snow white teeth bared and her hands upraised. Blue flames sat within the Lady's own hands. They flickered in her palms, like candle wisps; they were small and shapeless. But they were enough to signal that someone with the gift of dragons must be present, for flame ignites flame—or so went the lore.

There were none present that had such a gift. But the flames could also signal something momentous. She inspected the small blue dancers in her hands with curiosity, and then with outrage. They had never before appeared when with the king or his court. *Yes*, she thought, *something is different*. Then her face warped into an awful smile, like one who discovers a terrible truth. She locked eyes with Briar and growled like a beast ready to pounce.

Her voice punched through the crowd's growing murmurs. "Guards!" she shouted. "Take them!"

"It's too late," Sherman said. "Keep your hands hidden, if you can." Before Briar could respond, she, Dax, and Sherman were in the tight grips of Orpion's guard.

Chapter 19

The wolfguards dragged them with their rough black claws to the dim stone chambers beneath the palace. The walls were wet and moss-dripped, with the smell of bodily waste so thick that Briar could taste it on her tongue. Thick smoke from flickering wall torches hovered at the ceiling.

Dax and Sherman were shoved roughly into a rusty-barred cell. The ceiling was so low that Dax had to bend forward quickly to avoid knocking his head. Sherman skidded on his sleek coat and one of his hind legs was soiled with something slimy on the floor—blood or excrement—he couldn't tell.

One of the guards was especially harsh with Briar. He tore at her arms, bruising and cutting them, then he dragged her so often that her dress tattered and her elegant shoes became fallen casualties, lost down some dark corridor. He used such force to throw her into the cell with the others that she slipped on the sludge-slick floor and landed sharply against a stone wall. Barefoot and degraded, her eyes filled with tears. She slumped, exhausted from struggling against the guards, and afraid of what might happen next.

"Sweet dreams, talebreaker," the wolfguard said. He pulled off his masking helmet and Briar saw his grotesquely disfigured face contorted into a savage smile of yellowed broken fangs. It was the head of the wolfguard from the tavern. He laughed with a phlegmy cough, and then leered at Briar with his white glazed eye. "You'll be lucky if you get the mines." He spat on the floor and wiped his lips with the short hairs of his forepaw. "That's where all talebreakers go to rot."

He slammed shut the gates, which squealed with a shrill scream of iron on iron. He secured the padlock and then sat near the door. He muttered to himself, keeping a watchful eye on the group. He chuckled darkly and spat some more. Nearby him was a flagon of ale that he had dug out from beneath some rancid, oily hay in an abandoned jail cell. He polished it off with the contents trickling from the corners of his wolf-mouth down his pelt. It wasn't long after that he was sprawled out across the pile of straw, fast asleep and gurgling in his saliva.

Briar stared at the throbbing abrasions on her feet and ankles. She shivered—not from cold, but from residual fear and adrenaline. It was unbelievable, and Briar replayed the scene in the ballroom over and over. She stood face to face with the woman who had murdered her mother. She felt Orpion's evil breath and the burning chill of her touch. She confessed to murdering her mother, and she relished retelling the story.

Briar wanted to think about anything else, and she tried to force her mind to shift. She wanted to cry, but found that she couldn't. She told herself that now was not the time for tears. She didn't know what to do exactly, but she decided that tears would not help—not now, and maybe never.

The Lady Orpion saw through her disguise. She knew who Briar was, probably from the moment their eyes met in the ballroom. Perhaps she had some idea even before that. And now Briar knew, without a doubt, her mother's fate. She had always been alone in the world, but for the first time, she felt it fully. There was always the hope that there was a connection for her— somewhere in the world. But now that small shred of comfort was torn away. The pain in her ankles surged, but she could scarcely distinguish it from the ache in her soul.

Dax sat on the floor across from Briar, with his back against the moss-slicked wall. He stared at the stone floor with the look of an animal headed to the slaughterhouse. "This is it," he said. "We're toast." It wasn't in his nature to give up, to see only darkness—or nothing at all. But he couldn't help himself.

Sherman ignored that and trotted over to Briar. He sat beside her for a while quietly regarding her. Finally, he nuzzled her a bit and wrapped his fluffy tail around her. She looked up at him. He didn't return the look, but he nodded in silent approval. Now it was clear to both of them that Myrtle and Poplar were right. Briar was indeed the one named in the Omens—or at least everyone around here seemed to believe it. She didn't feel at all like the hero they imagined. And in the dank and the smell of decay in the cell, she couldn't understand how she would ever be able to save anyone—including herself. But whether or not the so-called Omens were true, it was clear that the Lady Orpion was not about to test them out. Briar realized that even if the Omens weren't true—and really, how could they be?—she was a sacrificial offering. She understood that once Orpion eliminated her, the Realmsfolk, would lose hope. And with hope gone, the Realms were a low-hanging fruit for the Lady.

The sound of stone grinding upon itself filled the cell. Briar and Dax looked in all directions for the source but saw nothing. Finally, one of the stones from the floor dropped down, away from the others. Tarfeather raised his head and peered around the cell with his ears tucked back.

He lifted himself from the hole with one hand, while in the other he carried a chunk of the floor-stone. He popped it into his mouth and crunched. Pebbles and sand cascaded down his rounded golden belly on to the floor. He licked his fingers and picked up the crumbs with his sticky saliva, smiling as he slurped them off. "Why Marge, I simply *must* have that recipe," he said like an old-time actress.

Dax said, "Now that's gonna require a dental plan."

"One more thing Tarfeather bringery," the dwaref said. His eyeholes glowed mischievously. He reached down into his tunnel and pulled out the king's pillbox that he had pilfered from the carriage. "With these little babies you'll have enough pep all day!" he said like a movie character. Briar Blackwood getery boyfriend," he said in his own rasp. Then he gave a proud fanged smile.

"Jeez, enough with the boyfriend," Briar said. "Even if we get out of here, the palace is crawling with Orpion's guard. We'd never be able to reach Leon and get out of here alive."

Dax's face lit up with realization. "Not necessarily," he said. He stood and then he paced. "I've seen you do this before," he said. No one could follow what he was talking about. "Do what?" Briar asked.

"Act. You can *act* like Lady Orpion," he said. Then a manic flair lit his eyes.

"If you were in your right mind, you would have never suggested this," Briar said.

"No, it can work," Dax said to Sherman. "I've seen her do this before. It's like she transforms into the character she's playing. You can't even recognize her."

"Remarkable," Sherman said. Then he sized Briar up once more with a squint.

"Dax, this is stupid. Let's think of a better plan than one that involves me *acting* like a murderous—"

"Wait a minute," Sherman said. "Your friend is right. This *might* work."

"Are you out of your minds? There's like a bazillion guards and monsters all waiting around for Lady Orpion to execute me so they can chew on my bones for an afternoon high-tea," Briar said. She caught herself saying it all too loudly, and she finished her thought in a loud whisper. "No way!"

The guard snorted himself half-awake. Everyone stood still, holding their breath. He grumbled something unintelligible while he leaned more, and then a bit more to one side. He finally drooped completely flat onto the straw and stone, and slept taking great whistling breaths.

"Hold out your hands," Sherman said. He seemed to have a glimmer of some secret in his eyes.

Briar shook her head. "Forget it."

"You know," Sherman said. "Myrtle and Poplar tried to convince me that you were the girl—the one we'd waited for. But

I couldn't see it. You were rough, cynical, sarcastic—"

"Hey, Pep-Squad, is this leading somewhere?" Briar asked.

Sherman continued, "—but when the Lady Orpion turned around with flames in her hands—I knew. Right then, I knew. Briar of the Black Woods, this is not how your Tale ends. And it need not end at all if you just survive past your sixteenth birthday. Prove the Three Omens and learn an enchantment from me. Give me your hands."

Briar exhaled like it was the last breath she'd ever release. She took off her long gloves and held out her hands. "Now I've never done this before, but in the books of dragon lore, I believe it goes something like this—"

Sherman drew a series of geometric shapes in her upturned hands with one of his claws. "Close your eyes," he said, "and imagine the Lady Orpion standing before you." It took Briar a few moments to settle down. But slowly, as though stepping through a fog, she saw the Lady Orpion, her finger again poised at her throat. Immediately Briar felt a burning sensation in her gut. The tingling moved to her hands. She felt her heart pumping until it was the only sensation she could feel. Suddenly the blue flames appeared, engulfing her hands like two torches.

Tarfeather audibly drew a deep breath, and he clutched the pillbox to his quivering golden chest.

"Look very carefully at the details of her face," Sherman said. His eyes were closed and tiny electrical currents, thin bolts of lightning, sparked from his paws toward Briar. "Allow her to come closer...closer... Let there be no gaps," he said in a trance-inducing tone. Dax began to fight a wave of sleep that suddenly overcame him.

Briar imagined herself standing closer to what she hoped was actually an imagined Orpion. Her pale skin, the color of death, seemed smooth, waxy, and unnatural without any flaws. It reminded Briar of marble statues she had seen in a mortuary. The Lady's eyes, pale green with slits for pupils, burned with an ice-cold rage. And yet, the more deeply Briar fastened her gaze and looked beneath Orpion's rage, the more clearly she saw something that seemed like pain, or hopelessness.

Then Sherman used his fuzzy snout to nudge Briar's flames toward her face. Like soap bubbles, the two translucent fires detached from her hands and became a single, luminous one that engulfed her head.

Dax and Tarfeather stood watching in amazement as Briar's face began to twist and warp inside the glowing blue fire. Then the flame worked its way down the rest of her body until it completely enclosed her. Briar's white silk corset and shimmering gown changed color, darkened, and transfigured into flowing black robes. Then she floated up off the cell floor, her limbs loose, her neck lolled back limply. The currents of shimmering blue flame swirled around her, twisting the robes tightly around her body so that they became a dark cocoon. The torches that once flickered outside the cell extinguished, and the world became as nothing in darkness.

"Briar," Sherman whispered. "Briar, answer me." But the cell was silent, save the guard's drunken snoring.

"What's happening?" Dax asked.

More stillness and silence.

The torches guttered and then flared back to life. Standing at the far end of the cell, gazing down upon them all with green reptilian eyes, was the Lady Orpion.

Tarfeather backed up against Dax. "Sweet Jesus. It's a monster!" he said like an old movie reel.

"Briar?" Dax asked. "Sherman what did you do?"

The Lady standing before them examined her robes and felt the skin of her face. "Dang Sherman. This feels so weird." Briar looked and sounded identical to Orpion and the others in the cell had trouble convincing themselves that it wasn't.

"I didn't do anything," Sherman replied, though he was as entranced as the others. "—except help Briar along. This is her magic alone."

Briar needed a few minutes for her mind to fathom her new appearance. It sickened her to inhabit the Lady's body. But she also realized that with Dax's plan and Tarfeather's seed-pills so that they could walk through the bars, this just might work. She looked up with Orpion's wicked smile. "Let's go kick some gargoyle ass."

The guard believed he was following Orpion's orders when Briar commanded him into the jail cell and told him to allow Sherman and Dax to tie him up with a thick jute rope. Then they gagged him with a rag that had, by the look of it, been used to mop up blood. They left him there, bound and muzzled and safely padlocked away, then sneaked down the lonely stone hallways, following Tarfeather.

Briar soon realized that no one wanted to cross the path of the Lady Orpion, not even her own wolfguards, so making progress down the hallways was easier than she initially thought. Doors slammed shut and people darted away when they saw her coming. Briar shivered from time to time as her bare feet met cold flat stone.

Dax walked alongside Tarfeather, who seemed certain of the way to Leon's hiding place, despite being blind. "There are so many hallways, doors, and staircases, Tarfeather. How is it possible that you know the way?"

Tarfeather grinned. "Are you sayin' I can't do it? Well, are ya'?" he mimicked an old movie actor. Then he said in his own gritty voice, "Usery nose, usery ears. Long time livery in palace."

They had journeyed through so many different passages that Briar lost track of how they might even return to the cell, let alone find their way out of Murbra Faire.

"It's almost as if Cole created this labyrinth of hallways to hide from something," Briar said.

"Or to keep something in," Sherman wondered. He pricked

up his ears and jogged with a nervous prance, scanning the halls in all directions.

Without slowing his pace, Tarfeather turned back to the three. "Just what are you trying to hide? You'll never get away with it!" he said, sounding like a daytime drama. Then he motioned with his claws like a tiny flicker, urging them to keep up. Finally, after several more stone corridors and short staircases, he stopped in a nondescript hallway next to an ordinary door, which seemed very much like dozens that they had already passed. "Sshh," Tarfeather said. He pressed one of his wrinkled ears to the door.

"Boy-friend inery Gelid room," he whispered in his gravel-voice. He pointed to the door with his sharp golden finger.

Briar reached into her robes and pulled out the cell phone that Myrtle and Poplar had returned to her. She turned it on, and miraculously it still had about half of its battery power left. She began thumbing the device and in a moment, Dax's pocket began to buzz.

"No way," he said. He pulled the phone from his knickers with a smile of amazement. "My mom's gonna kill me for these roaming charges," he said.

"Dax, Sherman, you two stay here. Hide behind these suits of armor near the door and text me if someone is coming," she whispered. "Tarfeather will come with me."

Tarfeather swallowed hard and his mouth went slack. Briar bent over to get closer to the floor and to Tarfeather's quivering face. "Don't be afraid. Everything will be okay," she said. She nodded to him and he hopped onto her shoulder and buried himself into the folds of her hood.

Then Sherman spoke with hushed, cracking voice. "Before you go, you must know something about this enchantment."

"What?"

"Most magic is done in short bursts," he said. "But a dragon's magic can last as long as one can physically bear it. Legends say the magic of transformation can tax the body and the mind."

"You're just full of good news today. Okay—whatever. I feel fine. But thanks." Briar turned to leave, feeling unsettled to her core.

"Wait!" Sherman said. "If you feel depleted, you must get out of that room immediately."

Briar rolled her eyes. "Thanks, Dad. I think I got this—"

Then she stood up, closed her eyes and inhaled deeply. She then imagined the sound, the voice of Lady Orpion. When she thought she had a good recollection of her voice, she opened her eyes and knocked on the chamber door.

A guard opened it. As soon as he saw her, he knelt low. "My Lady."

Briar lifted her chin, haughty and sedate. "I wish to speak with my ward," she said. She was surprised that the words came so naturally. Dax and Sherman, their backs pressed to the stone walls, exchanged looks of approval at Briar's performance.

"She said that *you* had summoned *her*, My Lady, and she left moments ago to your quarters," the guard said.

"Yes..." Briar replied. Then she stood silently for a long time, trying to figure out what to say next. She knew that if she said the wrong thing, she'd blow it for them all, and she started to choke. The guard, sensing something was wrong, decided to look up at the fake Orpion. He sniffed the air.

"My Lady?" he asked. Then he darted his eyes away as soon as he had spoken.

Briar lied with an imperious tone to save her mistake. "I meant that I came back for the frog." She took several confident strides into the room that sent her black cloak fluttering behind her. She searched with her eyes, but if Leon was in that chamber, he was nowhere in plain sight.

Tarfeather peeked out from behind her head and searched too. He whispered in her ear, "Not hearing, not smelling commons in here, Briar Blackwood."

"The frog is where you placed him last," the guard said. He

stood up now, closed the chamber door, and took a few dangerous steps toward her.

"Of course he is," she said. She turned to face the guard with a placid stare. "That will be all." But he wouldn't leave.

"Go ahead and take him...My Lady," he said, squinting, stepping closer.

"Take one more step and—" Briar began.

Now certain that he had caught a plot before it had fully hatched, the guard spoke. "And what? What will you do?"

Briar tried to figure out what to say next, but she drew a blank. She chose instead to stare defiantly, holding her serene facial expression in place the best that she could.

Then she heard buzzing coming from her robes. The guard flinched and began to cringe a bit from the sound. "What is that?" he asked.

It made sense. He didn't know about cellphones. Briar took it out and it lit up, buzzing some more. The guard rocked backward and fell to a kneeling posture.

"That's right," Briar said, "its magic. And I've got plenty of it. Lucky for you I only need one frog, fool—or you'd be next in line." Then she placed the buzzing phone on the guard's exposed neck and he shuddered with a whimper. "Now bring him to me before I decide that what I really want is a worm to squish beneath the soles of my shoes."

"Of course, My Lady," the guard said, and he ran to a faded tapestry on a far wall.

She read the text from Dax saying that Gelid was coming down the hall.

Briar watched him impatiently and her leg began to shake from anxiety. The guard reached up to the pale image of a cage that was embroidered into the whole scene. It was hidden among unicorns, pomegranate trees, and a host of courtly lords and ladies. As he touched the weaving depicting the cage, the actual cage with Leon in it pulled away in his hand, leaving a blank spot on the wall hanging. He hurried back and offered the cage to her with lowered eyes.

Leon hopped as far away as he could from who he thought was the Lady Orpion. Briar snatched the cage away, and the guard flinched at her quick gesture. The phone buzzed sharply in one of her hands. The guard cowered and backed away. The text just said, "Hurry."

"Why, all he needs is a little push to succeed," Tarfeather said, in one of his television voices.

"Stand up," she commanded.

As though he was shocked by a thousand volts of electricity, the guard sprang up and stood at attention. She held up the phone, its blue-gray light glowing in his face. He made a little whimpering noise and then he backed away from the strange object she held in front of his face.

"No, My Lady. Please."

"That's right, keep backing up and no one gets hurt," she said.

The door lock clinked.

Briar had no more time. With a burst of energy, she charged the guard and shoved him with every ounce of her strength into the tapestry.

Chapter 20

"My Lady," Gelid began. She made a slight bow, but never allowed her eyes to meet Orpion's. Briar could not sense the tone of their relationship, beyond this formality. She watched as Gelid secured the chamber door, then she folded her hands together at her waist like a prim cloistered nun awaiting orders from her Mother Superior. Her blue dreadlocks hung like ropes across her face as she lowered her chin. "You surprise me," she continued. "I was in your chamber not more than a moment ago."

"By now you should expect surprises," Briar said. She was shocked at how quickly she could come up with a bluff. She realized she was still holding the cell phone and she shoved it into her robes. She flicked her eyes to the cage with Leon inside. The eye movement, though subtle and relatively imperceptible in any other circumstance, gave away the purpose of her presence in Gelid's chamber.

"Ah, you came for the boy. So it is agreed, then. We shall complete Skull Sigil tonight," Gelid said. She glided over the frigid stone floors to the dressing table and standing mirror solemnly adorned with white taper candles, carved with filigree, and drenched in gilt. Briar noticed the magical jeweled hand mirror laying on the table.

"Yes, of course—the Skull Sigil," she replied. *There it was; but how to get it—* She gave a haughty chuckle, thinking that was probably just what Orpion would do.

Tarfeather whispered a movie line in her ear, "Run, child—like you've never run before!"

"My Lady," Gelid said. "It is as if the tides of time favor us. The moons dim and they are nearly concealed. No matter what becomes of the Blackwood girl, the Omens are null without the boy." Gelid sat and lifted the jeweled mirror with porcelain priestess' hands, reserved for tasks away from the sun or labor.

The she withdrew a glass vial from her belt. It was as long as a man's thumb, and in it, thick red blood. "Once I am wed to the prince, nothing will stand in your way." Briar watched as Gelid poured blood out in a thin sappy stream onto the mirror. It puddled, and she smeared it like finger paint.

She pointed the mirror at the chamber door. Just as before, the mirror illuminated with a strange white intensity. Countless pins of light, silver as moonlight, shot from its reflective surface across the room to the door. It glowed for a moment and then sealed up with stones. Like many of the other chambers, the builders had constructed no windows in order to maintain palace safety. But now there was no door. Briar suddenly felt dizzy. She teetered as though the floor had taken a slant.

"Too late, Briar Blackwood!" Tarfeather whimpered. Then he burrowed deeper into the hood.

"Yes," Briar replied. She swallowed hard and tried to control any quavering in her voice. But the danger of the situation made it clear that there was no control over anything now.

Gelid set the mirror down, gave a strange, hungry smile and then placed mechanical goggles over her eyes. "Now that none can intrude, clear the boy from his cage, dark Queen. Allow me to finish the last binding at my own hands, to rid this world of the Omens."

"This is no time to take chances," Briar said. "Unseal the door, and I alone shall complete the Skull Sigil in my chambers." She moved boldly to the wall where once was a door. A self-assured manner was even more necessary than before. She raised her chin expectantly.

But Gelid did not react as Briar hoped. She raised her eyebrows to the Lady Orpion. "Beg pardon, Lady, but this cannot be done alone. The Skull Sigil requires two. Have you abandoned your trust in me?" Gelid bowed her head, and her many knotted dreadlocks cascaded.

Briar noticed that although Gelid's head was bowed, she was

now following the Lady Orpion with suspicious eyes.

"I have not abandoned faith in you. But I have changed my mind," Briar said. She felt the churning in her stomach and the prickle of power building in her hands. She saw the lit candles at the dressing table and it occurred to her that she was usually near fire when her hand-flames appeared. If this was true, then they might appear at any moment.

Why had she listened to Sherman and Dax? As she thought back, she realized that they never really had a plan at all. It was a gamble from the start. But now there were few cards left to play, except to continue bluffing.

Gelid did not budge. "Why does the Lady Orpion walk in bare feet?"

Briar looked down and saw that one of her bare feet stuck out from beneath the long robes and she pulled it back. "I, um…felt hot flashes. You know what happens to women at my age—"

Gelid interrupted. "Where is the guard that was here before?" she asked. She took a vial of blood from the side of her boned corset and swallowed it down. A trickle oozed from the corner of her mouth. She raised her goggles while striding toward the false Orpion, and she stood close to Briar's face.

"I sent him to watch over the Blackwood girl and her companions," Briar said. She struggled to restrain the terror seizing her throat. She knew by now her hands must be fully ablaze and she tried to hide them inside her sleeves. "Now do as I say, and unseal this door."

Gelid's own eyes had changed to those of a reptile: cold, green, with slits where there ought to be pupils. She inspected Briar's face, as though trying to understand how a street conjurer's illusion had fooled her.

Gelid bowed reverently, "Of courssse." She stood upright and smiled. But now her teeth were sharp, ghoulish protrusions. Then she muttered something low, in an unfamiliar language that sounded like something caught in her throat. Suddenly she doubled over with a shriek. She toppled to the floor and writhed, curling like a worm that had been severed.

Briar backed up, her hands bursting with flames. She tightened her hold on the cage and then she whispered to Leon using her own voice, "It's me, Briar. Don't worry, I'll get you out of here." Leon nodded, but his eyes were distracted and full of doubt.

Gelid was completely still beneath her cloak. "This is no time for games, Gelid." Briar tried to still sound in charge. Was Gelid dead? Briar crept forward and reached out a toe to jab at the body. She lifted the cloak only to find a misshapen embryonic thing within a translucent fleshy membrane. Its head was long and horned and its body was sleek, scaled and glistening black. Whatever it was, it hadn't fully formed.

Briar's stomach dry-heaved and she backed up, falling over a footstool near the filigree table. Leon's cage rolled beneath. Briar felt her innards melt as the black creature clawed its way out of the filmy cocoon and unfurled to its full serpentine length. But it wasn't a snake. It was something more repulsive.

It stood on stubby, claw-footed legs, as tall as Gelid, but it seemed to continue growing. It opened its slimy black-within-black eyes and then hissed angrily at Briar, snapping its long toothy jaws. It craned its twisting neck and licked with its black reptilian tongue at two malformed buds on its back that Briar supposed were to be wings. Instead they looked like short webbed claws that had atrophied.

"Jeez, Gelid. That may not the best look for your wedding night." Briar grabbed the footstool in her blue-blazing hands, and held it like a shield against the giant black beastie.

The thing hissed and curled its claws downward, leaving gouges in the floor. Briar knelt down, grabbed Leon's cage, and ran to the far end of the room. But there was nowhere else to go.

The creature sidewound its way and stopped within striking distance. Briar threw the footstool at it, but the awful thing was quick to nab with its toothy jaws, and crush the furniture to splinters. The monster laughed with a sound like a punctured tire. It towered above Briar on its malformed hind legs, licking the air with its black forked tongue. Brownish saliva slavered from its sharp jaws and sizzled on the stone floor below.

With a boom and a crash the wall of stone behind the beast erupted and crumbled to a heap of rubble. There with his paws upraised in some magical gesture, stood Sherman. Dax stood behind, watching in astonishment.

The creature spun itself around and snapped its jaws. Then it lunged at Sherman with its massive body. But he quickly tucked into a ball and rolled aside. The enormous creature landed amid the rubble, scattering stones like toys around the room, then it coiled up to strike again.

"The flames," Sherman shouted. "Throw one at the dragon!"

Tarfeather, who had been clinging to the inside folds of Briar's cloak, saw the creature advancing on Sherman. He shouted, "The creeper, Briar Blackwood! Killery it!"

But before Briar had a chance to do anything, the reptile struck Sherman, sinking its fangs into his back. He yelped in a high-pitched canine cry.

"No!" Dax howled. He picked up a large piece of stone and slammed it down on the monster's scaly head. It unlocked its jaws and recoiled. Sherman flopped to the floor and did not move. He lay in the middle of a small blood-lake. The monster furiously sounded off with a noise like a hundred angry wildcats.

With a demonic, unstoppable rage, the beast slithered to strike Dax. He tried to back away, but tripped and fell onto the mountain of wall-stones piled just behind him.

"Behind!" Tarfeather insisted. "Takery from behind!"

Gelid rasped and bore down at Dax who rolled to one side. The creature's fangs scratched at the stone, sparking, gashing.

Briar charged up behind Gelid and struck her scaly back with one of the blue flames. There was a sound like raw meat sizzling on a grill, and the creature began twisting upon itself, like a great knot that kept tying. The monster screeched as electric strands of silvery lightning scorched between the crevices of her tangled body, causing her to wrench into a tightly constricted mass.

Dax scrambled to his feet while the dragon uncoiled with a final high-pitched cry. Then it sprawled, lifelessly, across the floor.

One of Briar's hands was normal again, but the other still blazed with power. She stood staring at it. Then she ogled the creature. Back and forth she did this, trying to understand what just happened. It wasn't until Dax picked up Leon's cage and ushered Briar toward the wall-opening, that she began to come back to her senses.

"Takery mirror," Tarfeather whispered. "Great powers it havery."

"Go," Briar said to Dax. She motioned to the opening. He hopped through it while she made a hasty detour to Gelid's dressing table. She seized the mirror and stuffed it into her robes. She knew Dax hadn't seen her do it, but she felt that it needed to be kept secret for now. *Who knows how it might help later on?* she reasoned. Then she dashed back to Dax, who stood looking down at something behind a rocky pile of wreckage.

There at his feet, Briar saw the fox lying with his red and white fur soaked through with blood. "Sherman!" Briar cried with such force that she was certain the remaining walls would crumble into dust.

Dax held her back. "It's too late. We have to get out of here."

Briar doubled over and sobbed. "We can't just leave him here." She knelt down and lifted Sherman's floppy body with her flameless hand. He felt lighter than she expected. And he was already getting cold. She pressed his form to her chest. His head lolled to one side and a strand of blood dripped from his mouth. Briar then listened to his chest. She felt like crying again, but this time from joy. Sherman's heart was still beating. It was faint. But he was alive.

"Come on!" Dax shouted. He was now in the outside hallway looking in all directions for guards, who probably heard the immense explosion and Gelid's gruesome shrieks.

Briar began to negotiate a path between the chunks of strewn stone. And when she passed Gelid's reptilian head, it lifted. Without Briar ever noticing, the thing widened its jaws, forming sticky saliva strings.

"Briar Blackwood!" Tarfeather screeched.

Instinctually, Briar slid down onto the rubble, trying to evade the creature. It bore down again, its sharp teeth gouging the rock-pile on either side of Briar's leg. She felt the dragon's wet mouth, but she was unharmed. Gelid slithered with all of her weight on Briar's robes, and pinning her to one spot. The creature raised itself for a final deadly bite, opening its mouth wide, when Briar whipped the remaining blue flame from her hand. The ball of fire propelled like a skyrocket, striking inside the dragon's mouth.

The creature bit down and tried to shake the flame out. But Briar watched the power from the flame glow through the creature's body and travel into its core. The reptile screamed and recoiled backward into a corner. It paced back and forth several times, like a mad, trapped animal, trying to expel the flame. It vibrated out of control when black smoke began to billow from its mouth. It slammed its own body to the floor, trying in vain to get the flame out. In desperation, the creature sank its claws into its belly and ripped itself apart with a wall-shaking howl that was filled with all the wildness of the world. Innards and black blood washed across the floor, soaking Briar's feet with a foul stench.

The dark creature finally lay without a sound, smoking and sizzling like doused campfire logs. Briar looked down at the slick black mess in which she stood and tried not to wretch.

"Now that's a perfectly cooked pot-roast," Tarfeather imper-sonated from a television cooking show.. "No time for wastery. Runnery!"

Chapter 21

Briar lost all sensation in her body and she wondered if it would ever return. Still, she cradled Sherman's blood-soaked, wilted frame like a child who recovered a long-lost doll. He had saved them, and paid for it with his life. But there might still be time, she hoped.

"Right this way, Madame," Tarfeather shouted in one of his many voices. He hopped weightless like a flea atop the scatter of broken stones. Then he scrambled down an empty hallway that faced an inner courtyard. It was different from others because it was lined with towering overhead windows.

Briar and Dax followed, their way lit by the haunting crescent moonlight that bled from above. Dax was not paying attention to the jangling of Leon's cage. "Let me out!" he yelled in a croaky voice.

"There's no time," Dax said back. "Just hang on."

"Is this a dream?" he asked Dax, looking with his green, bulging eyes.

Dax didn't know how to answer intelligently, so he didn't. "Yeah, I know it's hard to believe that I don't normally dress like a pop-star's backup dancer, circa 1990. But I don't—"

They managed to keep a fireball's pace behind Tarfeather, who streaked along, zigzagging through the maze of dim hallways.

"Is this the way out?" Briar asked. She was huffing and beginning to feel the weight of her many robes.

"The book? Why yes, darling, I know where it is," Tarfeather parroted from television. "Temple caves havery book of terrible things."

Finally the dwaref stopped and backed himself against a wall, droplets of sweat glistening on his golden skin. The others all came to a halt behind him and pressed their backs to the cold walls. Briar saw that just around the corner from where they stood were two of Orpion's wolfguard. Their helmets only allowed her to see their gray muzzles. Standing outside an open door, they bared long swords in a practiced military manner.

Briar and the others tried to control their huffing enough to remain unnoticed and to hear the conversation that echoed in the hollow corridors.

"I don't know how it happened," one wolf was trying to explain. His gruff voice sounded familiar.

"Have you searched the grounds?" This was unmistakably the Lady Orpion's cold, detached voice.

"We thought it important to report it first," the other wolf said. He had a cringing, rueful tone.

"Spread the word," Orpion said to one. "You stay here and guard my quarters," she said to the other. Then Briar heard the sound of hurried footsteps echoing into the distant halls.

Tarfeather peered around the corner, but the remaining guard saw him. "You there!" he shouted.

Briar knew what she had to do. She tried to hold back her inner trembling. It was the only way past this guard now. Briar set Sherman down at her feet. She took a moment to collect her thoughts. She realized that she was beginning to feel fatigued. Sherman had warned her that the spell could be physically taxing, and now she was beginning to feel it. Nevertheless, she knew it would be just a moment longer and then they would be out of the palace. She stepped out from behind the wall.

"I hope you were not shouting at *me*, fool," Briar said. Feigning Orpion's cold intensity, she came face to face with the head of the wolfguard again, with his decay and smell of sickness.

"I...I..." The wolf looked down the hall in the direction where he saw Orpion leave. Then he looked back at the Lady approaching him. "I thought I saw the escaped prisoners," he said. It made Briar feel powerful to see him backing up, his gray tail tucked between his legs.

Briar, hands clasped at her waist like Gelid, moved toward him with a dignified glide. "It sounds as though your judgment is impaired. Perhaps you should take your leave, soldier." She felt her legs trembling with weakness and a cold sweat forming across her brow.

"Forgiveness, Lady," he said. Then he tucked himself low and cringed like a beaten dog.

Briar felt woozy. Her heart pounded as though she had run a marathon, and her skin felt as though it were coming off. She could not speak or move or even stand for a moment longer. The hallway began to swirl, but in her haze she noticed two standing suits of armor flanking one of the soaring floor-to-ceiling windows. But as soon as she saw them, they seemed to blur. She felt herself sink toward the floor, nauseated, her consciousness sinking into a puddle of moonlight.

Briar dropped to her knees, pale as a viper's belly. The wolfguard dared to look up and his distorted, blind-eyed face twitched as he watched his Lady's features contort, blister, and re-shape themselves.

Tarfeather listened from around the corner and motioned for Dax to watch what was happening. As he peered around the corner, he watched the wolf stand above Briar, sword held out, afraid of what he saw. "My Lady?" he asked. But Briar did not respond.

The wolfguard watched as one of the Lady's arms reached out and changed from pale, death-white to flesh pink. The Lady's black robes transformed from somber black to the soft white and gold of Briar's tattered ball gown.

The wolf cracked a sinister smile. "So it's the talebreaker," he said. He growled and bent low so that he could be eye to eye with his prize. "Think you can just leave me in a prison, tied like a roasting pig?" Briar just wheezed and reeled, unable to do anything. He slapped her hard and her lips bled. Then he loomed over her and hoisted his sword with both of his paws gripping the sword tightly. "I've been wanting to taste your flesh since the Horn and Hold. Now it's time for a little slice."

He began to bring his heavy blade down, but it was met by another, blocking it just before it would have chopped at Briar's exposed neck.

It was Valrune. It shocked the wolfguard who was told by the others that the prince was as soft and dithering as his father. The wolf stood at his full height, towering over Valrune by a head or more and he lifted his sword. Valrune began to advance attempting to strike so that the wolf would move away from Briar. But the wolf was quick to meet Valrune's sword with his own and parried it away with a twisting motion of his body, giving him enough time to position himself so that his back was not to a wall.

Briar slowly began to lift herself from the ground. She looked at her tattered ball gown, and she registered the clanking of swords just a pace or two away from her. But she still felt incapable of standing.

"Crap on a stick!" Dax said to Tarfeather.

"What's happening?" Leon asked, from inside the cage.

Dax opened it up and Leon hopped out to Dax's shoulder in order to get a good enough view. "I can't take this anymore. Someone's got to help her," Dax said.

Something suddenly changed and Briar's eyes blazed with a focused fury. The torches along the walls dimmed and her hands glowed with blue, undulating fire. She noticed the unused sword propping up one of the coats of armor and she lurched for it—as though she knew what she was doing. Despite its weight and size—for it was nearly as long as Briar was tall—she wielded it as though it was a feather in her hands. She stood tall, an iron strength permeating her body, and without giving thought to her next move, she poised the sword like a trained warrior.

The prince and the wolfguard clanked swords in a fiery

frenzy. Blade met blade again and again. Swords sparked ferociously until finally, swoosh! The guard's blade passed close to Valrune's head, but he leaned back in time to dodge it. That was when the prince lost his balance and fell back. His sword skated away.

Leon sprang from Dax's shoulder and hopped madly across the floor. Dax charged behind him until they reached the wolf. Meanwhile Briar, hands tightening on her sword and jaws clenching enough to pulverize her molars, took a lunge at the wolf herself, and thwacked his sword away. It happened just as he was about to plunge it into Valrune's chest. The wolf's sword slid with a metallic scrape across the floor and he looked with eyes of disbelief. Leon hopped from elbow to shoulder and then to the guard's face where he slapped his webbed feet across the wolf's eyes. Dax stepped up and socked the wolf square on the muzzle.

"Ow! Shit that hurt!" Dax said, shaking his hand.

The soldier yipped and shook his head, then he tried to unseat Leon. Briar lifted her sword once more and jabbed it mightily it into the guard's leg. He howled while revolting black blood, like that of the dragon, spurted profusely. He fell backward, clutching his leg with a manic yowl. Then he realized Leon was still on his helmet and he tried to pull it off. But Leon quickly hopped away and averted the wolf who sunk one of his own claws into his blistered, exposed skin. He cried in pain once again, but it was only a moment before he turned the pain into a white-hot rage.

He managed to get up on all fours, tuck back his ears, and prepared to kill. But first he had to be rid of Briar's protectors. He turned with a poisonous rage to Dax, and with a single paw-swipe, backhanded him to the floor. Then he reached behind him and struck at the base of a suit of armor, causing it to tumble with a great crash and the weight of steel across Valrune.

The prince wheezed and his face turned purple. The wolf

realized that it didn't kill the prince so he turned to topple the second suit of armor. Briar lifted her sword once more, and this time she jabbed its point at the center of the wolf's chest. Valrune, meanwhile, clawed at the floor, trying to pull himself out from beneath the pile of armor parts.

The wolfguard backed away. "You'll be found," he croaked. A thin strand of drool dripped from his mouth.

"Shut up, you freak-ass dog," Briar shouted. Her eyes were focused and clear, and she continued to hold the sword point sharply at the wolf's heaving chest.

"Guards!" the wolf croaked. But as soon as he did, Briar shoved the sword into his other leg. He arched his whole body as more black blood gushed out. But then he clenched his mouth and gave Briar a defiant smile.

She lifted the sword back to his chest and shoved the sword in a bit deeper. Black blood began to run in a thin stream down his front side. He pressed himself against the window. "They say you're the one from the Omens," he sniggered. "But you're just an insignificant talebreaker. You're nothing. And you'll never be anything." He laughed with a snarl, his eyes wild and insolent.

"My, what big fuckin' eyes you've got," Briar said. She dropped the sword, then powerfully shoved him against the tall window. Her thrust was so great that he lifted from the ground and crashed backward through the window. He fell only halfway through, and jagged sheets of glass pierced his back. He screamed and wailed, his black blood running down the knife-edged pieces. Briar flicked the flames from her hands at the immense razor-sharp shards still dangling above him in the window frame. They loosened and fell, lodging deeply in the wolf's neck with an awful bone crack and a squish.

It was done. Beyond Briar's belief, she had killed twice now. A cold dread clutched her heart. Reeling backward from horror, she tripped on Valrune and the armor scattered across his body. Landing on her hands just beyond him, she blinked in astonishment.

Dax moaned and rubbed his jaw. Tarfeather stepped out from behind the wall and tried to help Dax to stand.

"How in the heck did you do all of that?" Dax asked.

Briar sat by Valrune, aiding him until he could stand. He was sore and winded, but he could still get up. "You don't go through six weeks of theater combat class without walking away with *something*," Briar said. She tried to sound fine. In fact, she was beginning to realize that her fear was because she felt fine. She shouldn't feel that way—not after killing twice. She wanted to feel badly about it all. But instead she felt nothing.

Valrune clasped a hand over his bruised chest. "Come with me, all of you," he said. Dax went back for Sherman, and then they all followed as Valrune, leaning on Briar, half-jogged down the halls.

"Why, it's my knight in shining armor!" Tarfeather said in a female southern drawl, while he and Leon hopped alongside the group. "Gates lockery. Long walkery by foot," he added in his own rough voice.

After a few short turns down several narrow passages, they arrived through a side entrance to the main throne room. The lion banners that formerly hung so grand and regal were shredded and torn. Cold night drafts stirred the frayed fringes of their remains.

With a face full of deep, unquiet pain, the prince surveyed the destruction of his home. "Hurry," he said. He limped with the group to the enormous main doors that had been split and left unhinged. None of Orpion's soldiers stood guard, which Briar counted as fortunate, but peculiar. "Before I found you, I told the wolfguard that you had escaped and headed south to the Ink Sea," Valrune said.

He scanned the great hall for possible stragglers or spies. Then to Tarfeather he said, "Go down to the carriage house. If it has not been ransacked and looted, tell them that Valrune requests a carriage with two of the king's fastest horses." Tarfeather nodded and ran quicker than Briar had ever seen him run. Out into the night past the torchlight of the palace he ran and disappeared into ruined shadows.

The prince turned to Briar, saying, "Take the carriage, all of you. The driver knows where there is safe hiding. Wait there. I will first see that my father is not harmed and then I will join you by horseback."

Briar shook her head slowly and looked into his deep, sturdy gaze. "We have further to go," she said. "We came to save Leon here." She glanced to the floor where Leon sat by her foot, his throat bloating with air. "But before we take him back to his home—our home—we must find the spell that can change him into his own form again. So we're going to the Towery Flowery Hill."

"I see," Valrune said. There was more than a hint of disappointment in his voice. He eyed Leon and then Briar. "You have endured these hardships to save this frog?"

"Hey, watch it, buddy," Leon said, feeling testy.

"Well, he's not really a frog. He's a friend of mine," Briar said.

"A friend?" Valrune asked.

Briar reiterated. "A friend."

"A friend?" Leon asked. The tone of his words almost sounded like Briar had slightly bruised his ego with her platonic definition of their relationship.

Briar held her breath a moment and felt mixed up. Leon had made it clear that he was interested in Megan. And now, if Briar read Valrune's intentions right, there was a prince on the horizon of her life. It made no sense to her that Leon should even care. She had already admitted her heart's secret to herself the same night Leon crushed it. No, there was no sense in fooling herself any longer. Leon should just stay a friend and nothing more.

"Yes Leon. A friend."

Dax piped up. "Can we change the subject? I'm feeling a little confused."

Briar heard the sound of hooves clattering on stone and she knew Tarfeather had returned with the coach. "Here," she said to Valrune. She reached into an inner pocket of her dress and produced the smooth stone given to her by Ash. "Take this and give it to your father. It's a powerful charm that can protect him."

She placed the stone in his broad hand and closed her fingers around his. Her hand rested on his for a moment and she found it difficult to take it away. It was heartfelt and safe. Whatever was happening between them was palpable to everyone standing nearby.

Valrune leaned in close, as though to kiss Briar in thanks for the charm.

Leon spoke up. "Hey, buddy, back off."

The prince glanced down at the smooth, glossy frog, so small and pathetic on the floor by her foot.

"Yeah, that's right. She doesn't want any part of your so called princely-charm, or your phony-baloney palace living..."

"—Or your sizzling good looks, or your wealth," Dax added.

"You're not helping," Leon said.

While looking at Leon, Valrune noticed Briar's bare toes protruding from beneath her gown. "Dame Titania," he said. "You cannot journey in bare feet." He reached down and slipped one then the other of his own long, black leather boots from his feet. Then he knelt down and helped Briar into one. It felt warm and slightly dewy. "They may not fit, but they can keep you from further injury," he said. Then he fitted her other foot with the second boot.

"Aren't those supposed to be glass slippers?" Dax asked. The prince gave him a bemused look, cocking one eyebrow. "Always amusing, Lord Bottom," he said.

"That's what they tell me," Dax replied.

"Dame Titania? Lord Bottom? Who is he talking about?" Leon asked. This whole thing was clearly not settling well with him.

A familiar voice dolefully called from the shadows. "Your Majesty." Then from behind a pillar stepped Damarius, a grave expression on his face. "I heard the sounds of battle in the great Halls of Murbra Faire. There was no protection for me, so I secreted away until all had quieted. There were murmurs of Cole going missing and of these, his guests in grave peril. And, by all the Legends, you have found them. A job well done."

The prince arose and faced the king's advisor. "Damarius, the Lady Orpion has taken control of the palace. You were right to hide. But now you must flee."

Damarius looked confused. "It is difficult to believe that with so many negotiations undertaken and sacrifices made that she would end things thusly—" Then he stood looking into the battle-worn faces of those before him. "Surely our own men can defeat the small number of troops she has in her retinue," he said. He saw Sherman lying in Dax's arms, bleeding, unconscious. "What madness is this?" Briar noticed that his voice changed suddenly in seeing Sherman. His usual detachment seemed rattled—almost emotional. A royal advisor who must observe certain precepts and formalities cannot overtly display such feelings, she thought, and it seemed peculiar.

"Yes. Orpion's work to be sure," Valrune shot back. "I have arranged to send these innocents to safety."

"Indeed," Damarius said. He established a firm, determined gaze upon Briar as though trusting her for the first time, and expecting that same trust in return. "And where in these Realms can these children hide? If Orpion has her eye fixed upon them as talebreakers, she will not stop until—" He cut his thoughts short and took in a short sharp breath. He bowed his head to the prince, but said no more.

"We journey south, to the Ink Sea," Briar said. She gave Valrune's hand a short squeeze to cue his silence.

"A wise choice. The Ink Sea is a considerable journey south of the Black Waste, and the Lady would not risk the dangers of night bandits she would surely encounter along the way," Damarius said. Then he noticed the jeweled mirror tucked into Briar's bodice boning.

"Great Goose," he said. His throttled emotions were now clearly on display. "Is that not—the Lady's mirror?"

"Gelid had it and used it to seal me in her chamber before she changed into a psycho-dragon that nearly ate me," Briar said. "I figure that it's probably safer with me."

Damarius swallowed and his face looked like fallen sacks of flour. "This is a foul artifact of blood magic; it's only purpose to harm. It should be destroyed at once. Give it to me…"

"Hold it right there," Briar said. She said putting a stopping hand against the man's chest.

Damarius was unaccustomed to anyone questioning him, it seemed clear to Briar. He clenched his jaw and drew his hands into tight clamps.

"I beg your pardon—" Damarius said.

Valrune watched Briar carefully, and then said, "You have no need for it, Damarius. Whatever Dame Titania needs, she shall have. And her purpose will be questioned by none."

Damarius' breathing became labored and his face was the color of stewed tomatoes. He withdrew his hand and bowed solemnly. Valrune spoke again. "Besides, without it, I trust, the Lady Orpion will have one less power at her disposal."

"Yes. Of course," Damarius said. He lowered his eyes in a practiced manner.

"Now please find my father and assure his safety," Valrune said. "I shall be along presently."

Damarius nodded his head gracefully, but he cast the rage in his eyes at Briar. Then he rushed away, his expression fevered.

Valrune steeled his voice like an officer giving a military command. "Take your leave, Dame Titania, Lord Bottom. You must not become embroiled in the contrivances of this palace." With that, Briar nodded and they all piled into the king's carriage that waited for them just outside the massive doors. "Be cautious along your journey, and stop for no one," Valrune ordered. Then he slammed shut the carriage door and the driver sped them away, furious hooves beating into the blackness.

Chapter 22

The carriage bumped along the rolling plains of the Black Waste for what seemed like an eternity. There were few features to the landscape: a rise in the road here and there, a black tumbleweed, a dark, endless horizon.

Briar pressed an ear to Sherman's soft white chest for the umpteenth time listening to his withered heartbeat. "He's not going to make it," she said. She reached down and ripped her dress from the hem up to her thighs, exposing the shiny black boots that went up past her knees. Then carefully she ripped the lower part of her gown in a straight horizontal line.

The mirror she had carefully tucked into her dress was not only in the way, it was jabbing her ribs. So she tucked it into one of her long boots where it could remain concealed and relatively safe. Carefully she took the fabric she had torn away and ripped it into a few manageable sections, which she then used to dress Sherman's wounds. "This will have to do," she said, looking at her work.

"Wow, you really do like a certain look," Dax said, admiring how the altered dress now seemed like another version of Briar's former cinched-up black Victorian and grunge boots.

Tarfeather, who sat on the tufted leather bench facing Sherman, had tears streaming from his tiny eyeholes. "I don't think he's gonna' make it. And then what'll I do without him?" he repeated from television.

"What is Tarfeather going on about?" Dax said.

"No, mister Dax not understandery. Magic flowers makery medicine for Sherman. But flowers at Towery Flowery Hill."

Dax looked at Briar perplexed. "But that's good news, Tarfeather. All we have to do is get there and we can help Sherman."

Tarfeather shook his head then buried it beneath Briar's

mounds of shredded petticoats. "It's such a long journey. I don't think we'll ever make it," he impersonated. Then he began to bawl, though it was muffled beneath Briar's dress.

"Don't worry, Briar," Dax said. "He'll be okay. My dog Mitzy was sick for a week before she...uh—"

"Wow Dax. Thanks for that message of sensitivity and hope," Briar said.

Leon sat next to Tarfeather silently fuming. "You know, you shouldn't take this out on Dax," he said. "The only reason we're here—the only reason why he's injured"—Leon pointed to Sherman with his small flipper—"is because of you, *Dame Titania!*"

"What? We're here because of you, dumb-ass." Briar said. She had had enough of Leon and his flip-flop loyalties.

"Me?" Leon asked. "I was handling things just fine, until you had to come and rile up Gelid. Oh, by the way, congratulations on killing Orpion's best friend. I'm sure we can all rest well tonight."

"Are you out of your mind?" Briar began to raise her voice. "You are a frog. A *frog*. You were stuck in a cage that was woven into a tapestry. That was your idea of handling things?"

"Yeah, I was better off there. I didn't need you or Prince Boredom—the Pussy in Boots—to rescue me."

"Oh, that's what this is about," Briar replied. "Nice. You're jealous of a storybook price—who is so incredibly, unnaturally gorgeous that he probably doesn't even really exist. Meanwhile, you keep Megan as a girlfriend for your image, and me on the side because I entertain you. You're a real piece of work."

Involuntarily Leon snapped his long pink tongue at an insect that had flown into the carriage and he sucked it into his mouth. "Oh crap, please tell me that I didn't just eat a bug."

"Okay, everyone to neutral corners," Dax said. "Leon, you'll be home soon and out of this mess. And Briar...this flirting with the prince is just off the charts, girl." Dax slapped a high five with approval. "Now that's what I'm talkin' about!"

The carriage unexpectedly stopped, sending Dax, Leon, and Tarfeather to the floor. The horses chuffed and the reigns slapped.

"What was that? No—no! I said don't come any closer," Tarfeather said like a movie scene. He cleared away Briar's layers of dress from his face.

"I don't know," Briar said. She looked out the window and saw a dark figure, black mask covering its eyes, holding a sword toward the carriage driver. She gasped and silently indicated for everyone to get down on the floor.

"Bandits," Briar whispered.

Then the carriage door flung open and Briar, who was cramped against it, fell to the dusty desert floor. At once she felt a cold knife at her throat. "Briar," Dax shouted, but he could not see who it was that held Briar hostage in the darkness.

"Stand up real slow or I'll slice out your throat," a resonant voice said. "The rest of you, get out."

Dax piled out of the cab. Leon and Tarfeather sprang out after, leaving Sherman inside. "Hands where I can see them," the bandit said. He shoved Briar toward Dax, where Leon stood on his hind flippers, his tiny green arms raised high. The carriage driver was forced down to stand with the others.

"Turn around," said another tough-sounding man. He jabbed something sharp into Dax's back. "Put your hands on the carriage."

The masked bandit, who seemed to be rather short in stature, called out. "Blessfang!"

"Yeah Boss?" Blessfang called from deeper in the shadows. He had a thicker, slower sounding voice.

"Check them for weapons. Vilesight, Thrash, check the carriage for valuables." Two caped creatures swooped from above into the carriage, while another stomped, heavy footed, behind Briar and the others and began to frisk them roughly.

"They're clean," Blessfang announced.

"What do you want?" Leon asked.

"I said hands on the carriage! Eyes down, everyone. Don't look up," the masked one said. Then he held the tip of the sword to Leon's green skin and said, "Unless you want to be the main course at our dinner tonight."

"Yeah Boss," the dull-voiced Blessfang replied. "Frog's legs with a little butter sauce would be utterly delightful."

"Shut up, Leon," Briar whispered. "You're going to get us killed."

"I'm not the one who got us into this mess in the first place," Leon snapped back.

"Both of you, be quiet," the masked bandit said. "I'll ask the questions. What are you doing here?"

"She's Briar Blackwood!" Dax shouted. "The redeemer of the Realms. The girl from the Three Omens."

The masked bandit chuckled. "Really? The girl from the Omens?" He laughed some more and then Blessfang followed suit, laughing a bit too enthusiastically. "Shut up, you dope," the masked one snapped. Blessfang went mute.

Vilesight and Thrash came out of the carriage but were too quick for Briar or the others to see who they were. "There's nothing in there but a sick fox," Vilesight said.

"Yeah, we checked everything," Thrash confirmed.

"Impossible!" the Boss said. "Is this not the king's coach?"

No one responded.

"Answer me!"

"Yes, it is," Dax said. Briar elbowed him. "What?!" The king's crest is right on the door."

"Then why is there no treasure?" the Boss asked.

"Prince Valrune sendery Briar Blackwood to safety from Murbra Faire," Tarfeather replied. "Is under attackery by Orpion and bad wolves."

"Boss," Blessfang said. "That's all part of the Omens."

"Oh, what do you know?" the masked bandit said. Blessfang

shut his mouth again and the masked bandit—the Boss—entered the carriage.

"Faywries and berries!" he exclaimed. "Sherman Herbclaw! It's Herbclaw come back." The Boss popped his smallish masked face from the door. "How do you know Herbclaw? He left this place long ago. Went with those three dillywigs, didn't he? What were their names?"

"Uh...uh—" Blessfang tried. He wanted to have an answer for his Boss.

"Myrtle was one of them," Thrash said from far away.

"That's right," the masked bandit said. "And Poplar. What was the other one's name?"

"Ash," Briar said.

"Hey, she knows them, Boss!" Blessfang sounded like a happy child.

The masked bandit hopped from the carriage and pressed the sword into the base of Briar's skull. "You'd best explain how you know them dillywigs." One of the bandits plucked some dried weeds, struck flints together, and lit them to get a better look at Briar.

Briar began to tremble. She felt in danger and now they were near an open flame. Her palms tingled and her guts tossed. "My friend told you already. My name is Briar of the Black Woods. I came in search of my friend here." She gestured to Leon. "I was sent by Myrtle, Poplar, and Ash. Sherman came as my teacher. But now he's hurt—badly."

"A likely story," the Boss said. "What do you think, boys? Shall we skin 'em and sell their bones to the ogres?"

With that, Briar's hands became fully engulfed with power. She tried to hide the flames, but it was no use. Out in the utter darkness of Waste, there was nowhere to hide such an obvious source of light.

Blessfang gasped. Then he recited aloud like an elementary school kid:

"The Dark One ever chases
What the winged three did tickery-take
To hish-hush secret places,
Dragon powers in her wicketty-wake..."

The others stopped talking—stopped moving altogether. Briar felt the sword fall from her neck and the blade landed in the soil with a little shushed dig. She turned around to face her attackers, glowing palms face out. And from their shifting gas-blue light, she could finally see the bandits' faces.

One was a deer, who stood on its hind legs, front hoofs to its mouth in a breath of horrified recognition. Two others were tiny dark-caped bluebirds that sat perched on the deer's antlers. Their shining black eyes and beaks were wide with amazement. Briar could finally see that the Boss was a white rabbit that stood perhaps as high as Briar's calves. Had he not just attempted to cut her throat out, she might have found him darling and tried to cuddle him a little.

"Boss, it's her," said Blessfang, the deer. "Just like it says in the *Lores of the Bramble*. It's the Black Woods girl, come with her Dragon Powers."

"Can it be?" the Boss asked. "The Black Woods girl, here?" He paused, as if to consider the question he posed. Then to the others he shouted, "Blessfang, bring Sherman out. Vilesight, Thrash, fly quickly and bring back the Dire Liquid."

The flames in Briar's hands died down and she could only assume it was because whatever danger they were in had passed.

The bluebirds shot away and Blessfang, large and ungainly as he was, still managed to carry Sherman respectfully out of the carriage. He lay the fox on the ground and his head slackened to one side like one who had already died—or was about to die. The Boss hopped to Sherman and cradled his head with his paws. His tall ears flopped forward as he opened the bandage Briar had made from her gown and examined the puncture holes.

"Black dragon," he said aloud. "One of Orpion's creatures." He spat upon the ground, a magical custom against abominations. Blessfang tried to imitate his Boss, but instead he just dribbled down the front of his pelt and giggled with embarrassment.

Vilesight and Thrash arrived back with a bounce in their flight, carrying a small knapsack. They alighted in Blessfang's antlers. "There ain't much left, Boss," Vilesight said.

Briar and Dax stood by watching in the darkness as the Boss opened the small knapsack and removed a silver container. He uncorked it and held it close to Sherman's wounds. He was careful to put no more than a single drip on each lesion. They sizzled, the smell was something foul—like garbage or rotting meat.

He covered the wound again with the bandage and looked up at Briar with his dewy bunny eyes. "Where were you headed so conspicuously?"

"Conspicuously?!" Dax asked. "It's the middle of the night in the Black Waste where you can't see anything unless it's pressed up against your face."

"The Black Waste is journeyed by Orpion's troops. It is the only route to Scarlocke that they can travel in concealment," the Boss replied.

"We are on our way to the Towery Flowery Hill," Briar said. "We have less than two days to get there. Can you help us?"

"Sherman is in very bad condition. He will be lucky if he can heal. The wounds are very deep and he has lost much of his gray mist. He can't go further," he said.

Then his ears stuck up and turned left and right like antennas picking up sounds unheard by others. "The road is not safe, Black Woods girl," he said. "You'd best come with us for the night. Call me Boss, and these two tough birds here are Vilesight and Thrash." He pointed then to the deer who was busy entertaining himself with the clip-clop noise he could make with his hooves. "And that there's Blessfang. You'll be safe with us for the night. But a night is all we can offer."

Blessfang charged up to the carriage and hopped inside like a puppy being taken for a car ride. He bounced up and down on the leather benches, slobbering and clapping his hooves. "Let's go in the pretty buggy," he said.

Briar and Dax picked up Sherman and carried him aboard. The others filed into the carriage after them, except for the Boss, who climbed up and seated himself beside the coachman. Then with a whip crack, they galloped away.

Chapter 23

The Boss' den consisted of little more than a short, weathered door stuck into the side of a hidden rise in the terrain. Briar noticed some puffs of smoke wafting from a hole at the top of the ridge. Two nearby boulders obscured anything from view until they were all well on top of it.

There was some worried chatter about the carriage giving away their location, so they camouflaged it with some of the giant black tumbleweeds that rolled across the plains.

Once they were all safely inside and the door shut, the Boss showed them around, though his den proved to be uncomfortably snug for them all. The ceilings hung quite low, so that Briar and Dax had to bend in half to fit. The coachman decided it was better to spend the night in the relative roominess of the carriage than to sleep with his limbs cramped. This left additional space for everyone else, for which Briar was grateful.

The den was a crudely hewn dugout. Dead black roots, left by whatever grew there before, decorated the unevenly formed walls. An ornately carved table with filigree touches and matching chairs, a few masterful works of art hanging on the crude walls, and a glittering gold candelabra, all the glorious remnants of previous heists, sat at one end of the room. The Boss and his posse seated themselves around the table, allowing Briar and the others to cozy up to the smallest fireplace Briar had ever seen, which had a miniature fire burning bundles of black offcuts and loose root fragments. On the floor before the fire was an embellished rug, plush, with fancy images woven into it, upon which they laid Sherman.

The Boss offered Briar and the others some flat brown bread that looked to Briar and Dax like pressed dirt. But they hadn't eaten since they left Myrtle, Poplar, and Ash at the birdhouse and they were starving. Leon unfortunately had, on instinct, snapped up another insect that looked like a small black pellet that the Boss called a scatter bug. So now he was full—and nauseous all at once. Tarfeather was happy to scratch out a few choice stones from the walls and crunch on them.

They all sat in the dim flicker of the fire for a long time before the Boss spoke. "We didn't always live like this." Briar had been looking down at Sherman, who shivered and twitched, and she was surprised when the Boss spoke. She did not respond, except to look up at him.

"No tellery this to Briar Blackwood," Tarfeather said. He sounded cross. "Now why would you go and say such a terrible thing?" he asked in the voice of a black-and-white film ingénue.

The Boss then pulled one of several brown bottles from the roughly made shelves set in the wall just above the table. He uncorked it with his prominent buckteeth and spat it out onto the floor. "You gotta be kiddin' me. She doesn't already know?" he asked.

He took a big swig. He passed the bottle to Blessfang, who tried his best to imitate the Boss' manly swagger but couldn't hold on to the bottle with his hooves. Most of the distilled drink ended up soaking and staining his matted pelt.

"What don't I know?" Briar asked. The faces of the animal gang were somber and their eyes, full of old wounds.

"We once lived in a great wood that went from the Ice Cap Mountains to the Ink Sea. It was the greatest forest of the Realms," the Boss said. He grabbed for the bottle and drank again. Dax looked at Leon who sat on the rug nearby Briar and he shrugged.

"Then why are you here in the Black Waste?" Briar asked.

"The woods were burned to the ground," he said. He directed the statement to Tarfeather and squinted his pink rabbit eyes. "Only ashes and memories remain." The room fell silent, save the spark and sputter of the burning roots. Transfixed by the thought, he gazed into the fireplace for some time before continuing. "Orpion, of course."

"That's...terrible," Briar said.

"It was terrible," the Boss shot back. It almost seemed like an accusation. But Briar couldn't understand it. He reached for a charred child's toy made of wood and metal that he kept near the bottles. "Everyone gone." He wiped a tear away. "That is except for these mooks here." He laughed bitterly and took another swig from the bottle.

"I'm so sorry," Briar said. It was unfathomable, senseless really, that Orpion would burn her own world.

"Yeah, me too," the Boss said. He looked down with his ears drooping.

Briar felt a surge of anger at the injustice. "Why would Orpion do such a thing?"

"That's the funny thing," he said.

Tarfeather sprang up and landed in one bound on the table. "I say enoughery! No tellery more!"

Briar spoke to Tarfeather calmly. "I want to know."

The dwaref hopped down from the table and lighted across the floor. Once he faced Briar, his eyeholes began to shed tears. Then he spoke in one of his television voices. "There's no one to blame, darling. There's just no one good to blame."

"Go on," Briar said to the Boss.

"Orpion came to burn down Blackwood Hall, which was hidden by charms in the deepest recesses of the forest," he said. An uncomfortable silence filled the room. "But the story is that she couldn't find what she came lookin' for. So instead, she decided to scorch everything else."

"You mean the Black Waste is what's left of the Black Woods?" Briar asked. She was hardly able to speak.

"My home," the Boss said. "And theirs, too." The bluebirds and the deer all looked down at the table; one of the birds spat upon the floor, hoping to avert further evil.

"She wants the twin kingdoms to herself. The Lady Orpion—

the selfish old cod," Vilesight said. He held up one of his small talons. "I'd like a turn at her eyes."

"That will be a pretty day," Thrash replied.

"What two kingdoms? I thought Murbra Faire was the only kingdom of the Realms," Briar said.

"Scarlocke, the Lady's palace, is its twin," the Boss said. "Once, the two lived in peace. But a wickett who saw no use for the Grand Design, rose to power. Her magic was so great—her force was so dark that none could stop it, neither by magic nor by might. That was when once good Realmsmen abandoned their homes, as if under a spell, and went to serve the Dark Lady."

"Wicketts?" Briar asked.

"They're bad. Real bad," Blessfang said.

"And the Black Woods?" Briar asked. "Why would she destroy them if all she wanted was one hidden thing?"

"It is almost sixteen years to the day that she went looking for the hiding place of three dillywigs and a baby—the girl-child whom the Omens foretold would end her reign and destroy her."

Briar couldn't swallow or breathe for a moment. It was she who had brought pain, horror and death to the Realms, not only for Thrash, Vilesight, and Blessfang, but for countless others whom she would never know.

"That's horrible. I...I don't know what to say," Briar mumbled.

The Boss took several more swallows and then slammed the finished bottle on the table. He stared into its emptiness for a moment, looking for something that might make things right. "There's only one thing left for us to do," he said. "Blessfang, bolt the door."

The deer stood up with an angry scowl, knocking over his chair. He muscled his way past Briar and the others and put a wooden bar across the door. As he stomped past, Briar backed away and huddled with Dax and Tarfeather.

Leon hopped forward, forgetting his size. "Now wait a minute," he said to the Boss. Trying his best to assert the tough-guy demeanor that worked so well for him on the school campus wasn't working out so well in his present condition. "This is Briar, you guys. The girl from the Omens. You said so yourselves."

The Boss sat in his chair and fixed his gaze upon the group of travelers. Briar couldn't read his rabbit face to understand what he might have planned. Then the Boss spoke. "That's why we're locking you in for your safety."

"Huh?" Dax blurted out.

"Get a good night's sleep. And in the morning," the Boss continued, "we will do whatever we can to help you."

Briar let go of the breath she found herself holding. "Thank you," she said.

"Nothing would please me more than to see the Lady Orpion's head stuck to the end of a sword," said the Boss.

Chapter 24

Freezing winds howled across the great lonely plains all night, kicking up ashes, blowing them through all the crevices. The tiny fire had long since blown out. Briar huddled for warmth next to Sherman, who shuddered under the effects of the Dire Liquid. At times he shook with such violence that Briar wondered if maybe, by accident, Thrash and Vilesight had brought something poisonous to drip into his wounds.

Or, perhaps it was done intentionally, and considered kindness to give someone a swift death, rather than see them suffer. Briar knew as well as they that few could survive Sherman's deep wounds. But she pushed such thoughts from her mind as soon as they entered.

There was nothing to do, except try to stay warm and sleep. But it wasn't exactly relaxing to have Dax behind her, holding as tightly as he did. She wanted to see how Tarfeather and Leon had kept themselves warm, but she didn't want to wake either Sherman or Dax, so she just laid there with little bursts of shivering in the dusty draughts of icy desert air. Still, given enough hours and fatigue, Briar finally drifted off into a black dreamless state.

She was awakened by sharp morning light streaming through the door slats and striking her eyes. She no longer felt Dax behind her, so she luxuriated in a well-needed stretch and she turned her body. The den was cold and stale.

The fireplace smoldered and sputtered. Its root bundles had fallen into soft ash heaps around the tiny grating. Then Briar realized how still the place had become. Last night was all snorts and wheezing, and now it was as silent as an undiscovered pond. Except for the clicks of morning scatter bugs, which rhythmically crescendoed and fell in unison, as though a master insect directed their choir, the whole place had fallen to stillness.

She pushed herself up so that she could see what was happening. Everyone was gone. She felt a spasm of uneasiness, and she swallowed hard. Was Orpion just outside, waiting for her to exit—to assure a dramatic and grand finale? Had the Boss and his posse done away with everyone, leaving her as a bargaining tool? Myrtle did say that she would fetch a price at market. She felt her blood coursing, warming her face. Her mind began to race.

The door opened and sunlight flooded in, suddenly blinding her. She squinted until she could finally see the outline of a man. He stepped closer and then she could see him clearly.

It was Leon. He was transformed back. He stood there naked, though she could see no more than the silhouette of his musculature and his handsome smile. She blushed. It surprised her that, despite everything, she still felt an undeniable force of attraction to him. She tried not to look at his physique too closely. It felt immodest, but her eyes seemed to act of their own accord. He squatted down on brawny thighs and brushed her cheek with the back of his hand.

She spoke in a whisper, scarcely able to mask her complicated feelings. "What happened?" she asked.

"I don't know. Gelid died. Maybe when you killed her, you erased her magic," he replied. Then he drew his face close to hers. "It doesn't matter how it happened." She felt his warm breath on her. Then his nose touched her throat and lightly tickled the length of her neck.

Her heart quickened and swirled with a storm of emotion.

"Where are the others?" she asked.

He smiled and touched his nose to hers. "Away," he said. Then very gently, like the wing of a moth, his lips touched hers. Her heart responded so fiercely that she thought he might feel it through her skin. She closed her eyes and he pressed his lips to her again.

When she opened her eyes, the room was filled with a gray

gritty light that filtered through the door planks. Leon was not crouching beside her. She was kissing nothing more than the foul morning stench of cinders and stale breath that filled the den.

Her heart ached and she clutched at her chest. It took her a few minutes before she could accept that it was only a dream. That was when she realized that Sherman was missing from his resting place. Dax hadn't moved a single muscle all night and was still gripping Briar from behind. Briar raised her head a bit and peered around the den.

The Boss and his posse were missing too. Then it occurred to her that Sherman might not have made it through the night, and that the Boss removed him to avoid Briar's upset, not to mention the stench of death.

Beginning to feel a strand of desperation arising within, she lifted up further and whispered to Dax. With a snort, he awakened. "Huh? What happened?" he asked.

Briar put a finger to her lips and pointed to where they had last seen Sherman. Dax made a face of disbelief and shrugged as if to say *where'd he go?* Then it clicked and he realized what Briar had thought: that Sherman had died and the forest creatures had taken him away. He tried not to show it on his face, not now.

But Dax's silence said it all. Briar drew herself into a ball, grabbing her knees tightly to her chest. Her eyes felt the sting of gathering tears and she wept silently.

Dax placed an arm around Briar's shoulders and scanned the room. He saw Tarfeather asleep near the fireplace, cradling Leon in his arms like a baby. Sherman was definitely gone.

The shabby little entrance opened. Briar and Dax looked up to see the silhouette of the Boss.

"You're finally awake," he said. "It's well past half of the day." Then he noticed Briar's distress. "Did Blessfang come in here already? I'm going to kill that idiot."

Briar wiped her tears. "No one told us. You don't have to explain," she said. She tightened her lips to put on a brave face.

"It would only feel worse if you did."

By now, Tarfeather and Leon had awakened. "What's going on?" Leon asked.

"He's gone, he's gone," Briar said, shaking her head, unable to refrain from a flood of tears.

"You shouldn't cry," the Boss said. "We didn't want you to see him how he was. So we took him to the watering hole to clean his body first."

"You told me that the Dire Liquid might not work," Briar nodded. She wanted to sound like she understood and blamed no one.

"That's true," he said. The Boss nodded, but had a look of confusion.

Tarfeather skittered over to Briar and hopped up on her shoulder. He petted her hair. "No worrily, Briar Blackwood. Tarfeather lead you to book. Tarfeather help you home."

A second figure approached the doorway from behind the Boss and spoke. "Why is everyone crying?"

It was Sherman.

Briar jumped up and ran to the door. She hugged him tightly. Sherman winced and Briar noticed that he still wore a bandage around his mid-section. Dax joined Briar and they both hugged the fox.

"My goodness," Sherman said. "Why all the fuss?"

Then Briar turned to the Boss angrily. "You said you took him to clean him up. I thought he was dead!"

"Now why would you think that?" the Boss asked. "I took him to the only watering hole in this stinkin' place so he could wash the blood off his coat. We can't have him travelin' with Briar of the Black Woods lookin' tattered and all."

"Dry your tears, child," Sherman said. "We have great lengths to travel, and our tasks are unfinished. Once you turn sixteen— well, I don't suppose I need to remind you..."

Sherman put a paw lightly on the key at Briar's throat. "But we still have time on our side," he said. Despite his surface optimism, darkness and worry filled his eyes. "Well then," he announced, seeming to change the subject. "There's one more surprise."

He limped outside holding a paw to his wounds. Then he turned back, gesturing for them all to follow. Once they stepped outside, Briar felt engulfed by the glare and the heat of the Black Waste at mid-day. It took some time for Briar's eyes to adjust, but once they did, she noticed Sherman gesturing toward the king's carriage. The tumbleweeds had been cleared away, and the coachman was seated in his usual place, whip at the ready. The shimmering black horses, now coated with dulling ashes, scuffed at the ground and snorted, ready to ride. The driver tipped his hat to Briar with a short smile.

Dax, Tarfeather, and Leon all crowded around Briar, trying to see why Sherman gestured to the carriage. Then, on the ridge above them, another horse reared back and landed. Then it galloped down to meet the group below, with a cloaked rider on its back. The rider stepped off and flung back his hood. It was Valrune.

Briar ran to him and flung her arms around his neck. The prince gave a wide smile and then wrapped his arms around her in return. "You couldn't very well leave with my boots," he said.

Leon rolled his amphibious eyes. "Oh please," he said.

"How did you find us?" Briar asked, flustered. This was truly a morning of surprises.

"Vilesight and Thrash spotted me riding horseback along the high road about a thousand-leg from here," he said.

"What about your father? Is he safe?" Briar asked.

"I sent him to the Westwolf Wall at the far side of the palace," Valrune said. "It was built to withstand intruders. He took all of his horses and all of his men. He shall be safe for now."

"Thanks for the update chief," Leon croaked. "We can take it from here."

Valrune ignored him and spoke. "We have far to go yet, and half a day has gone. It is best that we ride now while the sun is high and the wicketts to their dwellings."

The Boss and his posse helped Briar and the others into the carriage. Valrune mounted his black horse and he rode it beside the coachman. He gave Briar provisions of flat brown mud-bread and full bladders of water that he had drawn from the ember-filled watering hole. "To serve the great Briar Blackwood was to serve the Three Omens and the Realms," he said. Then he hopped away and stood with his friends, watching with eyes of approval.

To Briar he looked so bleak standing there: his white fur contrasted against the dunes of coal black dust stretching endlessly to the horizon. She couldn't bear the thought of the Boss and his friends living in the filth and chars of the Black Waste. It was because of her that it happened in the first place and she wanted to set things straight, if she could.

"Can't you come with us?" she asked him.

"What? And leave this paradise?" He laughed a bit. "No, this is our home."

"You could go where it was safer, to where there were better provisions."

Now Blessfang, Thrash, and Vilesight joined in the laughter. "And where would you have us go, Briar of the Black Woods?" Vilesight said.

"Well, for one thing, you *could* go to the Westwolf Wall at Murbra Faire and watch over King Cole," Briar replied.

Valrune nodded, realizing the wisdom of Briar's plan. "She's right. You could send Thrash or Vilesight to warn us at the Towery Flowery Hill should any harm come to the king or to Westwolf."

The Boss just stared with his head cocked to one side, watching from only one of his eyes.

"In the meantime," Valrune continued, "food and drink and

warm beds await you there. They are simple means, but you will be safe from the coming darkness that looms from Scarlocke."

The Boss tilted his head some more and he twitched his nose.

Blessfang began to chew at the tips of his hooves. "I don't like darkness, Boss," he said.

Valrune took off his royal ring and held it out to the Boss. "Take this as proof of our alliance. Give it to my father and he will honor my wishes. Take my horse as well." The Boss looked at each member of his posse, and then he hopped to Valrune. With one leap he mounted the horse and swiped the ring from the prince's leather-gloved hand.

Sitting behind Valrune, the Boss examined the ring's pale gold sparkle in the sun. He nibbled it a bit. "I never say no to royal gold."

Chapter 25

The coach rambled along through the heat of the Black Waste for hours. They journeyed for some lengths to the east amid the bleak forest remains. Briar ruminated miserably over the landscape. Orpion's job of incineration was more thorough in some places than in others. Occasionally, instead of far-reaching stretches of charred gray, Briar saw evidence of bones poking up through mounds of soot. She felt a quiet fury building in the heat of her stomach. Finally she could take her self-torment no more, and she decided to close her eyes.

The sway of the carriage eventually rocked the others to sleep. The prince had long ago given the Boss and his posse directions on how they might enter the Westwolf Wall from a secret passage. And Briar thought that they would be safe now. Only she and Sherman remained awake. Finally, Briar broke the silence. "Why didn't you use magic before?"

"I beg your pardon?" Sherman replied.

"You used magic to stop Gelid. Why didn't you use it any sooner?" Briar asked. "You could have changed — well every-thing."

Sherman looked away, an old pain lingering in his eyes. He gave a soft sigh as he cast his gaze out the window. "Magic is rarely the answer we seek," he replied. "It can lead to terrible things." Briar heard a whisper of choked emotion in what he said.

"The Black Woods were your home too," she guessed. She looked out again at the sickening terrain, imagining how Sherman must feel traveling through it.

Sherman nodded. "My Mara and my cub — both gone."

Sometimes there are no words, Briar realized. So instead of trying to say something of comfort, she sat and watched Sherman until he was able speak again without such a terrible stomach-wrenching warble.

"But sometimes—just sometimes—magic can make a difference," he said. He sniffed and wiped his eyes with a paw. "That's why I learned it. And that's why I hoped one day I would help the girl-child of the Omens to end the Orpion's reign." He gave Briar a short smile and an encouraging nod.

"You hated me when we met," she said. She gave Sherman a sly look.

"I didn't believe that you were the one," he admitted.

"But Poplar followed me since I was a baby. Ash came to rescue me—" she replied. She gave a little laugh.

"Ash has made his mistakes," Sherman said. Then he looked far away to the horizon with a bitterness she hadn't seen before. She wasn't sure what Sherman meant, but she knew that this wasn't the time to drag him through more unhappiness, no matter the cause of it.

She tried to change the subject. "Well, good news: I might be getting the hang of how to use these Dragon Powers."

Sherman sat upright in his seat, his ears stood on end. "Impossible," he said. "Magic, and especially that of the Dragon Powers, takes years, even lifetimes to master. You would be lucky to learn just a few simple enchantments to keep you alive should you ever go toe to toe with Orpion."

"I stopped Gelid, you know," she said.

"You have learned a simple transformation," Sherman replied. "And you were given rudimentary instructions about your Dragon Powers. But do not mistake these simple conjurations for the deeper mysteries. You will need more than a couple of tricks if you are to leave this place alive. It is time you learned, and in earnest."

He placed a paw on her hand and he closed his eyes. Briar watched as he squeezed his fuzzy eyelids shut in concentration and leveled his tufted ears. Her hands started to tingle, and it felt like there were bubbles in her fingers. Then Sherman's paw glowed with such intensity that it seemed to fill the entire carriage.

In a flash, within that dazzling moment of brightness, Briar saw a vision. Thousands of geometric patterns appeared before her, one after another in what seemed to be an intentional sequence: intricate spider's webs jeweled by morning's dew, each droplet reflecting the others, the delicate flourished structures of snowflakes branching elaborately, the connections between stars emblazoned across the deep night sky, and those of shadows as they elongated across the landscape. Briar was shown patterns seen everywhere in nature: in the budding flowers, the tides of shimmering oceans, the hives of bees, and even laughter. No matter what she was shown, she could see the design. It felt to Briar that she already knew these things, but now that Sherman was showing her, she was somehow awakened to their memory.

As unexpectedly as the visions arose, they faded away. Briar sat with her heart pounding from exhaustion. Sherman opened his eyes and nodded without saying more. After catching her breath Briar eventually spoke up. "What was all that?" She knew what they were. In her bones, she knew. But she couldn't put what she knew into words just yet.

"These are the structures of magic—the Grand Design," Sherman explained. With that, he spent a good deal of time describing to Briar the history of magic and the long, intricate theories that governed it. He drew complex patterns in the air with his paws, and now that Briar had seen the vision Sherman had given her, his designs looked like fine Irish lace, which hovered in front of him as patterns of light and shadow. And while this served to intrigue Briar at the start, the initial excitement of learning magic was sucked dry as Sherman's lengthy lectures continued for hours. Briar felt like she was back in school learning some convoluted trigonometry formulas. But not wanting to insult Sherman, she tried to give a few interested nods throughout his lengthy dissertations.

Finally, he began to teach her about the Dragon Powers, their rarity, and how the ancients harnessed their strength. He taught many complex magical passes, each of them a reflection of the Grand Design. These were only a handful of the thousand-and-one that a dillywig must know to master the art of enchantment. Since they all seemed alike to Briar, she found them confusing; a slight angle of the hand up or down could make worlds of difference in the magical outcome.

Nevertheless, while the others in the cab dozed to the rhythmic clip clop of hoof beats, Sherman continued to school his student. Then Briar drilled many of the most important passes, again and again, until Sherman felt that she had gained some precision and a few secrets of the art. But he would not teach her how she might summon the Dragon Powers at her will. "For now, these enchantments must only be used in your defense," he argued. He would say nothing more about it, no matter how much Briar tried to convince him otherwise.

"But I will tell you about the curses," Sherman said. Then he gazed distractedly out the window, as though deliberating if she should know what he was about to tell her.

Briar stopped her practice. "You mean, what happened to Poplar, Myrtle and Ash?" But it took a good long time before Sherman was able to respond. He faced the small cab window and surveyed the blackened landscape.

"They loved you very much," he finally said. "They put themselves in harm's way trying to protect the child they believed would save these Realms." He turned to face Briar.

Briar nodded, but didn't really know what he was talking about. It was clear that Poplar was cursed to eat rats and Ash's garments would change unexpectedly. "What happened to Myrtle?" Briar wanted to know, but felt a lump in the pit of her stomach.

"She was cursed far worse than the others with the *Unspeakable*," Sherman said. "Can you even know the suffering, or the disgrace of a dillywig who can no longer fly?" He shook his head and covered his eyes.

Briar looked out the window at the wasteland, imagining what might have happened as the Black Woods burned on those dark days. She knew that Poplar, Ash and Myrtle's curses were likely a painful humiliation for them. But she couldn't understand how Sherman could compare their seeming inconveniences to the ruin she witnessed outside the carriage.

"There is more," Sherman said. "The malignancy of these curses has spread."

"What do you mean?"

"Each of these curses is lethal. Yes, Poplar has done well staving off the worst of it with her teas and potions. But to be honest, I don't know how much longer any of them has—" He sounded as though his throat suddenly constricted, and words could come no more.

Briar placed a hand on Sherman's head to pet him, and he looked up with surprise. But he didn't resist Briar's smoothing hand. She decided not to ask anything more. She knew enough.

She knew that she was loved. Never feeling cared for as palpably as she did in that moment, she found herself confused. Perhaps that was the fourth curse. Sherman curled up on the bench and buried his face beneath his tail, and he allowed Briar to stroke his soft pelt.

It was late afternoon when they finally reached the green-vined base of Towery Flowery Hill, pungent with the perfume of roses and a sickly stench that reminded Briar of decaying bodies. She tried to breathe through her mouth, but it didn't help much.

"Okay, that wasn't me," Dax said. Then he tried to cover his nose in the crook of his elbow.

"What *is* that?" Briar asked. She tried not to gag from the smell.

Sherman pushed the carriage window open and stuck his head out. "I don't know, but I suggest that we proceed with caution."

Once upon the hill road, the soil was no longer hard and compact. Hooves did not make their usual noises, but sounded more like rocks thrown onto a haystack. The carriage continued to sway, but the ride was soft, as though the wheels turned on cushions.

She gazed upon the bases of thick green tree trunks that stood tall and proud, pushing upward to the sky. So high did they reach that Briar could not see their tops. The foliage seemed somehow familiar, yet unlike any Briar had ever seen before. She looked up at the branches and leaves noting how they had knitted together to form a thorny canvas for the road. It was a soothing contrast from the endless glare that they had endured in the Black Waste.

Finally Sherman opened the cab door a crack while the horses still trotted along, and he signaled the driver to stop. The sudden and shocking silence that filled the small space seemed to awaken the others, who stretched and looked and marveled at the scenery. The cab driver opened a door and they all stepped down onto the soft red mulch that was made of leaf mold, damp soil, and leathery, withered rose petals the color of dried blood and the size of a full grown man. The rancid smell made sense now. The area was like a compost heap.

Briar stood back a pace to see from where the petals were coming. She shielded her eyes and tipped her head back, but could only see vague puffy shapes silhouetted against tiny patches of bright blue sky.

Sherman stood behind Briar. "They say they reach as high as the clouds, and some even beyond that," he mused.

Dax looked up and gawked at the barbed spectacle and majesty of the forest. "What kind of trees are these?"

"Trees!" Sherman laughed. "These are roses."

"Roses?! Come on," Dax said. Then a giant petal, red as a ripe apple, drifted down and softly draped over his head.

"Come along this way, big boy," Tarfeather said, mimicking an old movie. He darted among the leaves and petals, his tiny feet stomping them down. Briar signaled to the others and they all followed Tarfeather, who clearly knew his way. Under fallen thorny stems and over boulders that appeared suddenly in their path, Tarfeather led them tirelessly up the hillside.

They finally reached a cave entrance, smooth and square, hewn from the rock and fitted with dark bronze doors the color of troubled storm clouds. The place seemed well tended, though it smelled like soil and animal droppings to Briar. As they got closer, Briar could see that the bronze entryway ornamented with hideous faces, dark, fanged and scowling. Two hoops served as the door-pulls. Valrune stepped up and assuredly pulled one, but it wouldn't budge. Leon hopped up and said, "A bit too heavy for you, huh?"

"Little frog, this door is locked," Valrune said.

The dwaref climbed up to Briar's shoulder. "Tarfeather noticery Briar Blackwood trinket."

"How did you know this was a trinket?" she asked.

Instead of saying, he tugged at her necklace chain until the key came out from beneath her neckline.

"Now let's be careful." Sherman put his paws up in a halting gesture. "We don't know if her key works at all. I've heard, ever since I was a cub, that this was a very dangerous place. It's riddled with traps."

Not listening, Tarfeather had already unclasped the necklace and held the key up on her shoulder like a prize. "Put the key in the lock and turn it, honey. We're all waitin'," he said like a 1920s gun-moll.

"See?" Leon asked. He was hoping Briar was paying attention to how stupid Valrune was for not thinking of the obvious.

"You've got to use a key." He hopped up past Tarfeather and nabbed it. "Now if you had used your head, you would know that," he said. Then he bounced up high enough to insert the key in the lock. But having no ability to turn it, he just dangled helplessly.

The prince flicked Leon aside with a finger. "Oh that's just cold," Dax noted. Leon landed roughly to the ground. Briar was too focused on their situation to pay attention to their ridiculous male domination behaviors.

Valrune smiled, satisfied that he had sufficiently humiliated Leon, then he turned the key. It clanked loudly and the sound echoed down what seemed like long passages. He took the key out and shrugged, since the door didn't open. Then several more metallic clanking noises occurred mechanically from either side of the cave entrance, above, and then below.

The ground under their feet opened up and they slid down through pebbles and clumps of soil. As she slipped through the opening, it felt to Briar that small roots sprung from the earth and grabbed at her while she slid past. Then they fell through a cave ceiling and landed on a tangled bed of something that felt soft and clammy. One after another they landed, each rolling away from the next one falling. The smell of moisture and minerals hung heavily in the air.

Briar landed feet-first into a bundle of sticky fibers and discovered that there was no place to stand; she was suspended up to her chin within the stringy mass. And try as she could to lift her arms or move her feet, her actions only served to sink her deeper into the knot. The only bit of light trickling into the deep darkness came from the trap door embedded high in the cave ceiling, and the small shaft of indirect light was not enough to help Briar understand on what they had landed.

"Rose roots!" Tarfeather shouted. He yelled the words with such alarm that he might as well have said, "hand grenades!" He had landed atop the heap. But because he was too light for the tendrils to grab him, he rolled himself far away and landed on solid stone.

"What the—?" Dax yelled. He landed flat next to Sherman on top of the root heap, so neither of them had sunk down into the sticky tangle.

"Rollery off," Tarfeather shouted. Dax took Sherman's paw and pulled him as he rolled to one side. It felt as though they were stuck to flypaper and his already tattered clothing from the ball finally ripped to pieces as he rolled away. Sherman gritted his teeth and groaned. His fur pulled out in several small clumps as he rolled off onto the stone floor.

He stood and made a gesture with his paws that left an intricate hologram design of silvery light hanging in the air before his face. The hologram merged into a single glowing ball that floated toward Briar. Sherman stood on the edge of the mound with his eyes closed, and he seemed to direct the light with his upraised hands.

Briar felt something like pinpricks, tiny and sharp, begin to invade her skin. She realized it was the roots, seeking nutrients. One of them crept and wound itself up over her face. Then it began to burrow into her ear.

"Sherman, help!" she shouted.

The glowing light began to drift above Briar and they could all see the rose roots, just as Tarfeather had warned. It was a tangle of hairy looking filaments, thick as fingers. They covered all but the crown of Briar's head, which stuck out of the top of the mound. Bones and skulls of various creatures, brown with age, were scattered across the floor and mixed into the root knot.

"The prince," Tarfeather shouted. "Where is he?"

"And Leon?" Dax asked.

"I'm here," Leon shouted back to the group. He was standing lightly atop Briar's head. He strained with his small flippers to pull the roots from her ear.

"Leon, jump off," Briar yelled at him. But as soon as she opened her mouth, a root entered and began to explore the inside of her cheek, pricking with its sharp ends. She screamed and began to struggle. She sank lower until her face slipped out of view.

"Briar! No!" Leon shouted.

"Sherman, do something!" Dax pleaded.

Sherman shouted to Leon. "Remove yourself at once!" His slimy skin slid past the sticky roots and he could easily hop from limb to limb until he reached the solid floor.

Quickly, Sherman made another gesture, as though sculpting something in midair. Then he slammed the invisible sculpture onto the floor. In response to his movements, the ball of light changed into a pair of ghostly gardening shears that suddenly dove into the root mass and started snipping pieces away.

The roots receded quickly, as though Sherman's enchantment were poison to it. The glowing scissors cut through roots, causing them to ooze a blood-red sap. Sherman kept his eyes closed and he continued to pantomime as though he were holding the shears in his paws. The roots continued to fall away and recede until a gap was opened.

There, on the bare rock below, Briar lay crumpled. Next to her was Valrune, who was on his knees, gasping for air and making gagging sounds. With both hands, he extracted a long root out from his mouth that had crawled down his throat. Dax rushed forward and helped both Briar and Valrune up and limped with them far away from the tangle. Together they collapsed against a cave wall.

Sherman made another gesture and the phantom shears vanished in a puff of glowing silver smoke. Sherman slumped forward, grabbing his side. Dax noticed that blood once again formed stains in his bandages.

The prince sat next to Briar and Leon hopped onto her lap. "Are you all right? Say something," he said.

Briar coughed up bits of dirt and she rested her head between her knees for a moment. Then she said, "I always thought roses were kind of creepy."

"Where is Sherman?" Dax asked.

Briar looked down one of the many cavern-tunnels and there,

hobbling away with a slow unsteady gait was the fox. The others stood up and followed, looking one to the other once they noticed the sopping red blood stain in his bandages.

"Sherman, stop," Briar said.

"We must...keep moving," the fox said. His voice was becoming labored, but he kept trudging forward.

Tarfeather spoke up. "Temple dwellers makery Dire Liquid. We findery."

"No," Sherman replied. "No time left...just the book. Then back home. Poplar has herbs—"

Tarfeather's face looked more withered than before when Sherman refused the obvious help he needed. The others exchanged glances and knew what this could mean for the fox. But no one said anything. Sherman was right. They had only a few hours to find the book. It was a choice that sickened them all: to risk Sherman's life for the sake of the book.

"Sherman, you can't go on like this. You don't even know where to go." Briar said.

But Sherman kept taking one limp step after another. Briar could not stop him in his duty. There was only one way out. It was to get the book and go home.

"Tarfeather," Briar said, "lead us to it."

Chapter 26

Briar and the others walked deep into the winding caverns, hands along the rough fissure walls in order to guide them through the darkness. So as not to get lost or trampled, Leon sat in one of Briar's hands. Sharp, cold, moist stones scraped their fingers as they descended the path. Finally Sherman drew another complex magical pattern in the darkness that erupted into sparks, which fused together and became the giant spider from the birdhouse.

"Mittens—" Briar exclaimed. She was grateful to see something familiar, but then after watching him click around, she thought otherwise. The spider took on its magical glow, which allowed them all to see where they were now, which was inside a cavern full of sharp crystals. Mittens' glow shimmered on the millions of glassy, reflective surfaces, and the whole cavern seemed illuminated. Mittens made an awful ticking noise, loud and abrasive, like it was crunching through the shell of another insect.

"Yes Mittens…happy to see…you too—" Sherman said. Above them, below their feet, in any direction they looked, the shimmer of amethyst, rubies, emeralds, and diamonds played in the glow of the spider's body, and whenever he moved, the jewels seemed to sparkle that much more.

Dax was enamored by the gleaming jewel display. "Cha-ching! What *is* all of this?"

"It's where my father sends prisoners and poachers," Valrune said. He examined the gems distractedly. "The Priests of the Tales live here in the darkness of the temple caves. They train their initiates here and maintain order among the prisoners."

"Then where is everyone?" Dax asked.

"Walk—" Sherman said. Then he spoke in the Old Language, guttural and incomprehensible to the others. But Mittens seemed to understand. It was the same language that Gelid used before she became the black slithering monster. It had a harsh, throaty sound, Briar thought. It also held some strange familiarity that left Briar uneasy. The ghostly spider, listening to Sherman, began to click again, then crawled ahead of them down the path. The group had to hurry to keep up.

Briar kept pace with Sherman, and even tried to help him walk, but he refused.

The further along they paced, the warmer and smokier the cave became. It smelled of sulfur and burning coal—perhaps the smell, Briar wondered, of some ancient land during the Industrial Age. The heat and the odor became so thick and acrid that everyone had to cover their mouths in order to catch a breath. The ground vibrated and the group stopped, wondering if it may have been a tremor before a full volcanic eruption, or a cave collapse.

"Mining," Valrune said. He stepped ahead of the group. He had never been to this place. As a boy, Valrune asked again and again if he could see it. But Cole would always brush aside his son's queries. "It's no place for a son of mine," his father would often tell him. But he'd say no more than that.

As a child Valrune always imagined the mines were a place for adventure, and he could never understand why his father would want to keep him from the fun of it. But as time passed, he heard rumors, whispered words from the mouths of servants.

Words like "slavery," and "coercion," they'd say in hushed tones. But the palace servants knew better than to openly admit anything. Cole must have had his reasons for his secrecy, Valrune believed. And now his eyes were wide and hungry to know what lay ahead in these hellish depths.

Mittens crept further ahead of them into the catacombs. Just beyond the bend in the path they saw light moving, burning red, undulating upon the cavern walls. They could hear the tick-tick-tick of countless pick axes chipping away at stone in a deeper chamber. Once Mittens reached the glowing red light, he popped like a soap bubble into a shower of tiny sparks that evaporated before they could reach the ground.

The Briar and the others followed behind Valrune to the red glow, until they reached an opening that led to an immense vaulted structure. The rough cave walls were replaced by smooth, polished marble slabs that were carefully engineered, lining the towering cavern.

The domed ceiling was supported by pale beveled columns as tall as city buildings. The cavern interior was like a layered cake that had seven or eight tiers with countless rows of arches leading to what Briar assumed were jewel-filled caverns. Standing before the caverns were Priests of the Tales that had tattooed blue markings on their faces, like Gelid and Damarius.

Heaped on the floor of the central cavern were piles of jewels, as tall and as deep as desert sand dunes. They shimmered in the light of a thousand torches that flanked the smaller cave entrances. Dwarefs—hundreds, perhaps thousands of them, dressed in tatters—emerged from the lower arched tunnels with wheelbarrows filled with precious stones that they dumped into the jewel piles. Then back up ramps they would trudge in lines until they reentered the smaller caves.

The Priests, dressed in long, wooly, earth-colored robes, stood at the edges, near the smaller cave entrances. Each grasped a staff and pointed it from time to time to discharge a silvery electric current at a stray or stumbling slave worker. Anyone hit by the flashing current fell to the ground and screamed as though being seared by a hot poker. Fellow slaves would assist the fallen workers and prop them back up into the line.

In the middle of the chamber was another set of columns that supported a central platform high above the cave floor. A curve of earthen stairs hugged the columns and led to the platform. Whatever was upon it seemed to be the energy source for the priests' staves.

Valrune walked to the edge of the terrace on which they stood and stared with eyes fixed upon the scene. "What has my father done?" he asked. His voice was full of loathing and regret. Sherman grabbed Valrune by the back of his clothes and pulled him back to the group that stood in the shadows of the smaller cave, where he would be less likely noticed.

"No." Valrune shook his head. "I don't believe this is my father's work. He would never—"

Sherman placed a paw over Valrune's mouth.

Dax asked, "Why are they all dwarefs?"

"Built for diggery," Tarfeather said. He held up his long golden claws and his face seemed to crumple from sadness.

Dax glanced up at the ceiling and was taken aback. He grabbed Briar by the shoulder and pointed. The ceilings, high and wide enough to fit a small city below them, were painted with three ornate panels. Accented with gold leaf, like the illustrations from an illuminated manuscript, they depicted distinct scenes that featured a girl with long black hair who wore a torn white ball gown and thigh-high boots.

In one panel, the girl touched her hand to a spinning wheel. In the next, she bit into something handed to her by a hooded figure. The third panel depicted her holding a sword up to a dark, cloudy image.

Briar was overcome, and tears flooded her eyes. It was true what the Omens said. She wondered how many lives had been lost in the name of either maintaining the Omens or ending them. To think of this frightened her.

Sherman stood alongside Briar gazing up at the paintings, and he placed a paw on her cheek. "Do not be afraid, Briar of the Black Woods."

"These are the Three Omens," Briar said. Sherman nodded and drew her chin down so that he could look her in the eyes.

"Yes," he said.

"But it shows me pricking my finger," Briar said. Just saying so caused her to lose balance and fall against the pillar behind her.

"Yes," Sherman replied.

"Then, no matter what we do, I'll die." Briar felt like the cave walls, and the smoke and heat were closing in around her throat.

"If you believe the Tale that others tell. Then you are cursed to live by it," he said. "There are omens and prophecies to fill a thousand halls. Live by your own Tale, Briar, not theirs." She did not feel better by him saying this. She knew nothing of their ways. He could be filling her head so that she'd continue to take risks. Who was she to them? Perhaps nothing but a pawn.

Tarfeather started down the path that sloped to the cave floor. He turned back for a moment. "Book of bad things—" He pointed one of his golden claws to the central columns.

They followed along behind. Leon was no longer in Briar's hands since she and Dax now had to support Sherman between them. Instead he hopped alongside them, being careful that no one stepped on him in the shadows.

As Briar and Dax walked with Sherman along the cavern wall, they noticed that he had begun to drag his feet as he walked and his eyelids drooped. There was, perhaps, more blood outside of his body than there was inside it by now. "Sherman, how will we get the book?" Briar asked him mostly to keep him from drifting into unconsciousness. "It's in the middle of everything."

"Disguise yourself as Orpion again," Dax suggested.

Sherman tried to refocused his eyes. "Disguises will not work here," Sherman replied. His voice was barely audible. "The Priests of the Tales know these magics... Many prisoners have tried to leave this place by way of magical disguise. Their Tales...do not end well. I will camouflage you... Get the book. Bring it back."

Briar looked at Dax. "But Sherman, it may take some time to get up and down those steps, let alone steal the book without anyone noticing. It will drain you."

"Climb the steps. Take the book. It is the only way," he replied.

"I will protect you, Dame Titania," Valrune said. Then from his belt he withdrew a dagger with a stubby blade.

"Wow. We'll call you when we need a letter opened," Leon said.

"Sherman, this is crazy," Briar said. "You need the Dire Liquid now."

"There is no Dire Liquid...without...book," he replied. Briar didn't want to argue with him any longer, but she knew that none of this was about saving Leon, changing him back, or making Dire Liquid. Sherman wanted that book. Perhaps Myrtle, Poplar, Ash, and he had plotted this all along. *There are Tales within Tales*, Ash had warned her.

They hiked down to the lowest level and they hid behind the enormous pillars and a collection of rusted mining carts. Sherman stumbled back but then steadied himself. He raised his paws unsteadily, and drew another of his intricate enchantments. The design enlarged and dropped like a net around Briar who then vanished.

"Go," Sherman said. He held his shaking arms up to maintain the spell.

Now unseen by any, Briar bolted out from behind the carts and ran as fast as she could toward the central pillars. Through the mountainous jewel piles she wound along a narrow path that was just big enough for a slave worker and his wheel barrow to fit through. She heard someone coming and she climbed out of the path onto the side of a pile, rubies and emeralds cascading below her feet.

"Hello?" A familiar voice was calling from just beyond her view. She held still so that no more jewels would tumble. Then the slave came around the bend.

It was King Cole. His royal robes were shredded, his crown was gone, and his curl-toed shoes barely held together. He also had a prominent fracture in his shell that started at the top of his head and cracked down the front of his face. "Is there someone there?" he whispered. He maintained visual contact of the watchful Priests along the walls, hoping they hadn't noticed him speak.

Briar covered her mouth so that her breathing would not be heard. Cole looked around some more. But seeing no one, he overturned his cart of jewels onto the pile and trudged away. He glanced back over his shoulder to where he heard the sounds, but sighed and went on his way.

When Briar was certain he was gone, she ran for the columns at a greater speed, dashing around mounds and making her own path through them. When she reached the steps, a priest stood guard with his staff planted in the ground. She picked up a large ruby, which vanished as soon as she held it in her hand. She threw it with great force and it struck the priest's face. Then she ran around to the other side of the jewel pile.

The priest fell back, and his hood slipped off, exposing his pale, bald head. He reached up with a hand and wiped a trickle of blood from his face. He gnashed his teeth and held up his staff to zap whomever it was. Briar could see a flurry of silvery electrical currents storming the area and she lay against one of the tall piles out of harm's way.

Then she heard his footsteps approaching. "Where are you, filthy slave?" She slipped around the opposite side and headed back to the stairs, which were now unguarded. Up the steps she climbed for what seemed like several stories of a building. Her footsteps sounded up the stairs, and the priest who searched for her followed up after them. "Come back here, talebreaker!" he shouted, forks of electrical power shooting along the curve of the stairs, but never reaching Briar. She finally made it to the upper platform and stood perfectly still.

High above the cave floor, Briar got a better view of the vast jewel stockpiles amassed by the slaves. And there, on the far end of the platform on a dais between two standing incense urns churning out thick gray smoke, beneath a domed bell jar, was the *Book of Cinder and Blight*. It was an unassuming little thing: black leather bound its yellowing parchment pages together. And it was no bigger than a slim school book. It was propped open on intricately carved bones. Two trim black chains with ball weights at their ends were draped across the pages, keeping them spread apart.

The priest huffed as he ascended the stairs and when he arrived at the top of the platform, he shot more power from the tip of his staff. It swept with long crackling branches in every direction, but did not seem to expose the intruder the priest thought was there.

Briar crouched safely behind the dais. When everything went quiet, she peered secretly from one side. The priest was gone. But she noticed that Gelid's jeweled mirror had fallen from her boot in the process of finding safety. It lay in the middle of the platform. She stood up and looked around more. If she moved quickly and quietly enough, she could easily recover it. Unexpectedly from behind, the priest leveled his staff to her throat he began to choke her with it.

Sherman's spell must have worn off. She knew he could not keep up his energy for long. Now she was visible and defenseless.

Briar put her hands up to push the staff away and she saw the glowing flames forming in her hands. She would have touched the flames to the priest, as she was taught, but her hands were the only buffer between her throat and the priest's staff, which clamped tighter against her flesh.

She began to lose consciousness, her coughing and gagging the only things that kept her alert. She tried to kick at him, but it was useless. She had grown too weary. Through her daze, she could hear voices and footsteps of other priests who were watching from their posts along the cavern.

"You little fool," the priest snarled. She saw his thick doughy hands, knuckles whitening on the staff, small magical sigils tattooed on his fingers.

The jewel stockpiles were likely the last thing she would see, she realized. Her eyes began to flutter closed. Images flashed in her mind: her foster sisters laughing at her, the spinning wheel, the Lady Orpion touching her trinket, Valrune holding her. She saw herself back on stage the night Leon disappeared. He stood there shirtless, leaning in to kiss her.

She felt a sudden surge of power. She opened her eyes and leaned all the way forward, flipping the priest into the air. He landed with a crash, overturning the dais and the bell jar. The book slammed to the ground and shut. His staff fell to the floor dead of its power. Where the priest choked so tightly, she still felt her muscles compressed.

Briar flung one of her flames at him where he lay already writhing. It attached to his face and engulfed it, turning pale skin into a blistering mass of charring meat. He clutched at what was left of his face, screaming, kicking his legs around, trying to stop the pain and the spell.

She staggered away, coughing violently, clutching her neck. But he had choked her so tightly that she was having trouble catching a breath. More priests stomped up the stairs and Briar flung her remaining flame at them. But masters of defense, two of the priests used their staffs to block it and even batted it back at her. She surprised herself again with a dropping floor-roll in order to escape the flame.

As she rolled, she landed close to the jeweled mirror. It was coved in blood that oozed from the dead priest's body. The three remaining priests barreled for her. They surrounded her and pointed the tips of their staffs. But the book was closed, and the source of their power had been cut off. Unable to use magic, the priests began to swing their staves, aiming for Briar's head.

Unexpectedly, she leapt into the air, vaulting into a backward flip over one staff, then forward flipping over another. She had never been trained in gymnastics, but she was performing aerial acrobatics she never knew she could do. One of the priests, missing Briar with his swing, brained one of the others who stood close to the platform edge. The struck priest's head buckled, and he tumbled onto a jewel pile below.

Briar turned toward the other two priests, the bloodied mirror still in her hand. By accident, she shone the mirror toward one of the unholy priests. The effect was sudden and unexpected. He vaporized into nothing but gray clouds of dust that arose with heat and then settled on the ground with a sound like sand scattering.

Tarfeather was right about the mirror, and Briar thought it fitting that those who formed it and used it for such dark purposes should taste its wrath.

The remaining priest was stunned only for a moment. He tried to run, but Briar caught him in the mirror's reflection. He too vaporized and dropped to the floor not as a man, but as a scatter of dust.

She stood there coughing, holding her neck, shocked by what had happened. Then she realized what else the mirror might do. She stood and shone the mirror on priests who were stationed around the cavern perimeter. Each one whom the mirror faced became charred dust that got sucked away by the outgoing airflow of the smaller caves. The few remaining priests who had evaded the mirror, fled through the catacombs, leaving the dwaref-slaves behind.

The captives began to revolt once they saw the few remaining priests running. The larger dwarefs chased close behind them with pickaxes and torches they seized from the cavern sconces.

Others ran out from the smaller caves, shouting jubilantly. Some of them, who had witnessed Briar's feat, pointed to her and cheered. Pandemonium ensued as the freed slaves began to shove and push through the main cavern. Some filled small bags with jewels, others fled though smaller caves, following the priests who knew the secret ways out. Carts were overturned, and those dwarefs who had been too weakened by exhaustion or starvation got trampled in the chaos.

Leon, Valrune, and Sherman, followed by Tarfeather and Dax, ascended the steps at a frantic pace.

"Briar!" Dax shouted. "Are you all right?"

"I'm fine," she said. She seemed unable to focus her eyes and her head throbbed. Sherman said nothing, but watched Briar, who still held the mirror in her hand, a look of dread on his face. He hobbled to the book at her feet and he snapped it up.

"How did you do all of that?" Sherman asked.

"I don't know, I just..." Briar looked down at the mirror and felt a sickness overcome her. She doubled over and vomited. Valrune rushed to her side and Leon hopped up to her shoulder.

"Drop the mirror. It—it is dangerous," Sherman said. He eyed the thing like it was radioactive waste.

"I can't," Briar said. Her hand could not unclench from the handle.

"Do something," Dax shouted to Valrune. He immediately rushed Briar to the edge of the platform and forced her to crouch down. He gripped her arm and swung it so that the mirror caught on the hard edge. Again and again he swung her arm until the mirror cracked and fell from her grip down into the cavern depths where it struck the stones below and shattered to pieces.

"This cannot be," Sherman said. He looked stricken. "The mirror was Orpion's wickett magic. You are dillywig. This was not in the Omens."

Briar did not understand Sherman's concern. The priests were defeated and the dwarefs freed. Why was he so worried? Then she remembered Cole. "Val...rune," she tried to call his name through her violent coughs. "Your father. They brought him here. He was with...the slaves." Valrune gazed in stunned silence down to the cavern floor, at the riots taking place. Saying nothing, he turned from the group and raced back down the stairs to find his father.

Chapter 27

King Cole was dead. Briar and the others found Valrune among the rioters, slumped on a boulder. His father lay cracked in half, fallen from a high wall in the caves. The raw, clear goop with a swirl of bright yolk oozed from his shattered shell.

Valrune looked detached, as though he was thinking of something else—not of the king. It took time before he even noticed that Briar and the others were standing around him, looking at the gruesome mess. "We must do something to save him," Valrune said. "The Dire Liquid—we can prepare it."

Sherman shook his head and placed a paw on Valrune. "Magic has its limits before it becomes something dark and regrettable. We cannot put him together again."

There were no tears in Valrune's eyes. He returned to his silent, far-away gaze. Briar and the others were at a loss, but they remained standing by Valrune's side, waiting for him to awaken from his cocoon of pain. "You have your book," he suddenly said. "You have your friend." He would not look at them. "You had best be on your way."

"We cannot leave," Sherman said. Briar and Dax exchanged stares and noticed that Sherman was unable to lift his gaze from the ground.

"What?" Dax finally said.

"She touched Orpion's mirror, and what's more, she used it," he said. There was a great hollow pain ringing in Sherman's voice. "I don't know how, but she used Orpion's mirror."

"So what? Let's go," Dax said.

"You don't understand. Briar's power may not be dillywig after all," he said. "She cannot truly use her trinket, the key. I still don't understand how she used it to enter these Realms. It may have been sheer luck. Perhaps Myrtle and Poplar aided in some way. I just don't know. But now that she has used Orpion's mirror, the key will never be able to protect or even help us back. Using a dark object of magic makes all else turn to the dark. And without that key, there is no going back." He shook his head.

"But once the sun sets tomorrow, I turn sixteen," Briar said. "I won't be protected anymore. There must be something we can do."

Sherman gazed upon the ground and at the book in his hand. "There may be one last effort, but it risks all." He held up the small black book. "We do have this," he said. "It is the source of much of Orpion's power. Without it, she cannot completely carry out her plans."

"We should burn that sucker," Dax said.

"No!" Leon and Tarfeather shouted together.

"We still need it, Dax," Briar said. "And besides, Orpion will want that book above all. We can bargain with it."

"As I see it, she will do as you ask," Sherman said. "For without the book, great turmoil in the Realms would begin. Her seat of darkness would be challenged. Her own death would be inevitable."

Leon hopped up into Briar's hands with something to say. "So what? We're supposed to go back to the palace, confront her with the book and hope she plays nice? May I remind you all that this bitch has done battle among other kingdoms—*and won*. Drinking blood is a self-improvement course for her. How would we ever stop her from turning us all into frogs and then simply taking the book from us?"

Tarfeather spoke up in his movie voice. "I'll help. Why, we'll all help if it makes things better, darling." He was surrounded now by the seven other dwarefs that Damarius had caged and sent to the mines two days prior. Briar hadn't recognized it until now, but the rioting in the caverns had stopped, and many more of the freed dwarefs crowded around to see the Black Woods girl. Throngs of small golden creatures, as far as Briar could see, stood among and atop the cavern rocks and peered from the cavern tiers above.

"What's happening, Tarfeather?" she asked.

"Dwarefs comery to see special girl, Three Omens girl," he said. "Freery family. Freery friends. They helpery now."

"Will you translate what I say, Tarfeather?" she asked. Tarfeather nodded.

Briar stood tall and full of a confidence she never had before. She recognized this newfound strength and it felt right. "Friends, we need your help," she began. Sherman nodded encouragement to her. "If the Realms are to be free for everyone, we need you to stand with us and fight."

After Tarfeather translated, the crowd murmured. The dwarefs to either side of Tarfeather huddled with him, all of them nodding, speaking in the same guttural language she had heard Sherman and Gelid speak. Then one to another, they spoke the ancient language, passing along Briar's message.

Then a noise sounded throughout the cavern. It started out small, in the deep recesses of the cavern. But then it grew, widespread, across the vast crowd. It was a sound like bees buzzing. But it was a noise dwarefs made when they were about to march into battle. Louder and louder the noise grew until it felt as though the entire cavern was vibrating with the focused, righteous anger of an oppressed people.

"Battle for you they makery, Briar Blackwood," Tarfeather said. Then the buzzing changed to a sweeping ocean of cheers, while the dwarefs swung torches and their tiny pickaxes in the air.

Through the commotion, Valrune remained fixed upon his father, who lay shattered. Sherman put a paw on his shoulder and urged him away. "Come, Valrune," he said. "We all need rest now. I'll cast a little spell on you to help you sleep through the night. And then, in the morning, we can give him a proper burial."

"I cannot go further with you," Valrune said.

Briar stepped close to him and took his hands. "Valrune, please. How can we do this without you?"

He could not meet her eyes. Instead, he looked downward, and finally tears began to flow. He seemed to lose his strength. His knees buckled, and he crouched to the ground. Putting his hands to his face, he sobbed while Briar, Sherman, and the others stood watch.

It was dawn by the time the grave was completed for Cole not far from the temple cave entrance. Briar was surprised by the care the dwarefs exercised in bringing Cole's remains from the caverns. They had placed his enormous shell on a wheelbarrow, which they pushed slowly and solemnly—as though he were one of their own who had fallen.

Briar watched with admiring eyes, knowing that they had somehow looked beyond their imprisonment. Whether Cole knew it openly, or endorsed it tacitly, he was to blame for their sorrow. But rancor was not in a dwaref's blood. They lived freely, moment to moment, like wind blowing across the grassy plains, and like water gurgling over stones in a brook. One moment they were prisoners and laborers, the next they were free. And they did not hold themselves to the past, for what good would it serve?

Briar watched the tiny torchbearers flanking Cole's remains, keeping pace with the funeral procession. And once they were all outside the caves, the dwarefs spent the night on a bare slope of the Towery Flowery Hill with their pickaxes and their sharp claws, digging a grave for the king, singing a mournful dirge. Briar and the others slept near the coach that night, too exhausted to do anything else. But throughout the night, Briar would awaken from time to time, and wonder if she could live as the dwarefs, forgiving without hesitation. It seemed impossible, and it troubled her that she could not find the same freedom in her own heart.

In the morning, Briar awakened to the discomfort of sleeping in the cramped coach. She had spent the night leaning against Valrune's shoulder. And now she was stiff and achy. Leon had nestled himself into her lap, and she found it comforting to have been wanted, even desired by two such beautiful men. True, one of them was yet a frog. But it was still nice to be wanted by these two in this way, and she thought she could grow accustomed to it.

She looked out the coach window and saw Tarfeather standing at the edge of the grave, staring into the pit with his empty black eyeholes. Without disturbing the others, she left the coach, first placing Leon in Valrune's lap. She watched the two of them, resting comfortably together, and she wondered if there would ever be a way to have them both remain in her life.

She left them and approached Tarfeather from behind. The grassy slope was illuminated by the sun, and dew gleamed on the small white dandelion blossoms that looked like scattered kettle corn. Once she was close to Tarfeather, she saw that the other dwarefs had lined the grave with fallen rose petals. The king's shell was already cleaned and lowered down to its soft bedding. She knelt next to Tarfeather, but said nothing.

"Ha'tua innery king belly," Tarfeather said. He shook his head slowly. "King bad man," he said.

"I'm so sorry, Tarfeather," she said.

"No cryery for Tarfeather, Briar Blackwood," he replied. "King Ha'tua gonnery now. Bad things no more happenry now."

Briar sat with Tarfeather, the two of them watching over the grave, sitting without words. But Briar's mind went to dark places. Today was her sixteenth birthday and the curse of the sleepdeath loomed like heavy rainclouds. Poplar and Myrtle said they'd softened the curse so that Briar would sleep. But how did they know what would happen? There would no longer be protections. Perhaps she'd die. Briar tried not to think of these things, but the beauty of the hills, and the roses, and the dwarefs all working side by side, made the idea of death almost too much for her to bear.

One by one the others from the carriage awakened, and they gathered around the grave of King Cole. Valrune stood alone at the head of the ditch and spoke.

"Old King Cole was a merry old soul..." He tried to say more, but his voice caught on his pain and left him.

The dwarefs, too many of them to count, worked in teams to brush more rose petals down into the pit and to fill the rest with soft dark soil.

When all was completed, Briar and the others piled into the coach. There was little left to say. All that remained was their momentous task ahead. Valrune mounted his horse and rode alongside the coach as they journeyed back to Murbra Faire. The dwarefs marched behind Valrune with their pickaxes and hammers, ready for them to put to a far better use.

Chapter 28

After a slow day's journey, Murbra Faire loomed in the distance. The vast numbers in their troop made movement slow. Sherman and Valrune agreed that the route least traveled by Lady Orpion or her spies was to the north, through the Oaktangle Woods at the base of the Ice Cap Mountains. But it took them almost the whole of the day to make their way through the treacherous passes and impossibly tangled trees darkening the paths of their passage.

The dwarefs munched on stray pebbles of granite that cluttered the sides of the road. Briar and the others hadn't eaten since their meal of mud bread from the Boss and his posse. As revolting as it had tasted before, the hard flat loaves with the flavor of soil along with some water sounded good to Briar and Dax halfway through the day. Leon was lucky to snap up a flying insect from time to time. Even though the very act of eating a bug was loathsome to him, and even though they tasted disgusting, he knew it was better than starving.

Once they were well into the woods, Valrune called for the caravan to stop, and he ushered Briar and the others down a soft fern-covered bank that sloped from the side of the road. There, beneath a stand of oaks, was a ring of red berries the size of peas. Skilled in knowledge of the woods, Valrune called the shiny things Imp Weave, and said they tasted good. Briar and the others picked them and stuffed themselves with the sweet things, which tasted like crisp apples.

By the time they emerged from the woods and saw Murbra Faire up close, its windows glinted from the last rays of the setting sun. The forest was behind them, and Briar looked back at the spectacular western horizon, red and orange, reflecting brilliant pink and purple on the low-slung clouds.

As Briar gazed out, the final rays coloring her face, she knew that the protecting enchantments would soon end, if they hadn't ended once she used that mirror. She wondered if she might feel any different once the spells were gone. But as of now, all she felt was a growing sickness in her heart, knowing that things might end for her in this land.

Sherman's comments in the cave still haunted her. If she was not dillywig but had power, what was she? She felt lost—perhaps just as lost as she felt before coming to these Realms. Sherman wasn't convinced from the very beginning that she was the girl from the Omens. And what if he was right? What if she was not Briar the savior—Briar the hero? What if she was just the same as before: Briar the hopeless, Briar the nothing?

Or worse, what if she were wickett? There were undeniable clues. Her powers seemed to surge out of control whenever she sensed danger. Her entire being became a weapon in those moments, killing both soldiers and priests. If she were a child of the darkness, not of the light, there would be too much to lose. She had so little in her life up until this moment—so suppressing whatever was budding within her was a fast ranking priority.

Once they arrived at the Westwolf Wall, the farthest and most secret of the palace's wings, Valrune dismounted and instructed Briar and the others on how they might enter through the lower tunnels that were created to serve as an escape for the king in times of war. Westwolf was partitioned by the natural jagged mountain formations that jutted suddenly from the landscape. The upswept rock upon which Murbra Faire was perched extended farther west than most travelers or warriors suspected. So it had long served as a natural barrier for intruders.

Valrune mapped out his plan. He would go by horse to the main gates, to see if he could create a diversion while Briar, Sherman, Dax, Leon, and Tarfeather entered the secret passages below. The dwarefs remained in hiding below the Oaktangle Woods' snarled, camouflaging branches. They awaited Valrune's signal, a flaming arrow, if indeed it became necessary for them to be called to action.

The path to the secret passages of Westwolf proved a treacherous journey through a dried thicket of spike-length thorns. Whether or not the king had planned this as a defense, Briar did not know. But she did see the skeletons of rodents and other small creatures that must have accidentally ventured into the thorns and could not find a way out. Without telling Briar why, Valrune had given her his sword before he rode up the winding palace road. And now Briar found herself using it like a machete to hack at the branches, some of them thick as a child's arm.

Leon and Tarfeather could easily fit beneath or between most of the dangerous branches, and proved to be useful scouts for Briar, Dax, and Sherman. They would call out to them to turn left, right, or go back depending on the thinness of the chaparral.

The secret passage was not so difficult to find, and Briar wondered why it was touted a secret. The door that led into Westwolf was as tall and wide as Cole, with a small window near the top of it, barricaded by crisscrossing wrought iron. The door was not locked as they had suspected, But Sherman reminded them that Cole had likely tried to escape through it, and was apprehended, then taken to the mines.

The passage was a series of stone steps leading through a narrow stairwell that smelled dank and mossy. Small openings in the wall about the size of bricks served as windows and helped illuminate the stairs in the otherwise dim passages.

Finally they reached an old door set between the narrow gray stone walls. Briar used her sword to push it open, and it squealed on its ornate iron cast hinges. The chamber on the other side was cold and high. Like the rest of the palace, there were no windows set in the smooth stone walls, but this made sense, given it was the king's refuge in times of war. A fire roared in the room's sculpted stone fireplace, which was large enough for someone to stand within.

The place was sparsely, though regally appointed. A polished table, long and plain, was at the center of the room. Papers of curling parchment were unrolled on it, pinned down by numerous weighty metal markers. Two leather wingback chairs with backrests of exaggerated height were arranged near the fireplace. The room was still, but something about the place made everyone feel a bit uneasy.

"Hello?" Briar called out. She held Valrune's sword up. More stillness and silence.

"Why is there a fire burning?" Leon asked. He flopped next to Briar and gazed around with his bugged out eyes. Briar looked around, and it occurred to her that Tarfeather was missing.

"Tarfeather," she called out. "What happened to him?"

"Didn't he come up with you?" Dax asked.

"I haven't seen him since we started climbing the stairs," Briar said.

Sherman said nothing, but padded over to the solid, planky table and looked at the scrolls. "This is a map of the Realms," he said. "These look like battle markers."

Leon hopped over and up on to the table. "Oh, Briar, we need to get out of here now," he said.

"But Cole was planning no war—he had no enemies," Sherman said. "So whose plans are these?"

"Why they are mine, of course," said a familiar voice from behind them.

They all turned to face Damarius, who stood with his stone cold countenance, eyes cast down. From behind his robes, Tarfeather emerged. He faced Briar and the others with a long face, his claws clutched together and jangling at his throat.

"Givery reward," Tarfeather said to Damarius. "Givery now."

"In good time, my friend," Damarius said. Then he entered the chamber. He made a gesture with one hand, his fingers drawing a magical symbol in the air. The door behind him slammed and the lock clinked in place.

"No, givery now!" Tarfeather demanded. "Girl takery mirror, touchery mirror like you askery," he said. He now made fists and began tearing at his jester's clothes. "Givery back Tarfeather eyes. Givery back Ha'tua!"

"So demanding, for a traitor. Wouldn't you agree?" Damarius asked Briar. Then he drew another magic sigil in the air, and the *Book of Cinder and Blight* disappeared from Sherman's paws and re-appeared in his open hands in a burst of black smoke. Before Sherman had time to react, Damarius made another gesture and Sherman froze in place.

"Sherman!" Dax shouted. The fox fell to one side, like a taxidermied creature that had not yet been mounted to its base. Dax tried to revive him, but Sherman remained stiff, his mouth open in a gasp of surprise. Briar raised Valrune's sword toward Damarius, but it trembled visibly in her grip.

"Not as quick as the old fox used to be," Damarius said. But his voice was no longer high and effete, the affectation of a courtly presence. This voice was huskier, and starting to sound familiar. Facial hair started growing on Damarius' jaw at an alarming rate.

Briar's Dragon Powers seemed to have failed her. If ever there were a moment to use them, it was now. But the flames did not arise.

As Damarius moved to the other side of the table, his face began to shift and distort. He grew taller. A full length of salt and pepper hair fell to his shoulders.

"Ash," Briar said. She felt like her heart was trying to escape her chest.

"Time's up," he said. He pulled the hood from his head and placed the black book on the table. "The sun has set on your little adventure, I'm afraid. Oh, and by the way—happy birthday."

Briar backed up a step though she still held the sword up and tried to seem menacing. "You planned this moment from the start," she said. She realized now why Sherman looked frightened when he knew she had touched Gelid's mirror. "You wanted me vulnerable to Lady Orpion so she could end the

Omens. You used Tarfeather to get me to touch the mirror and then to bring me here."

"Why didn't you listen? I tried to warn you," Ash said. While he spoke, he made a complex magical gesture above the book.

"The stone you gave me. That wasn't protection," she said.

"Imagine our disappointment when we found King Cole instead of you holding it," Ash said. He made another complex pattern in the air that glowed blood red. The pattern became a mist that lighted over the book and caused it to take on the red glow.

"You used it to track me?" Briar said.

"And Tarfeather followed your every move in the commons. You would have found your way to this place one way or another." Ash looked at Tarfeather. "He is a useful little flit."

"That's how he knew so much about television and movies. That's all my stepmother does all day."

"Clever girl. But not clever enough, I'm afraid. There are Tales within Tales... You should have listened when you had the chance. But now—now things are out of my hands." He shook his head, and his eyes looked almost melancholy. "—And the Tale must be told as it must."

Tarfeather rushed to Ash's feet and seemed ready to dig his claws into the man. "You givery eyes, givery Ha'tua. Givery Tarfeather just reward! You makery promise!"

"As you wish," Ash said. The dwaref levitated from the floor with Ash's hand guiding him. The book creaked open. Then Ash whispered to the book, "A just reward." Then he took several cautious paces back.

The pages began to turn by themselves, and finally a luminous column shot up, scorching the stone ceiling. Ash held his tinted brass goggles up to shield his eyes.

Dax took out his phone, fumbled with it for a moment, then began to video record what was happening.

Tarfeather smiled wide, showing his terrible sharp fangs, as he became engulfed in the light. He raised his arms high above his head as though receiving a blissful, unseen gift. His missing eyes then appeared in his black eye sockets and he blinked with wonder at everyone. "Yes!" he screamed and laughed.

But then his laughter stopped, and a sickening silence overcame him. His face twisted into a look of terrible surprise as the enveloping light blazed, giving off an intense heat. The dwaref began melting like glops of molten steel into the book. Fused into the column of light and torn fragment by fragment, he shrieked until there was nothing left. The book then snapped shut.

Ash picked the book up and clutched it to his chest with a twisted smile. "And they all lived happily ever after," he said.

Briar suddenly realized that Dax was recording with his cell phone and she didn't want the—perhaps—one remaining lifeline to be taken away from them. So she stood in front of Dax, first snapping the phone away and shoving it into one of her boots before it was noticed.

Then Ash rushed past them to the door, his cloak billowing behind as he ran. He turned one last time to face Briar, his hand in the air, ready to wave. Briar braced herself, thinking he was aiming a spell toward her.

"Farewell, Briar of the Black Woods," he said. "You shall be missed." He gestured in the air and the door unlocked and opened.

In stepped the Lady Orpion. "Well done, Ash," she cooed. "You have your book." But then she was fixed upon Briar. She stepped toward Briar and Dax, who backed away. "Now our little Tale may conclude, unbroken," she said. Her eyes filled with the darkness of death.

"Of course, My Lady," Ash said. Then he made a quick hand gesture, and he disappeared in cloud of black smoke that floated out the door past Orpion.

Briar held the sword with both hands and backed away.

"Don't come near," she said. Dax grasped Leon tightly and ran for the other side of the room, hoping to find something to use as a weapon.

Briar swung the sword in front of her to keep Orpion away. But with a simple finger flick, Orpion caused the sword to fly from her hands and skid over to the burning fireplace—too far for Briar to run, to turn her back on the Lady.

Briar backed up until she bumped into one of the leather wingback chairs. Orpion sauntered toward Briar, holding up a glass vial full of blood, and then she swallowed its contents down. She passed by the immobilized Sherman and kicked his rigid body away as though it were a throw-pillow. "I told you long ago Herbclaw, that you and your pathetic dillywigs would never win." She licked her bloodstained lips as though she were tasting honey. "And I hate to say 'I told you so,' but, well, here we are." Then she smashed the empty vial in the fireplace. She raised her palms, and burning within them were small blue flames.

Just then, the fireplace pivoted part way from the wall, and from a secret passage behind it came Valrune. "Briar!" he shouted, "The Lady Orpion and her troops—" He stopped short once he saw what was happening. Like a spark from a flint, Valrune instantly went into action. He scooped up his sword and inched toward Orpion. He brandished the sword easily, trained warrior that he was.

"Get behind me," he shouted to Briar and Dax.

Orpion laughed. "Poor little Prince Valrune," she said. "Or should I say King Valrune now? Did Daddy fall down and break his crown?"

Valrune clenched his teeth, and inched closer to Orpion. "You're a monster," he said.

"Not quite yet. But soon," she smiled. Her eyes were wide with perverse delight, and she looked completely unhinged. Then she wildly flung one of her flames at Valrune. He lifted his sword and managed to block it. The flame pinged off the blade back toward her. She arose into the air, and the flame hissed below her feet. It slammed into the long table at the far side of the room, and it flared up into a rage of blue flame. Valrune looked at his sword and saw that the corrosive flame took a sizzling chunk from one side.

"Every Tale must end, Valrune," Orpion smiled.

But now that Orpion was rising up toward the ceiling, Briar ran to secure Sherman's safety. Dax ran with Leon and placed him beneath one of the wingback chairs. "Just stay low," he said. Leon nodded and then Dax bolted back to help Briar do something to protect Sherman.

Twirling high in the air and laughing at some joke that no one else heard, Orpion motioned to lob her second flame at Briar. But with her attention focused on her wicked task, she didn't see Valrune who had positioned himself below her. He swung the still-broiling sword, and allowed it to fling into the air, and managed to take a slice from her cheek. She dropped suddenly to the floor along with the sword. She staggered back a few paces, and covered her black-blooded wound with a pale hand.

She growled like an animal. With her full fury unleashed, she glared at Briar and Valrune with unstoppable hatred. She opened her mouth wide and swallowed down the second flame. A mass of thick black smoke and churning orange fire engulfed her and she shrieked within the inferno.

To protect the petrified Sherman, Briar and Dax grabbed him, and between them they carried him through the opening behind the fireplace. The churning smoke and fire from Orpion's spell dissipated, and where the Lady Orpion stood was now a black dragon, tall as a full-grown man, hissing with its reptilian head tossed back.

Embers and smoke burst from its nostrils. It looked like the creature Gelid had attempted to become, but this one was fully formed. Its scales seemed thick and metallic. They shimmered blue-black in the firelight. It craned its long snake-like neck and snapped its narrow beaked mouth, as though the very air were an enemy.

The creature arched its leathery black wings, translucent and red with veins and capillaries. It flapped, filling the great hall with its wingspan and gusts, while it ascended to the high ceiling. It bore its meaty claws and aimed them for Valrune. Briar and Dax shouted, "Run." The creature dropped down with its full weight to crush and shred the prince with its powerful talons.

Valrune dropped his sword and tipped an overstuffed wingback chair for cover. The dragon landed, full force, on the exposed back of the chair and ripped halfway though it with its sharp claws. But the talons got tripped up in the chair's thick stuffing and it lost its balance. It fell to one side, and furiously beat its wings against the hard stone floor. The beast had lost control and slammed its head against the fireplace wall a stomach-churning screech. It let loose a furious cloud of red-yellow fire from its mouth that singed the stone walls.

With the dragon down, Briar ran for Valrune's sword, which lay only a few lengths away. But once she had it, she realized that it might not be able to pierce through the creature's thick armor of scales. So she swung the blade and stabbed it through the dragon's soft leathery wings, ripping a long gaping gash in one of them. The dragon let out a shivering nerve-splitting cry, and it hissed angrily. "That's for my mother!" she shouted.

With the dragon tangled and unable to fly, it was everyone's chance to escape. Valrune crawled out from beneath the chair, picked up Leon and commanded Briar to run. But it seemed like she could not hear. Instead, she stood staring at the creature with an odd intensity in her eyes. With Briar not budging, Valrune shouted to Dax, "Hurry!" Dax had been standing mesmerized by the scene and Valrune's shout shocked him into action. Valrune dashed with Leon to stash him behind the fireplace passage for safety and Dax slid in with him.

Meanwhile the dragon splattered black blood everywhere in the room, especially as it tried to beat its sliced, fleshy wings. As Valrune hastened away with Leon, the dragon used the bony parts of its wings to right itself and brace against the wall while it ripped its claws from the chair's innards.

It stomped after Valrune with a leaden sound. And just as he slipped behind the fireplace passage, the dragon leaned onto the marble with its long neck. Briar heard the heavy grinding of stone upon stone. The dragon shoved the opening shut with its head, sealing it with a sound of finality and doom.

The dragon hissed and turned its attention to Briar, who was left alone in the chamber. Briar held up the damaged sword, making quick warning stabs toward the fiend. Then she ran for the second leather wingback chair to get cover.

The monster snapped its jaws and with them, it seized the sword in Briar's hand and yanked it away. The metal melted like a chocolate bar in its smoking mouth. The dragon grinned, exposing its pencil-long sharp teeth. Drips of molten steel fell from its jaws with fizzling metallic clanks to the floor.

Briar ran to the chair and curled up in a ball on the seat. The dragon drew back the skin from its fangs with a long inhalation. Then screaming like nails on glass, it let go a tremendous stream of fire. It blew across the chair like an atomic bomb blast, completely incinerating all that it engulfed.

When it passed, the chair collapsed in a heap of cinders and smoke. Briar sat amid the ruins, blinking, but unharmed.

The dragon hissed in hysterical frustration. But Briar arose to her feet, and felt something release inside of her that felt just as ferocious and frightening as the black beast.

Her hands suddenly glowed with blue flames. There was no use in fighting whatever it was that overcame her, she realized. She may not have been the girl from the Omens, and she may not have known what she was at all. But if she could withstand the flames of a dragon, she knew she was at least a creature with whom to be reckoned.

Briar watched how Orpion had done it, and now it was her turn. She held her arms out like wings and she levitated into the air. Hovering midair, Briar swallowed one, then the other of her blue flames. She felt something molten and unforgiving arising in her stomach.

The black beast hesitated and withdrew, looking for a place it might go. It began using its wings to beat at the swiveling fireplace, but it would not budge.

Briar floated across the room, above the awful black monster. It barred its fangs and snapped its beak at her, but unable to fly, it found that Briar was out of reach. It stomped heavily toward the chamber door, which would be its only way of escape. Briar did nothing in response but stare with an awful, deadly fury. As terrible as it was, Briar realized how liberating it felt to finally allow whatever it was within her to run unbridled.

Aerially, Briar followed the beast as it tried to escape. The creature wound its neck backward, ready to bite, when Briar doubled over and spewed out a stream of vomit onto the dragon's face. The creature shrieked sharply, expecting it might burn, but then roared with defiant laughter when it did nothing at all.

The dragon then turned to finish Briar off. It inhaled deeply, preparing to spew its flames. Then it savagely released its orange burst of crematory fire. At the same time, Briar opened her mouth. The burning logs in the fireplace guttered while Briar exhaled her own torrent of flames, blue and vibrant as the open sky. The two flame streams collided and exploded in the middle of the room with a heat that caused the stone walls to glow red.

Orpion shut her putrid dragon-mouth, stunned.

Briar landed on the ground and smiled at the dragon, with an awful, delicious smile. Thinking quick, she remembered that Dax had recorded Tarfeather engulfed by the dark magic of the book.

She reached into her boot and fished out the device. She pressed "play" and pointed the screen toward the creature.

Her guess about the recording was right. Instantly the phone took on an eerie glow and a radiated a beam of light that locked onto the dragon.

The monster squinted, hissed, and stepped back a pace. Then Ash's recorded voice said, "Just reward." The dragon's eyes opened wide and its long reptilian mouth hung dumbly. The beast was entranced.

Then the phone's emanating light formed into a glowing heat that enveloped the dragon's body. Realizing it had been caught, it tried to flap and scrape away with its one good wing. Then it was pulled into the light bit by bit, bellowing and shaking in a fruitless effort to escape. Finally, the creature was sucked completely into the screen.

Briar then dropped the phone and stomped on it with her heel, grinding it into the floor. It sparked and popped, and a slight whiff of bluish smoke floated up like a little electronic soul.

"Taste that twenty-first-century magic, bitch!"

Chapter 29

Briar wasted no time brooding over the fate of the Lady Orpion. But it took a few minutes for her body to stop vibrating with power and adrenaline. Using the residual strength of her Dragon Powers, she grasped the mantle of the marble fireplace and pulled it until it swiveled open with a sound like a grinding millstone.

Valrune, Dax and Leon all stood on the other side of the fireplace staring at her with wide eyes. They had been trying all this time to open the fireplace, but Orpion had closed it so soundly that the fireplace would not dislodge for them.

Valrune broke their blinking silence. "Dame Titania—thank the Tales you're all right," he said. He rushed past the others and embraced Briar.

Dax slipped past into the chamber and gazed around at the fire-singed walls and the char-heaps where furniture once stood. "Jeez, what the hell happened in here?"

"Orpion—she's gone now," Briar said.

"Gone, like, 'catch you on the flipside' gone? Or like—gone-gone?" Dax blinked.

"Gone-gone," Briar said. She didn't sound proud of what she had done. It just was a matter of fact.

"You stopped the Lady Orpion?" Valrune asked.

"But—but how?" Dax asked.

"I don't know. But what's most important now is that we get out of Murbra Faire." Briar said.

Valrune looked at Briar as though noticing her in a crowd for the first time. She understood. She felt like a stranger to herself right now.

He paced back and forth with a hand to his mouth. "Dame Titania is right. The Lady's wolfguard doesn't yet know what has happened—nor do others of their kind," he said. "But it won't be long before this is discovered. No doubt her plans were known by many. And once she does not return to them, none of us will be safe."

Leon hopped up to Briar's hand. "What about staying here in Westwolf until the worst of it has died down?"

"Grab the fox," Valrune said to Dax. And between them they carried the petrified Sherman down the long fireplace corridor. Briar slipped in behind the fireplace and used her strength to seal it shut. She scooped up Leon and carried him with her as she followed Valrune and Dax.

"This is ridiculous," Dax finally said. "How will we ever get out of here carrying Sherman like this?"

"Come this way," Valrune said. "There is more than one safe room in Westwolf. Let's try the hidden stair along the south corridor. We can place Sherman safely there and come back for him once we've defeated Orpion's guard."

"Someone's been hitting the self-esteem curriculum a little too hard," Dax said. "There's only the three of us plus Leon, who's busy sucking up bugs. And in case you haven't guessed, I'm not exactly cut out for battles."

Valrune smiled. "We're not alone. Before I found you here, I gave the signal to the dwarefs. They'll be here by now. Come on, let's get moving."

They started down the narrow stone tunnels and were soon covered in cobwebs. There were more of the small brick-sized window openings that allowed some waning daylight to into the tunnels. But it wasn't long before the sun was completely set, and they found themselves in an unforgiving darkness.

Abruptly, Briar's hands took on the glow of her Dragon Powers. "Great. *Now* you light up—" Dax groused. Briar knew that the flames never appeared unless there was some danger nearby.

"We must be near the main palace and Orpion's guard," Valrune said. Briar lifted one of her glowing hands and used it to light their way through the passages.

They came to an intersection that Valrune recognized as the entrance to a secret stair leading to the high turret. He felt the wall for a moveable brick. He pressed in on it, and a narrow section of the wall swung inward.

"The main palace is right over here," he said. He nodded his head toward a longer tunnel that seemed to dead-end. "Leon and I will see if it is yet safe to leave." He set Sherman down and took Leon from Briar.

"Hey, wait a minute," Leon complained. "Why do I have to go?"

Valrune placed a hand on Dax's shoulder. "I am trusting you Bottom, to watch over Dame Titania and keep her safe."

Dax put his own hand on Valrune's shoulder. "I can't assure she won't distribute any more bogus aliases. But I will do my best," he said.

"Take Sherman up to the turret as well," Valrune instructed. "We will come back for you when it is safe."

Briar and Dax lifted Sherman and headed up a twisting set of squeaky wooden planks held up by metal brackets set in the turret wall. They had to exercise caution; the stairs were so narrow and steep that the two of them could no longer hold Sherman as they had before, beneath their arms. The narrowness of the stairs required that they stand him upright and lift him step by step. Briar's hands still glowed, and that puzzled her. She assumed that they must have moved a safe distance from Orpion's guard by now.

At the top of the stairs, they came to a locked door. But Briar knew with a growing sense of certainty that it would easily open with her trinket key. She tried it in the door and the latch clinked open. "I'm telling you," Dax said. "Once we get out of here, I don't care where we go, so long as that key comes along."

She swung the door open and she felt her heart beat at in her throat. But nothing special was there. The room was yet another stone chamber, sparsely arranged with long stained glass windows. Briar raised her flame-glowing hands and looked around. Several items large enough to be furniture were stored beneath draping cloths. She and Dax propped Sherman against a wall, and Briar said they should look for candles and flints. Briar knew that if the royal family had used this for shelter during perilous times, they would have kept such provisions.

Briar and Dax spread out and looked in the various corners of the room. Briar's heart sank into her stomach and soon she could no longer tell if her body was moving. She felt dizzy and thought she might faint. She propped herself against one of the covered furniture pieces.

She pulled the cloth away and discovered her basinet. Briar lost her ability to speak. They had found their way to the spinning wheel chamber she discovered long ago. She knew what was there just a few paces away. It was her prized possession, the thing she most desired in the whole world.

Dax shouted, "Hey, look what I found." He struck flints together and lit a beeswax candle. When he went to show Briar, he saw her walking, entranced, toward a spinning wheel that was spinning as though someone was there making the thing go.

Dax rushed. "Briar, stop!" He tried to grab her by her arm, but Briar shouted back in a voice that did not seem like her own, "Leave us alone!" Then she cast one of her flames at Dax. It knocked him clear to the far side of the chamber where he slammed against the wall and slid down unconscious.

Now we are alone, Briar thought while gazing at the spindle and the spinning wheel. She reached out her hand, aching, anticipating the sting.

There was no weeping once Briar drew a drop of her own blood. There was only a moment of realization and regret. Then there was the sweet, silent darkness.

Chapter 30

Ash told me I'd forget—and that idea has haunted me since the words fell from his lips. I couldn't figure out what it meant—or why it might be so important. I mean, if you had my life, forgetting might sound like less of a problem and more of a solution, right? Maybe it's because I'm dead, but I think I understand it now: the grand realization that sums up the wisdom of the ages and defines the destiny of the universe. Okay, I'm really yanking your chain because I don't really know if I'm just talking out of my ass.

But it seems to me that there will always be dragons to slay, curses to undo, omens and wicked queens to face. That's fuckin' life. And they don't have power over you, unless you forget. You can forget who you are, what your life has been up to now, and you can forget this very moment if you spend your life worrying about if and when they might come.

Yeah, of course we all like to act like we've got things all figured out. But maybe that's just because we're afraid of being in the dark. But I'm telling you the dark isn't so bad. I mean, maybe there's nothing really to figure out. What if everything's happening on its own? I can hear the world just screaming, "Let go—please let go—" But we're all too busy looking ahead, forgetting, to listen. Life has its own plans, its own gravity. And in the end, it kicks our asses and we all die.

I mustn't forget. None of us should ever forget.

It was a wonderful place. Her bedchamber, though small, was finely ornamented in carved dark woods and gauzy linens. She heard birdsongs on a gentle breeze that wafted in through her tower window. It carried in the intoxicating scent of vine roses and sweet meadow grass. She leaned out and inhaled the lush white climbing blossoms, tiny, fragile things that opened gracefully and framed the window in the shade of the tower eaves.

She still wore her ball gown of pretty pale satin. She twirled around at the sunny window with a bliss she had never before experienced. But that was when she spotted a dark smudge in the oval mirror at the far end of the chamber. The blemish was unmistakable, smaller than a coin, at the center of her stomach, and that cherub-framed mirror dared to expose it, as if these carved winged creatures were sent to spoil the day.

She touched the spot and frowned. A white dove flitted through the chamber window and perched upon one of her uplifted fingers. But she couldn't take her eyes from the stain, as it appeared to have grown like a cancer in just those few short moments. It was now as large as a muddy puddle.

She tried to rub at it, and the dove flew away, disturbed. But still that sickening blackness crept, and Briar felt helpless to stop it. The growing stain sparked other changes too. Briar's sleeves dropped from her shoulders down past her wrists in large bell cuffs. The neckline rose to form a high black collar that fanned out and became a hood that swooped down and shadowed her changing face. She felt her skin loosen and her fingers become knobby and twisted. Briar's heart pounded with dread as she lifted an arm only to find it now sagging like that of an old woman.

Perhaps this was a trick of the light. The mirror would know. Briar looked up and was shocked to see Valrune there, standing in her place, wearing the same black robe as she. She paced back, a quiet dread overcoming her.

But the image of Valrune did not do what a mirror image ought to do. Instead he came forward and out beyond the glass. He stood with his broad shoulders filling the black robes, his golden hair glistening. He reached out for her, and he smiled, dark clouds behind his laughing eyes.

Delicately, she reached to him. She touched the tip of her fingers to his hand and he pulled her close. She felt his breath, his heartbeat, his strength, and she melted into his embrace. He drew his lips close to hers and then lightly—very, very lightly—their lips brushed together. She closed her eyes and they kissed.

She had never kissed a boy, but it wasn't what she had expected. His lips felt cold and thin. The firmness of his embrace began to feel like crushing, and she squirmed with discomfort. She opened her eyes and instead of Valrune, an old woman held her. She could not see the face; it seemed somehow blurred. Briar winced in pain and fright; she struggled against the old woman's powerful arms.

With a gasp, she awakened.

In the cold of the tower chamber, Briar lay still on her back for a moment, scanning the place for the old woman, but she was gone. The room was dim, lit only by a few flickering candles, and beyond that, it was midnight dark. She lay in a heap of white muslin furniture covers puffed up all around her where her body had not flattened them. Valrune was there, kneeling by her side, his warm breath on her cheek, his eyes sparkling in the candle-light.

He spoke gently to her. "Dame Titania?"

"Valrune," Briar whispered. But then she remembered Orpion, the wolfguard and their present danger and she sat suddenly upright. He held her hand, but she couldn't understand why he seemed unafraid. "What happened?" she asked. But then it all flooded back. "The spinning wheel, the spindle, I pricked my finger." She held up her hands and found there was no mark.

"I told you that all it would take was a kiss," Poplar said. She smiled and clasped her black lace gloves together. "It's so romantic."

Myrtle was there, frowning. "Sister, please do get a hold of yourself." She pushed Poplar aside and leaned in to inspect Briar, her spectacles sprung to mechanical attention. "Awakening from death—particularly a sleepdeath—due to a kiss is utter nonsense."

"Poplar? Myrtle? How did you get here?" she asked. And

seeing them caused her to burst into tears. But then she suddenly stopped. "Wait a minute. A kiss? There was a kiss involved here?"

Valrune smiled at Briar. "Yes," he said.

Leon pushed his way through the others so that he could see Briar. He was fully restored and wearing one of the white muslin covers like a cloak. "Yes," he said too.

"Leon!" Briar exclaimed. She threw her arms around him, but then she pulled back just a bit when she noticed Valrune darken.

"Wait—what what's going on?" Briar asked.

"I told you frog-boy, it was my kiss that awakened her," Valrune said.

"It might have been your bad breath," Leon said. "But it was more likely my kiss that worked."

"How? How?" she asked.

Poplar flounced over to Briar and nudged Valrune aside with her pumpkin-round hip. She took Briar's hands. "I'll say it again: it was true love's kiss that brought you back, dearie."

Myrtle seemed quite perturbed. "Poppycock," she announced.

"And what's more," Poplar said, "once you killed Orpion, *all* of her curses lifted!"

Myrtle levitated from the ground and landed on the other side of Briar. She took Briar's hand and nodded with appreciation. Briar felt a flood of joy. Myrtle and Poplar were cured. Then Sherman stepped into view. There were no words left. She sobbed into her hands while he hopped up to her shoulders and hung around them like a fox stole.

"Listen here, Briar of the Black Woods, champion of the Realms," he said, "there are many sleeping beauties here in these lands who have pricked their fingers and who shall never awaken. But you—you have defied the Tales. You came of your own free will and could not be bound by them. Instead you awakened, not by enchantments nor by the kiss of love, but by your own accord. You and your friends have weakened the grip of the Tales. The rule of darkness cannot survive in the wake of your doings."

Briar looked at Poplar and Myrtle, confused. "I can't be the one. I can't be the girl from the Omens. I...I..." But she stopped her words. She realized that none saw that she had burned with a wrath greater than Orpion's, and breathed fire like the black dragon. She switched the topic. "But how did you all get here? How did you know where I was?"

"I brought them here, from the other side of the portal," said the Boss. Briar hadn't noticed him until he hopped out from behind Valrune. Then she noticed that Vilesight, Thrash, and Blessfang were there too. But they kept close to the wall behind Briar's bedding, not wanting to crowd the recovering Black Woods girl. "Vilesight here saw you through the window," said the Boss.

The eye-patched bluebird flitted over and perched onto Briar's boot. "This tower was dark for sixteen years, but tonight I saw lights," he said, looking back at the long stained glass windows. "When I came to see what was going on, I saw you both on the floor, out cold."

Then Briar asked, "Dax...where is he?" Then Dax stepped into view from behind everyone crowding in. His head was wrapped with muslin strips. "Oh my God, Dax—are you all right?"

"I'm a little sore," he said. "I would never have guessed you would pack such a mean punch. But hey, six weeks of theater combat class—right?"

Myrtle snapped her spectacles shut with a curt nod to Dax. "Indeed, Orpion is gone for now. But there is more to come, I fear."

"What do you mean?" Poplar asked.

"Ash has the book," Myrtle replied. "He commands its power now." She shook her head. "He has proven to be a disappointment. War and ruin in these Realms has only begun."

"Then we have to fight, don't we?" Briar asked. She surprised herself. There was strength ringing in her voice now—and she knew that she was a far cry from the girl who was freaked out by a school audition.

"Tell her, Myrtle," Sherman said as he popped down from Briar's shoulders. Myrtle nodded her agreement, but seemed to have trouble coming up with the words.

"You cannot stay," Myrtle finally said. Her pronouncement rang like a bell through the room.

"What?" asked Briar.

"You are the one who would sleep," Myrtle said. "But instead, you awakened. And now it is not Orpion whom we must guard against, but the powers that rule in the shadows behind her throne."

Briar looked confused. "There's someone else? Someone worse?"

"Far worse," Sherman said. Briar suddenly recalled the cloaked old woman from her vision.

"But we can't just leave you all here by yourselves," Leon said.

"We have the dwarefs," Valrune said. "They helped battle off those of Orpion's guard who hadn't run off at news of her death. There will be others who will join us too."

Myrtle nodded at Valrune and then turned her attention to Briar once more. "There is no argument. It is far too dangerous for you to stay. The enchantments that once protected you are gone and the legions that now scramble for Orpion's throne will use anything in their power to destroy you."

Briar knew it was all a lie. There were never likely any enchantments protecting her, except for her own hidden dark powers. They would never know if she kept it to herself. "But what about the Three Omens? There's only been one," Briar protested.

Sherman smiled, crinkling his foxy muzzle and exposing his pointy canines. "The future changes, young one. A drop in the pond carries ripples to the shore."

Poplar clasped Briar's hands. "Child, you did well. You have changed the Tales. But we have to finish what's begun without endangering you or your friends further."

Briar felt no triumph in the moment. What they were proposing was a return to her miserable life.

Valrune, still kneeling by Briar's side, helped her to stand. "They are right, Dame Titania."

Leon rolled his eyes.

"I could not bear it if you were to come to any harm," Valrune continued. He fixed his gaze with hers. "Do as they say. And should our Tales align, we will meet again."

Leon interrupted, "Yeah—and just remember whose kiss broke the spell."

"And remember whose kiss shall last forever," Valrune said.

Without warning, without letting one know what is about to transpire, as abruptly as the words "Once upon a time" arise from the page, the chamber door opened. It swung wide at Myrtle's command. A cloud of mist roiled just beyond.

Briar could not help herself when she ran to Sherman, Poplar, and Myrtle and hugged them all with tears streaming from her eyes. For the first time, perhaps ever, she felt love. It felt soft and vulnerable, happy and fearsome—all at once. Even as she held each of them and felt the sureness of their embrace, she knew she must leave and that she would have to one day come back to fight. But that moment was not now. Now was the moment of knowing that she would be kept safe from harm, and that they could fend for themselves.

And just as final as the words "happily ever after" in children's tales was the sound of the chamber door as it swung behind Briar and her friends, sealing them safely away from the Realms, from curses and dragons, from the crone just past the mirror, and from the gathering darkness in the distant sky.

Epilogue

The doorbell rang at midnight. Briar was wide awake when it happened—so it wasn't a disturbance as much as it was a curiosity. She found sleep elusive for the past weeks, and whoever had the misfortune of ringing the Saulk's bell after hours provided her a welcome distraction from her usual brooding thoughts. Though, she knew someone would catch hell for the late-night commotion. She just hoped it wouldn't be her.

Briar could tell how angry this made Matilda. She heard her standard heavy-footed stomp become so loud that it shuddered the basement ceiling. She heard raised voices and then without warning her basement door slammed open against the wall.

"I'm sorry, Mrs. Saulk, but I assure you this is customary," said a woman who sounded familiar. Footsteps fell on the stairs down to the basement, and Briar sat up in her creaky bed to see who might be coming.

"There you are, dear," said Poplar. "Come, come. Stand up straight. You've company."

A young woman, pretty, with a simple kindness in her eyes trailed down the steps behind Poplar, followed by a man who held the pretty woman's hand. They were dressed humbly, and they had sincerity in their wake. The man looked to Poplar, hesitant, but then grinned at Briar sheepishly. "We're sorry if we woke you up," he said. He turned to the pretty woman. "She's everything Mrs. Poplar said."

Poplar corralled them then stood by Briar's side. "Mr. and Mrs. Grant—this is Briar Blackwood."

"Poplar, what's going on?" Briar asked.

"Briar dear, say hello to your new mother and father," Poplar replied.

"What? You're changing my foster home?" Briar asked. There was a terrible look of sickness on her face. Living at the Saulk's was miserable, but what would a new foster placement bring?

"Not exactly, dear," Poplar said. She gave Briar a quick squeeze.

"We'd love for you to come live with us—for as long as you'd like—as our daughter," Mrs. Grant said.

Before Briar had a chance to respond, Matilda clomped down the stairs with Megan and Marnie following behind. "Over my dead body," Matilda barked. All three of the Saulks wore fuzzy slippers and sleepwear that belonged in a rummage sale.

"Mother, they can't take Briar," Megan said. She rushed down the steps and sidled up to her foster sister with forced tears. "She's my very best friend in the whole world."

Another voice at the head of the stairs spoke, but Briar couldn't hear what was being said. This was followed by more footsteps down the basement stairs.

"Yes, officers—right this way," Myrtle said. She gestured toward Matilda who stood looking like someone had poured ice water down her pants. Myrtle was followed down by several strapping policemen. "This is the woman in question. The charges are in the full body of my report."

"Are you Matilda Saulk?" one of the officers asked.

"I'm afraid she's not here at the moment," Matilda said.

Two of the officers turned her around and cuffed her. "You're under arrest for fraud, child abuse, and endangerment." They led her up the stairs and she struggled defiantly in their grip. "Briar! Tell them how good I've been to you! Tell them! If it weren't for me, you'd be locked up in some orphanage or workhouse, you little throw-away—"

"Oh dear," Poplar said. "Did I lose track of the centuries? Is Charles Dickens around here somewhere—?"

Megan and Marnie stood gawking at the scene. Myrtle walked up and slung her black-laced gloves around their shoulders. "Chin up, girls. I know it isn't easy to have come from the home of a criminal. But, I've found suitable foster homes for you both while your mother serves—well, there's no easy way to say it—but she'll serve hard time."

Megan and Marnie looked like a couple of compulsive gamblers who lost their last dollar.

"Come along," Myrtle said. The remaining officer escorted the girls up the stairs with Poplar following behind. "And if things don't work out, we can always find you a nice workhouse."

Mrs. Grant took Briar by the hand and squeezed it. "Let's go home," she said. There was a sparkle of mischief in her eyes. "I bet you need a good night's sleep."

LODESTONE
BOOKS

Lodestone Books is a new imprint, which offers a broad spectrum of subjects in YA/NA literature. Compelling reading, the Teen/Young/New Adult reader is sure to find something edgy, enticing and innovative. From dystopian societies, through a whole range of fantasy, horror, science fiction and paranormal fiction, all the way to the other end of the sphere, historical drama, steam-punk adventure, and everything in between. You'll find stories of crime, coming of age and contemporary romance. Whatever your preference you will discover it here.